CATHEDRAL CHASE

"Hooligan!" cursed a babushka as Nick pushed past her to follow Olga into the cathedral.

Women groaned, heads turned. *"Molodi chelovek!"* Young man. *"Skandal, skandal!"*

Frantic, Nick looked all around, spinning, searching. Where could she be? He broke into a run. Out of the dense crowd, he ran to where he had seen her. He lunged through a small group of women, shoving them aside. Some cried out, thinking that he was militia, or that he was KGB. He jumped again. Olga had disappeared.

Then he spotted her covered head bobbing furtively through the congregation, like an animal running in fright. She was heading toward an obscure chapel off the side of the cathedral. She was trying to get away from him! It didn't make any sense. Then he started to understand. He was becoming involved—in something dangerous. . . .

THE SURVIVALIST SERIES
by Jerry Ahern

#1: TOTAL WAR (960, $2.50)
The first in the shocking series that follows the unrelenting search for ex-CIA covert operations officer John Thomas Rourke to locate his missing famly—after the button is pressed, the missiles launched and the multimegaton bombs unleashed . . .

#2: THE NIGHTMARE BEGINS (810, $2.50)
After WW III, the United States is just a memory. But ex-CIA covert operations officer Rourke hasn't forgotten his family. While hiding from the Soviet forces, he adheres to his search!

#3: THE QUEST (851, $2.50)
Not even a deadly game of intrigue within the Soviet High Command, and a highly placed traitor in the U.S. government can deter Rourke from continuing his desperate search for his family.

#4: THE DOOMSAYER (893, $2.50)
The most massive earthquake in history is only hours away, and Communist-Cuban troops, Soviet-Cuban rivalry, and a traitor in the inner circle of U.S. II block Rourke's path.

#5: THE WEB (1145, $2.50)
Blizzards rage around Rourke as he picks up the trail of his family and is forced to take shelter in a strangely quiet Tennessee valley town. But the quiet isn't going to last for long!

#6: THE SAVAGE HORDE (1243, $2.50)
Rourke's search for his wife and family gets sidetracked when he's forced to help a military unit locate a cache of eighty megaton warhead missiles. But the weapons are hidden on the New West Coast—and the only way of getting to them is by submarine!

Available wherever paperbacks are sold, or order direct from the Publisher. Send cover price plus 50¢ per copy for mailing and handling to Zebra Books, 475 Park Avenue South, New York, N.Y. 10016. DO NOT SEND CASH.

THE CROSS AND THE SICKLE

BY R.D. ZIMMERMAN

ZEBRA BOOKS
KENSINGTON PUBLISHING CORP.

ZEBRA BOOKS

are published by

KENSINGTON PUBLISHING CORP.
475 Park Avenue South
New York, N.Y. 10016

First Printing: January, 1984

Printed in the United States of America.

In memory of my dad,
Charles Wacker Zimmerman

PROLOGUE

New York City, May 1978

Vladimir Pavlovich Zamyatin spent the majority of his free time in America eating. When the Soviet diplomat was not on duty at the United Nations, he could usually be found combing the streets of New York City for yet another novel, edible item. It was in this way that Vladimir Pavlovich passed the lonely hours, for food eased the pain of being separated from his darling wife, Lidochka, who remained behind in their expansive Moscow apartment. It was also in this way that instructions for his covert activities were communicated to him.

Accustomed to an earthy diet, Vladimir Pavlovich thought Americans ate far too many fresh fruits and vegetables, and dismissed American bread as little more than spun chemicals. He prided himself on being open-minded, however, and was quite willing to try anything he could swallow. Big Macs were his favorite food discovery since his arrival in New York, though he considered the ubiquitous sauce a trifle too sweet. He also liked chili dogs, and the best one he had found was served at a food stand on the corner of Fifty-fourth and Lexington. He had also developed a particular weakness for fresh, hot donuts, and without a doubt all of his clothes—his one black suit, his other coat, his two pairs of pants, and his three shirts—had recently developed stretch marks.

Zamyatin left the United Nations on a pleasant May afternoon under the pretense of going out for a short stroll and a bite to eat. Some twenty minutes later, satisfied that he was not being followed, he came to a cheerful white and yellow food stand. Hot pretzels. His eyes widened.

"Please to give," he said, raising a single finger. "One."

The vendor, a thick black mustache curling into his mouth, reached for the tongs.

"Have you no beer?" asked Zamyatin. "It's a pleasant day for a beer."

The vendor, without so much as glancing at Zamyatin, recognized the words. Offering their counterpart, he said, "No beer. Only soft drinks, ice cold just for you."

The Russian's frown gave way to a condescending smile. "Then please to give one pretzel and that is all."

"As you like." He reached below for the napkin.

Zamyatin received his pretzel, squirted mustard all over it, took a large bite, and was on his way again. A quarter of a block later he slipped the concealed car key from under the pretzel. Then he dabbed the corners of his mouth with the napkin and noted the address, which was faintly written in pencil. Cramming the remainder of the food into his mouth, he pitched the paper into an overflowing garbage can, and reached the indicated parking ramp several minutes later.

Most of the other drops had been made along the Garden State Parkway. This one was in Darien, Connecticut, and the trip took Zamyatin twice as long as it should have with all his sudden turns and double-tracking. He proceeded only when it was perfectly obvious that he wasn't being tailed and he arrived in the small town just before four in the afternoon. Slowing in front of the Baskin-Robbins ice cream store, he winced when the driver behind him honked with incessant irritation. He put on the emergency flashers and stopped. Two large men in their mid-thirties, Stugachevsky and Polovko, rushed out of the store. They threw their ice cream cones to the ground and hopped into the car.

"Problems?" asked Zamyatin, maneuvering the Ford into the stream of traffic.

"Nyet." Stugachevsky passed Polovko the paper towel.

"Thanks," muttered the other, wiping his mouth. "You're late."

"There was a lot of traffic. You know these Americans and their automobiles." Zamyatin lied. His last detour had taken him through the drive-in lane at MacDonald's and the service had been terribly slow.

Two miles later Vladimir Pavlovich turned into a dilapidated suburban shopping center and drove to the phone booth in the far corner. Routinely—this was their sixth such venture—Stugachevsky reached into the back seat for the red coffee can and Polovko removed the envelope from the glove compartment.

Stugachevsky was already out the door and hurrying

toward the phone booth by the time the car had stopped. He deposited the coins, dialed the number, and hung up after two rings. Leaving the coffee can and the envelope on the grimy floor—the can containing four thousand dollars, the envelope instructions for the next drop—they trotted back to the car. The trio was on their way again within the moment.

Zamyatin drove to the other end of the shopping center and parked by the last store. He looked across the deteriorating pavement and spotted the crumpled milk carton at the base of a telephone pole. It appeared to be nothing more than litter on the side of a busy road.

"There it is," he said.

Stugachevsky and Polovko clambered out and went in opposite directions. Several minutes later, assured by discreet nods from the two men that all was safe, Zamyatin also got out. Ignoring the drone of a distant highway, he listened to the carefree chirping of a handful of birds as he calmly walked to the milk carton. He loved nature and yearned for his little dacha outside of Moscow. Daydreaming of his wife and cottage, he was shocked at how uncomfortable it was to bend over and pick up the carton. Could he have gained more weight?

Seated once again behind the wheel of the car, Vladimir Pavlovich, unable to restrain himself any further, shook the carton. A soft rattle came from inside and he smirked. He adored success, particularly when so little effort was required. Prying open the carton with his stubby fingers, he was hit with the strong stench of sour milk. His delight could not be so easily muffled, however, for inside seemed to be just what the American had promised: the schematic diagrams of the acoustic system the U.S. Navy used to identify Soviet submarines.

Suddenly, out of the corner of his eye, a shadow moved. Frightened, he crammed the diagrams back in the container. Zamyatin lurched for the ignition just as a large fist pounded on the car window—once, twice, three times.

"Okay, buddy, you can get out nice and easy. We don't want a scene now, do we?"

Vladimir jerked his head to the left, to the right. He covered his mouth with his fat fingers and gasped when he saw Stugachevsky and Polovko being led away by four F.B.I. agents.

Zamyatin had diplomatic immunity and was swiftly returned to the U.S.S.R. Stugachevsky and Polovko, as minor Soviet employees of the United Nations, lacked this protection and were punishable according to U.S. laws. Under orders from the new and righteous White House administration, a longstanding gentlemen's agreement was broken and the two Soviets were indicted by a grand jury.

Moscow, June 1978

One warm evening, Frank and Judy Korman came down from their apartment and got in their brown Camaro. Leaving the fenced parking lot reserved for Americans working in the U.S.S.R.—he was the IBM representative and she was with the embassy—Frank waved as they passed the armed Soviet guard posted at the gate.

"Have you ever noticed that he kind of looks like

your Uncle Mike?''

''Yeah, I suppose he does.'' Judy looked out the rear window and saw the soldier picking up the telephone in the guardhouse.

Going to a cocktail party, he turned north on Ordynka Street and was halted by a red light several intersections later. On the sidewalk to their right was a long line of over a hundred Russians filing out of Meat Store Number 103. As always, people gawked when they drove the gleaming metallic brown Chevy through the streets. This summer night was no exception. Word buzzed up and down the queue, and one by one heads turned and voices whispered about the beautiful foreign car. *Babushkas*—grandmothers—their heads covered with scarves, cosmopolitan Moscow housewives in their fashionable American *''jeanzie,''* and men in their dark, baggy garb all craned for a better view. Soon the attention of the entire line was focused not on how many people were waiting nor if there would be enough meat to go around, but on Frank and Judy's sleek American automobile.

Sometimes Judy shocked Russians by waving as they admired the car. Sometimes she put on a cassette tape and played music loudly. This time, however, she just wanted to get to the cocktail party, have a Scotch, eat some nachos, and do what Moscow embassy people do best: pretend they are not in the Soviet Union.

''Just once,'' said Judy, sinking in her seat, ''I'd like to go out in public and not be gawked at as if I were from Mars.''

The light turned green and he accelerated like a teenager trying to impress his high school friends. Speeding along, they passed through one of Moscow's oldest quarters.

Admiring the ancient buildings with crumbling baroque detail and faded paint, Judy said, "With a little renovation this could be Moscow's trendiest section."

"Oh, come on . . ." His attitude toward the Soviet Union had been slipping for some time. "I'm sure these places don't even have indoor plumbing and I'd bet you anything the people who live here are dying to get out."

They crossed one bridge, another, and the Kremlin magically filled the horizon.

Frank was quick. "Spare me. Don't tell me how beautiful you think it is," he said, pointing to the imposing fortress of the tsars above the Moscow River. "Granted, all those steeples and their silly golden onion domes are impressive, but . . . but what about that?" He gestured to the enormous Rossiya Hotel. "Hideous!"

"Yeah, yeah, yeah," she said, brushing off the remark.

They passed through the center of Moscow and headed for Leningrad Prospect. Heads turned, people stared; it was impossible for them to go out without being noticed. They hit another light.

"Damn. I'm missing them all tonight."

A husky man, his attention focused on them, stepped off the curb and hurried around the back of the car.

"Shit," said Frank, his eyes on the rearview mirror. "I'm going to get a Soviet car just so people will leave us alone."

Judy laughed. "I'll bet."

The stillness of the empty Moscow street was suddenly destroyed. Making a powerful arc in their direction, a black sedan roared around the corner and barreled down on the Chevy.

Rubber tore against pavement in a painful squeal as the sedan braked, but it failed to come to a complete halt until its metal grill gently collided against the Camaro's rubber bumper.

"What the hell . . ." said Frank, stunned by the jolt.

He and his wife tensed as if they had just touched a live wire. Speechless, they watched as another Soviet car sped in from a side street, focused on them, and came to a noisy halt only inches away. A handful of muscular men jumped out of each vehicle.

"Oh, shit," said Frank, his fingers in a deathly lock on the steering wheel.

The husky man who had been on the sidewalk raced along the side of the car and threw open Frank's door. The sounds of the other Russians rapidly converged on Frank and Judy.

"We're Americans!" yelled Judy. "Leave us alone!" She slammed down the door lock.

The squad of Soviet men reached the Chevrolet and a mass of thick, threatening hands reached in and grabbed hold of Frank Korman.

"Get your fucking hands off me!" More shocked than frightened, he let go of the wheel and tried to fight back.

Several of the men latched onto his left arm; Frank hung onto the steering wheel with his right. One of them hit him in the jaw and Frank's grip loosened. Three Russians tugged on him and one by one his fingers slipped off the wheel. They pulled his writhing torso out of the car.

"Judy!"

She dove on top of his leg and wrapped her body around it. "Get away! We're Americans! *Amerikantsi!*" she screamed.

One of them extended an arm into the Camaro and toward her. She lost hold of her husband and they dragged him out, struggling and fighting even though he was already defeated. With the way now free, the Russian climbed into the car and shot an open hand toward Judy. She pulled herself back and cowered against the door.

"Get away!" She couldn't remember an obscenity in Russian. "You son of a bitch, we're Americans! *Amerikantsi!*" She raised her foot and plunged it at his face.

From outside she heard the racket of a desperate commotion. Through the windshield she saw a half-dozen Russian men trying to restrain her husband.

"Frank!" she cried.

His arms held back by two men, he twisted and yelled. He threw his head back and tried to lift a leg. A fist was raised above the group and then plunged into Frank Korman's stomach. Gasping for air, Korman doubled over and emitted a high-pitched squeal. The Russians, their target now quite manageable, tossed the American into the back seat of the waiting sedan.

Judy realized that the man in the car was trying to get the keys from the ignition.

"No!" she said, ramming her heel into the back of his hand.

"Sukka!" he yelled.

Full of rage, he lifted his fist back. He closed in on her and was about to strike when his commanding officer called him. Resentfully obeying orders, the man scowled at Judy as he withdrew, rubbing his wounded hand. He backed out of the Camaro and then ran to the black sedan. The shrill sound of spinning tires pierced the air even before his door was shut.

It was over.

Judy Korman sat alone in her Camaro on a deserted Moscow street, the car door wide open. Her husband was gone, torn from the car, stuffed into another, and whisked away. Trembling and fighting back tears, she crawled into the driver's seat, shut the door and started the engine. Reflexively, she headed directly for the American Embassy on the Sadovoye Ring, fully aware that she hadn't been taken because, as part of the embassy, she had diplomatic immunity. Her husband, however, as an employee of an American corporation, lacked this protection.

I

Kiev, September 1978

Elizaveta was reminded of her age whenever she unwittingly glanced at a calendar or, as she occasionally did, picked up a newspaper. Born three months after the turn of the century, she was confronted by her age each time she noticed what year it was. This had never upset her, however, and now, fully aware that she was in the final stage of her life, she had never been happier. It was not that morbidity had overwhelmed her, but that she felt a triumphant sense of peace with the world; she had survived World War I, the Russian Revolution, Stalin, and World War II, and the white-haired Russian woman knew she had accomplished a great deal. Soon her largest task in life would be complete. It was difficult for her to imagine this . . . that after all these years she would succeed. She was overcome with relaxation, with warmth, with sadness.

Elizaveta, whose round merry face was aged not with wrinkles but with sagging pockets of soft flesh, sat in an ancient monastic catacomb deep beneath the city of Kiev. There were miles of such forgotten catacombs, tunnels, and caverns in the city's hills overlooking the Dneiper River, and Elizaveta knew them well for they had safeguarded her and kept secret her work. She thought of her widowed father, a Russian Orthodox priest, and of how proud he would have been of his little Liza. He had been dead almost sixty years now, shot for his religious convictions soon after the Revolution. This had been his room.

Elizaveta raised her deep-set eyes. His room. Dozens of beeswax candles flickered, showering the craggy rock walls with dancing light and giving life to the icons all around her. This had been her father's private cell, his secret place of worship, passed on to him like a great gift from his religious instructor and mentor. It was here, in a forgotten chamber of the catacombs—a room roughly the size of a large living room—that he had buried himself away for days and weeks at a time seeking spiritual solace and understanding.

Cranking her stiff neck, she looked over her right shoulder. One. Two. Three. Then, grunting, over her left shoulder. Four. Five. Six. Six decaying coffins. Tucked neatly into the roughly sculpted arches of the caves, they held the rotted remains of nearly all the priests and monks who had used these chambers over the past two hundred and fifty years. How comforting, she thought.

"But so dirty! I must clean them."

She scolded herself, as she had been doing since the last time she cleaned them thirty years earlier.

A sad, gurgling sound came from her throat. Only one coffin was missing. Her father's. She had no idea where his remains were, and she had cried for decades over this. All she wanted was a grave or a marker or some kind of link which she could physically touch. Now the only memory of him she could cling to was his anguished face that day before he was led away. He knew even then. Sensing the impending danger, he broke tradition and revealed the chambers to his twenty-year-old daughter. Torch in hand, he declared, "Soon you will be the only living person with knowledge of this place of worship, Liza. It is from this source that you shall fulfill God's will. Never, never let die the eternal wisdom of our Lord." As he spoke, she focused on the blazing torch in his hand and on his long graying beard, unable to grasp what was to come.

Elizaveta rocked her portly figure, gathered momentum, and rose. She went to the rock wall and stared adoringly at a faded icon of Mother and Child. It was not the finest, but of the scores of icons in the room, she loved this one most. It had been a gift from her father the year before the Revolution. She crossed herself and kissed the icon, part of its egg tempera paint flaking off on her lips. Remorsefully she recalled how she had brought this along with her father's papers and Bible to the catacombs for safekeeping the day he was shot.

How quickly the world had been changing then. No sooner had Lenin seized power and swept away the Provisional Government than Civil War broke out. Anarchy prevailed and the Tsar and the Royal Family were soon executed, their mutilated bodies, like Elizaveta's father's, never to be found. Even as the revolutionaries were fighting for control of Kiev and the Ukraine, the Russian Orthodox Church, once the backbone of Holy Mother Russia, began to crumble. It was only a short time before all active Christians such as Elizaveta were classed "counterrevolutionaries" and treated accordingly.

She grinned, thinking of it in retrospect. That's how it had all begun. With an unusual burst of energy she whirled around and around on her swollen legs. Icons sheathed in gold. Icons covered in silver. Gilt religious screens. Stacks of Bibles. Brass candlesticks. Ancient gold incense burners. All around her from the dirt floor to the chiselled stone ceiling. Committed to her father's wishes and her own beliefs, Elizaveta had turned away from the world above and over the years had transformed her father's simple monastic cell into a glowing place of worship. What had once been a timeless cavern now seemed an elaborate Seventeenth century Russian Orthodox chapel.

She stumbled. "Oi." Her head was spinning.

She sat down with a thud and remembered those years that had been filled with so much tragedy and even excitement.

"A legend I was."

For it was Elizaveta's self-proclaimed pacifist mission to gather religious artifacts and preserve them for future generations of Believers. Even as the Bolsheviks were destroying church after church and burning icon after icon, Elizaveta was there, one step ahead of them, clandestinely collecting church relics and storing them in her rooms below the city. It was not long before the Bolsheviks had closed all but two of Kiev's 1,710 churches and her subterranean chambers were overflowing. Meanwhile word of Elizaveta's mission had spread and others who secretly practiced their beliefs made contact.

For Elizaveta, the break with the outer world was made complete when the official Russian Orthodox Church issued a declaration pledging complete loyalty to the Soviet government. An underground religious movement was immediately formed. Claiming to represent the only true Russian Orthodox Church, they vowed never to compromise with the Communists. It was under the sanction of this "Church of the Catacombs" that Elizaveta, a nurse above, became Sister Elizaveta below.

Those years had been filled with such bloodshed and turmoil that only the great fire within Elizaveta's soul had given her the strength to survive. They had murdered her father, disposed of his body, then denied it all—just as they had done to the Tsar—but she had not and would not stoop to their level. To do so would only be a denial of the Holy Father. Not once had she compromised herself, and now she knew she had been right in her convictions. Orthodoxy would prevail. Soon her greatest task in life would be complete and she would be at peace to further withdraw into her spiritual studies and meditations.

The catacomb chapel sparkled with candles, icons, brass, silver, and gold. Hunched over on a wooden stool, Elizaveta's gnarled hands reached for the simple red tin box. She caressed it, thinking of the precious contents.

She remembered. Word had spread so quickly. Tsar Nicholas II and his family were dead, the Bolsheviks had cheered, long live the Revolution! But when the Monarchists had captured Ekaterinburg, where the Imperial Family was supposedly murdered, nothing more conclusive than some terribly mutilated and burned remnants of corpses could be found. The Monarchists rallied. Perhaps the Tsar was still alive and there was hope in the battle against Bolshevism.

"But all along there were the documents," said Elizaveta gently.

Tsarist generals had kept them hidden so as not to demoralize their armies. Then the Civil War was lost and the papers were all but forgotten in the struggle to survive. It was many years before, via the underground church network, they reached Elizaveta. And now, at last, the time had come: they would be set free. Bishop Tikhon had made the irrevocable decision: the documents would be sent to the West. They would cause a great stir and much would be written about the Church of the Catacombs. Finally the world would learn conclusively of the Tsar's death and that real religion was not extinct in the U.S.S.R.

She tapped the box with her fingertips and got up. Olga would be coming soon and she had to get back to the house. Shuffling to the far corner, she put the tin box back in its hiding place—a buried steel case—and then returned to the iconostasis. She crossed herself, wondering if the documents still had enough power to affect the living, and kissed the icon of Mother and Child. She took a single beeswax candle, leaving the others to burn out, and slowly left the catacomb chapel. Wax dripped and splattered unnoticed onto her weathered skin.

Having made the trip thousands of times, Elizaveta's feet carried her automatically and steadfastly through the mazelike catacombs. The first narrow tunnel, less than two feet wide, twisted along for some thirty yards until it emptied into a small damp room. Crouching,

Elizaveta took the smallest passage that branched off from this. She next followed a tube-shaped corridor and descended into the Great Hall, a vast cavern containing a motionless lake.

Elizaveta froze. A creature, lapping from the waters of the lake, blocked her path. It was the mad dog—the same dog she had come across a week earlier—that had somehow fallen into the caves but had been unable to find its way out.

"Hello, little puppy," said Elizaveta, her voice slipping through the stillness.

Crazed from starvation and from living in the black caves, the black and white creature raised its filthy head. Too hungry to be frightened, the dog bared its teeth and stared at Elizaveta. One of its eyes, however, was smashed and encrusted with black rot. Low and deep, a determined growl rumbled from the dog's throat and was amplified by the curved and expansive ceiling of the Great Hall.

"I won't hurt you, but you mustn't hurt me, either." Troll-like, Elizaveta bent over and extended a friendly hand toward the dog. "Follow me and I'll show you the way out. Show you the way out, I will."

A stream of bloody saliva drooled from the dog's mouth, and it took a reckless, stalking step forward, hampered only by a broken front leg. Elizaveta flinched. Slowly, she bent down and picked up a handful of small rocks. With the other hand she held out the candle. The light, which was barely enough to cut through the deep dark and reflect upon the waters, was her only real protection.

"I must pass you by and you must leave me alone!"

Elizaveta, her figure old and plump, walked directly

toward the dog. As the candlelight reached the animal's eyes, it began to cower. Gradually, the growl diminished.

"Let me pass!" demanded Elizaveta.

Elizaveta held out the candle with one hand and pitched several pebbles at the dog with the other. The dog flinched, turned its head away, and retreated into the dark.

This was her chance, and Elizaveta scurried on. She made her way along the lake shore and then, at the other end, clambered up a ridge toward a soaring gap in the cavern wall. As she entered a tunnel, she heard the dog's distant growl rise and fill the Great Hall. Elizaveta glanced behind and crossed herself. She prayed that the dog would soon find a rat or a bat to eat or that it would find eternal peace in death.

Elizaveta wasted no time as her candle melted down. She followed the tunnel, which proceeded from the inner catacombs. The passage twisted and turned, and finally led to the back of her hillside house. A few minutes later, she reached the exit. Forcing herself to forget about the starving dog and concentrate on the world above ground, she stooped over and crawled out of the tunnel. Three awkward steps later she was in the rear of her house's fireplace; with the false backing in place and a fire blazing, the tunnel was virtually undetectable.

"Aunt Elizaveta?"

"*Da, da.* It's me, Olga," she said waddling across the ashes.

The tall young woman bent over and, holding back

her thick blond hair in one hand, gazed into the large fireplace. She was a sturdy woman with a handsome Slavic face—broad with the faintest hint of Mongolian ancestry—and a smooth complexion that looked as if she spent more time outside than she really did. Her Asiatic eyes were so deeply set behind prominent cheek bones that it was difficult to tell that they were dark blue.

"Really," said Olga, her smooth voice muted, "I wish there were a better way." She helped her great-aunt into the central room of the old wooden house. "You're getting far too old."

Elizaveta paid no attention. "So, are you ready?"

"Yes." Olga dusted off Elizaveta as one would a child. "Let's just get you cleaned up a bit first."

"I'll hurry. I'm excited. I've never been to an American exhibition before. Just let me put on my other dress."

"I've never even seen a person from America before. Have you?"

Elizaveta put a finger to her mouth. "A few, just a few. And all so terribly thin." She lifted her dress from a hook on the wall. It was gray with faded red roses. "My how this dress has aged . . . but what a pretty dress you have."

Not wanting to appear vain, Olga smiled only slightly. "It's my favorite."

She lifted up the simple white cotton dress printed with a green and blue floral pattern. The old woman, always one to touch something, took a hunk of the dress in her hand and admired it further. And again Olga realized how much she loved her aunt. After her mother had died and her father had done nothing but drink vodka, Olga had come to live with the maiden woman. She had stayed with Elizaveta for eight years—until she was twenty—and then six years ago moved closer to work. Olga still visited her aunt three times a week, and now felt as responsible and protective of Elizaveta as Elizaveta had felt for her as a suffering child.

"Tell me, Olga, does this boy, this young man, know anything about it yet? Does he know what he's going to do for us?"

"Turn around. Stand still." Olga unzipped Elizaveta's soiled dress. Even though it was necessary, Olga disliked lying to her aunt. "A bit."

"But you're sure he'll do it?"

"As sure as we can be." Her words were terse. She hoped her aunt would not ask too many questions. "Bishop Tikhon has great faith."

Elizaveta stood dream-like as Olga undressed her. "Good. So nice. So simple. This is how I always wanted it to be. Peaceful. Still, I'll be glad when it's all over, when the documents are in the West."

"Of course. Here," she said, changing the subject. "let's get you into your clean dress." The less her aunt knew the better, and there was much Olga hadn't told her in the past few years. Although she had found it difficult at first, Olga now accepted this role reversal as the natural course of life. The once strong and unshakeable Elizaveta had slipped into the weaker, needier position, and Olga, who owed her aunt so much, felt that the least she could do was shelter the old woman in these, her final years. "Here, put your arm through the sleeve."

"I just . . . I just want to have a look at him. A silly whim after all this time. I suppose it really doesn't matter so long as the documents get out, but all the same . . ." She stared off into the distance, then turned to her niece. "Olga, do you have any idea what he looks like?"

"In a way. Bishop Tikhon showed me his photograph."

"And?"

"And?"

"Well, tell me, Olga." She clenched her hands and shook them. "He's one of the most important people in my whole life. He's like a son to me, but I don't even know what he looks like. Tell me!"

"Well . . ." Amused, Olga buttoned up the back of Elizaveta's dress. "He's pleasant to look at." From the color photo, such a contrast to the typical black and white Soviet picture, the American seemed quite approachable. "He has an angular face with a small mouth, thick brown hair, and green eyes. I don't think he's particularly tall, but I could be mistaken. Bishop Tikhon has seen him at the exhibit. He said his Russian is quite good. Apparently, he's rather opinionated, too, and does not hesitate to express his thoughts." Olga found this intriguing. Evidently, it was also this outspoken quality that had already caused the American a good share of trouble; on a number of occasions he had offended the Soviet authorities with his blunt words.

"He's young, isn't he?"

"Late twenties."

"Is he from New York or California?" Those were the only places Elizaveta had heard of in the United States.

"Michigan."

"What's that?" asked Elizaveta, confused.

"A state—a region—in the middle of the country."

"Oh. Olga, you will point him out to me, won't you?"

"Of course, but you and I shouldn't be seen together at the exhibit. Not openly, I mean."

"Yes, I know, but still . . ."

Olga sighed. "Don't worry."

"Bozhe moi," gasped Elizaveta to her Lord. "I don't even know his name! Tell me his name just in case we lose each other."

Olga smoothed the old woman's collar. She had told Elizaveta the American's name just the evening before. "We won't lose each other," she said calmly. "And we are not to ask for him by name." It could all be so easily thrown off balance in these early stages.

Elizaveta wrinkled her nose and then turned around to kiss her neice. "Yes, yes, yes . . . such is youth. I remember it well, my dear Olga, the most conservative years of my life. You think I know nothing after all this time?"

"I'm sorry. I guess I'm the nervous one. I just hope everything goes all right."

"Do not worry, child. God is with you." She reached up and ran her aged fingers through Olga's thick blond hair.

"Yes, I'll . . . I'll let my convictions give me strength." She smiled. "His name is Nicholas Miller, Aunt Elizaveta. Nicholas Miller."

II

Nick was not a diplomat's diplomat. Deluged with questions about higher education, unemployment, the Pentagon, and agriculture, Nick pulled at his hair, and said, "For Christ's sake, I don't know. I don't know everything there is to know about agriculture and I don't know how many teeth the President has either."

Fifty or so Russians stared up at Nick, a guide on the FARMING U.S.A. exhibition. Their questions had been nonstop for over an hour. They were, however, a relatively small group. That day another crowd of twenty thousand Soviets was expected—more than 600,000 had already visited the exhibit in the other two cities—and by mid-afternoon a hundred or two hundred would be packed around Nick firing questions for hours on end.

A woman before him called out. *"Molodoi chelovek."* Young man, she innocently asked, tugging at the scarf on her head. "Do Americans want war?"

In the irrigation area, Nick, who had an aversion to

crowds and enclosed spaces, stood on an eight inch platform that protected him from the crushing number of visitors. Ten pounds overweight with a lethargical tendency toward things that demanded more talk than action, Nick struggled to appear both fresh and polite. This was, after all, probably the first and last meeting the woman would have with an American.

"No. No, no, no." He could have been more congenial, but how many times had he been asked this question—six, seven hundred times? "Americans do not want war. As a matter of fact, I've heard more talk about war here than at home."

She smiled, genuinely relieved, and took hold of his arm with typical Russian warmth. "Good." Her contact had been successful. "Now, when you go home, you be sure and tell all your friends, all your family—every American you meet—that we don't want war. We are a peaceful nation. *Mir i droozhba*—peace and friendship—that's what we want."

A stocky, older man, his face covered with a two-day beard, burst uninvited into the conversation. "What do you mean you've heard more about war here? We've done away," he said, waving his callused hand in the air, "with all the capitalists, all the warmongers who make money through the selling of arms. Our government stands for peace."

The other Russians in the crowd similarly perceived their government and nodded their approval. They waited with deep-seated curiosity for the American's reaction.

"Do you have any idea," the worker said, inching closer, "how many Soviets were killed in World War II? Do Americans know or . . . or . . ."—he let the words drag out—"is that kept secret?"

Insulted, Nick shook his head. "Hey, give me a break. Of course I know. Twenty million."

"Can you imagine?" He poked his face forward so close that Nick could see the individual gray and black hairs poking out of his craggy face. "Twenty million . . . dead, killed by the Fascists. Twenty million Soviet citizens sacrificed their lives during the Great Fatherland War. The Fascists were here, right here in Kiev. . . ."

The small Russian woman tried to step in front of the worker. "But we are a strong people and we have rebuilt." Changing the topic to a less heated one, she said, "Kiev is a clean city, a green city, don't you think?"

"Yes, a clean city, a green city," righteously continued the worker. He put a massive hand on the woman's shoulder and moved her aside. "But it was eighty percent destroyed. The Fascists were right here, can you imagine? Even my own parents were . . ."

Nick crossed his arms and the words faded. He glanced around the crowd, and from their wide, emotion-filled eyes, it was obvious that each and every one of them had lost a family member in the war. Because of this he restrained himself from telling them that he felt the real horrors of World War II had been turned into nationalistic propaganda.

Wanting them to know that he did understand their personal pain, Nick said, "Let me start over. What I meant was only that the war took place here, as you say. That was unfortunate. Extremely unfortunate. The Germans were on this very ground, so naturally you are more familiar with it." Albeit an honest stance, it was bland, and if the worker pressed him anymore, Nick decided he would ask him who killed more people, Hitler or Stalin?

"True, true, true," said the woman, wanting everyone to be friendly.

The worker was silent, his breath spewing out. Past him, Nick noticed an old white-haired *babushka* staring at him rather, he thought, affectionately. She stood by the drip irrigation display on the other side of the room and beamed an approving, even admiring, smile when their eyes met. Fiddling with a cross that hung from her neck, the *babushka* moved her stiff fingers up and down. Was she waving?

"What about the neutron bomb?" said the persistent worker. "How can a civilized country even consider making such a terrible, awful thing? I mean . . ."

Nick covered his eyes and shook his head. It just wasn't worth it. The guy probably was another "agent provocateur" sent to discredit him. Trying to get away from him, Nick moved to the side and gazed out over the heads of the crowd. The *babushka* was gone. Almost in the same spot stood a tall young woman with a predominant head of thick blond hair. By no means coy, she surveyed him with atypical directness and intensity.

"I mean," continued the worker with indignation, "a bomb designed just to kill people? How disgusting!"

War and peace. Unemployment. Crime in America. The price and availability of any item from an appendectomy to lipstick. The cost of higher education. The number of kernels on the average ear of corn. The questions had been nonstop for six months now and

Nick's head began to pound.

He turned on the man. "Are you trying to tick me off or something? Of course I agree. I think the neutron bomb's disgusting."

"You . . . you . . . ?" The worker, expecting a confrontation, was caught off guard.

After they had lost a third guide—a KGB agent had romantically approached her and she was consequently ordered home by the CIA—Nick had become the favorite victim. Hecklers found him an easy target, and he had been constantly followed in Dushanbe and Tselinograd, the first two cities visited by the exhibit.

"Listen, I gotta check one of the displays." He couldn't get into an argument this early in the day. "There's lots more of the exhibit to see and twenty more guides, too, in case you have any more questions. Just move right along. The dairy parlor's right over there."

The worker grumbled and dejectedly turned to go. The crowd mumbled its appreciation to Nick, broke up, and moved on to see what other interesting American items were on display. When most of the crowd was gone, the small woman came up to Nick and took him by the wrist.

"Thank you for coming," she quietly said, "and sharing this bright, beautiful exhibit with us. It's like a little piece of America, and you know this is as close as we'll get. Thank you for the information about your country. It's so important that we learn about each other's country and that we as people get to know one another personally." She looked scornfully after the worker, who had melted into the orange and yellow dairy area. "And don't pay any attention to that one."

It was what he needed to hear. "Thank you. I appreciate that. Really." He hesitated. "It's just that people like that . . ."

The woman shut her eyes and nodded. "Of course." She squeezed Nick's arm and drifted away.

She was right about the exhibit, though. It was like a Madison Avenue combination of a flashy suburban shopping mall and the Texas State Fair. From the gold carpeting to the orange tentlike canopies covering the entire exhibit, FARMING U.S.A. was as American as anything could possibly be in the Soviet Union. Three bright, sawed-off silos housed slide shows, followed by an array of equipment; a pickup truck, two tractors, a hydrostatic loader, a seeder, and even a country music stand. Just past Nick's irrigation display was a fully equipped dairy parlor with a fake cow—its hide a wild paisley—which in turn adjoined a pig shelter with a whole slew of piglets done in snappy plaid. Elaborate, extensive, designed more with color in mind than agriculture, FARMING U.S.A. was the seventeenth in a series of cultural exchange exhibits to visit the U.S.S.R.

Nick turned around. A young man from the crowd was lingering next to the lawn sprinkler display. He was proudly sporting a new pair of blue jeans and Nick knew from experience what he wanted. Like many others, this man hadn't come to the exhibit to learn about agriculture or necessarily about the United States.

"Greetings, friend," said the Russian stroking his thin beard. "I was wondering"—aware of the dangers, he looked around—"if . . ." He checked the other side. "If you have any . . ."

"No," said Nick nonchalantly. "I don't have any

jeanzie for sale. I have nothing for sale." He glanced about for the blond woman.

The Russian grinned, amused that Nick had known what he wanted. "But why? You have so many in America. You can get them again so easily. I'll give you good money."

"Hey, what do you think I am? A walking display of Western goods?" Nick scowled. "You've got *jeanzie*. . . What do you need another pair for? What kind are those? American, aren't they?"

"Oh, absolutely. They're *'Vrangleri.'* Do you like them? Are they in style now?"

"Of course they are," he said impatiently. "You know it's people like you who have taught me materialism isn't a byproduct of capitalism."

The Russian shrugged off the criticism. "*Jeanzie* aren't only fashionable. They're good solid clothing. And I got my pair at great price in Moscow. Only $160. Listen," he said almost whining, "perhaps you want to meet sometime. Perhaps we could get together. Have you seen Kiev? I know the city well. Have you been to the Monastery of the Catacombs? It's a museum now and the caves are most interesting. We could go there, then to my friend's to hear a little music."

For months now people had been asking Nick for foreign goods, from fish-eye camera lenses to mirrored sunglasses to American fashion magazines. He was sick of it.

"Say," said Nick, "you're not a *farsovchick*—a black marketeer—are you?"

"Sh-h-h!" He put his fingers to his mouth and peered around.

"Well, are you?" Nick spoke loudly, trying to eliminate any intimacy.

"No . . . no . . ." he said. "Please, friend, that's quite serious . . . and very dangerous. I just wanted to get a pair of jeanzie for . . . for my younger brother."

"It's dangerous for me, too, you know."

"Well, would you like to meet?" persisted the Russian.

"No, I . . ."

One of the Soviet crowd controllers, Viktor Yezhov, was staring at them from across the room. A little over thirty, he had a tall, narrow build, a fair face, chestnut brown hair, and wore square, steel-rimmed glasses from East Germany.

The Russian turned and eyed him, too. "Is he yours?"

"No, yours."

"Ah-hah." He fully understood the situation and that his jeans made him stick out.

The man's confidence dissolved rapidly, and Nick was again amazed at how Russians instantly perceived who the controllers were and what their function at the exhibit was. The naïve American guides, were dumfounded when they first observed the controllers harassing and checking the internal passports of those visitors who spoke too openly.

"Well," said the Russian. "I should be going. After all . . ."

"Pleasant, isn't it?" said Nick facetiously.

"Well . . . bye."

The Russian, as fast as he could, dissolved into the crowd. Nick edged around the corner to see what Yezhov would do. The crowd controller, however, had already slipped into the blue silo where the slide show on

American grain was presented.

Someone spoke from behind.

"Excuse me."

He turned. It was the blond woman, pulling her thick hair behind her head with one hand. In shoes with a pronounced heel, she was a fraction taller than he. She glanced to either side and then looked directly at Nick.

"My name is Olga."

He was intrigued. "I'm Nick." For once there didn't seem to be any games.

"It's a pleasure to meet you." Without hesitation, she said, "I was wondering if you might have some free time after work to meet with me. It's not so comfortable to talk here."

His small mouth formed a narrow grin. "I've never had an easier time meeting people than I have in this country."

The invitations were so frequent that it was rather like being a movie star. It forced all the guides—and in particular Nick because he had been followed so much—to become rather selective. Yet with this woman his decision was automatic.

"Sure. I can't tonight, but I can tomorrow."

"Good. At seven?" She lowered her eyes only briefly.

"Where?"

"Do you know the Metro station on Kreshatik Street?"

"Yes."

"At seven, tomorrow evening. I'll meet you inside, at the top of the escalator." She betrayed her relief with a small, barely noticeable smile, and then looked to either side. Satisfied that they were not being observed, she extended her hand. "Until our meeting."

Impressed, Nick shook her hand. "Good-bye."

So quick. So simple. She might want to buy something. She might want to practice English. Or she might merely want to try an American man. But Nick didn't think so.

"Too direct," said Nick to himself.

And while he accepted it as standard that she wanted something, which he would more than likely refuse to provide unless it was something totally innocuous, he guessed that her inevitable request would be out of the ordinary and in any case more interesting than blue jeans.

He watched her go, her simple cotton print dress shifting rhythmically from side to side as she walked. She paused in the dairy parlor, evidently impressed by the flashing digital lights and the stainless steel tubes shooting every which way. The small International Harvester tractor was next to catch her eye, followed by the Dodge pickup truck, that was totally engulfed by curious Russians. Then, as soon as possible, she was gone.

She was gone and the warning Mr. Thomas, the exhibit director, had given Nick several months ago returned to trouble him: "Just remember, Nick, the shit's really flying between our two countries right now and you guides are as big as they come without diplomatic immunity."

But even as Nick made his way across the crowded exhibit floor and back to the irrigation stand, he wanted to forget the warning. He was tired of being paranoid, of looking for hidden TV cameras and microphones.

Problems at the exhibit had peaked almost three months ago, and as Nick was quick to point out, he hadn't been followed once since his arrival in Kiev.

As he stepped onto the irrigation stand he was overcome with a sense of amusement. When he'd seen KGB agents slither around corners and take shelter in black shadows, he'd envisaged his arrest and imprisonment in a Soviet jail. Or worse. Perhaps being framed as a drug smuggler and banished to Siberia. Or even given the death sentence. How absurd he'd been. An American sentenced to death in the Soviet Union. Impossible. They wouldn't do that for a drug charge. He'd have to do something much more severe—such as commit murder—and that would never happen. Could never happen.

A murder charge. Nick grinned.

III

After he ate a meal of peanut butter and potato chips—rather than wait in food lines, he preferred these hoarded items from the American embassy—Nick came down from his room on the fourth floor of the Dneipro Hotel. As if it were a stolen item, he clutched a box closely against his side, half hiding it underneath his corduroy sportscoat. Passing through the hotel lobby, the only sign of life came from the hotel entrance where the short, uniformed doorman stood angrily shouting at two Russian women.

"*Nyet! Nyet! Nyet!*" he cried, roughly pushing them back. As soon as he saw Nick, an *Amerikanets,* he moved aside deferentially.

"Excuse me," said Nick.

Not wanting to attract attention, he ducked and quickly slipped by. Outside on the front steps, he heard the doorman continue his assault on the women.

"Foreigners only! We don't allow your kind in here!"

"But we just want to go to the restaurant."

"I said, no Soviets!"

Nick ran his hand through his hair and gazed around from his stance on the hotel steps. Before him lay the Leninist Komsomol Square, a broad traffic circle in the center of which rose the bright red slogan THE TENTH FIVE-YEAR PLAN IS THE PLAN OF QUALITY AND PRODUCTIVITY. This in turn was surrounded by a ring of photographs of somber local Party leaders, awards and medals pinned proudly to their left breasts. Beyond that, on the other side of the street, was the Park of the Glory of the Dneiper Hills overlooking the river, a tinge of early fall color on the tops of a few trees.

Nick was not concentrating on the view, however. Instead, he was taking note of every person loitering on the sidewalk before him. Satisfied that he'd later be able to recognize the faces, he headed for the pedestrian tunnel that crossed beneath the street.

Still tightly holding the parcel, he descended step by step into the tunnel and turned right down the long, deserted branch that crossed beneath Komsomol Square. His footsteps reverberated flagrantly off the white-tiled walls. Stealing a glance behind, he spotted a woman with a string bag of green apples and, farther back, a man carrying something wrapped in *Pravda*. In the distance he saw the shadow of a third figure.

The tunnel was supported in the center by a series of pillars. At the other end, to the rumble of an unknown number of feet and with his view obstructed by the columns, Nick doubled back. He passed the woman. He passed the man. They went on their own way, however, and Nick's eyes followed them out of the passage.

"Huh," he said, perplexed. He shrugged and continued back toward the hotel, eventually walking by a man who, bent over at the waist, was blowing his nose on the sidewalk.

Instead of taking the left branch, which led back to the Hotel Dneipro, Nick turned right and followed the tunnel beneath Kreshatik Street. As he climbed the stairs out of the tunnel and to the sidewalk, his ears were pierced by the shrieking of three fat *babushkas.* Scarves on their heads, they stood on the steps selling flowers, and their voices were shrill and vicious as they chastised a drunk man stumbling down the stairs.

"Aren't you ashamed of yourself?" yelled one.

"What about your poor wife and children? Who will feed them after you've spent it all on vodka?" cried another.

When the third pelted the drunk with a lump of dirt, she accidentally hit Nick instead.

"Hey!" Nick called out, not stopping. He walked beneath the large trees along the sidewalk, making an attempt to casually look in the store windows. A few people stood in Shoe Store while a line extended out of Fruit and Vegetable Store Number 22, where the window was filled with a pile of little green apples.

He turned left without a warning. He briskly walked up a steep, narrow pedestrian alley, pulling himself along using the railing attached to the side of a building. Halfway up he stopped and set the cumbersome parcel down. Using one of his standard techniques, he bent over as if to tie his shoe, but instead looked behind in the same motion. A shadow lingered, then disappeared. He picked up the parcel and went on immediately.

At the top of the hill, breathing heavily, Nick went straight up a connecting street. He looked to his right, over the red tin roof tops, and saw the evening sun flickering lazily on the Dneiper River in the distance. He pivoted abruptly and retraced his steps. Two young women, a young man—all slim and their arms looped snugly in an unbreakable show of friendship and affection—walked by. They stared at Nick's waist and admired his jeans. An anxious and stiff-looking man passed next. He wore an ill-fitting suit and white cotton shirt, and moved on without so much as glancing at Nick. They were, however, none of the faces Nick had noted in front of the hotel.

He turned right and started down another street. An instant later he heard footsteps in rhythm with his own. He halted. Again he bent over as if to tie his shoe. Seconds later a man moved quickly past. Crouched over, Nick could only focus on a worn briefcase. He stood and saw the back of a man with cropped blond hair who hastily turned at the next corner. The man's steps faded in the distance, and the darkening street was deserted, the gray plastered apartment buildings offering no sign of life. There was no one, not even a single figure out for a stroll. Then, in the distance he heard an engine start. Down the street he spotted a car crawling along the curb.

Still unsure, Nick knew he must not linger. The light rustling of the leaves overhead was all that caught his attention. He turned right at the first street and immediately threw himself against the cold stone wall. An instant later he peered around the edge of the building. No one, to his relief, came down the street he had just traveled.

Then he heard it. Steps from behind. He tensed with fear and spun around. Someone was grabbing for him, their fingernails already sinking through his corduroy coat and into his arm.

"Jesus Christ!" he cried. Was this the moment of arrest he so feared?

"Oi!" moaned the woman as he smashed full front into her, jabbing his parcel into her stomach.

"Molodoi chelovek!"

"Oh . . . excuse me."

The clawed feet of a dead chicken poked out from her large purse and left bright red scratches across his arm.

She sneered at him, gathered herself together, and brusquely marched on.

From then on the tension subsided and Nick began to search for a phone. He was, however, still hesitant, still unsure of the situation. It had been so obvious before. So blatant. The men observing him had walked with him, stood in line with him, admired books with him. Once, smashed together on an overcrowded bus, Nick had even read the grocery list in the pocket of the man who had been following him.

They had doggedly tailed him for more than four months. So why stop now? Each time Nick went out he still expected the KGB goons to be there, perhaps not visible at first, but detectable with his simple tricks. But they weren't. So why had they stopped? Why after so long? Nick shrugged. Perhaps the political climate really was improving. Or perhaps it was just Kiev. Foreigners were a more familiar sight here and maybe the local Party wasn't so paranoid about capitalists infiltrating their city. Still . . .

Nick assumed that his room phone as well as the pay

phones in the immediate vicinity of the hotel were monitored. Satisfied that he was now a safe distance from the hotel, he found a public phone on the next block. He stepped into the glass booth, setting his package on the floor, and searched his pocket for the carefully saved two-kopeck piece, another item in shortage. After he had located it, he scanned the street. No one. Suddenly, breaking the stillness, a light green taxi shot by, its long antenna bobbing in the wind. Then all was more quiet than before.

He reluctantly accepted his good fortune, positioned his coin, and dialed 37-54-32. The receiver was picked up on the third ring.

"Da," grumbled a deep male voice.

He released the coin and it fell into the telephone. The static-filled connection clicked on.

"This is Nicholas Miller."

Silence. The voice, making no pretense at being friendly, asked, "Who?"

"Nicholas Miller. I'm an American—with the exhibit—and Margie Ander—"

"Ah!" The introduction was complete and the Russian relieved. "You're a friend of our Margie? From America?"

"Yes." Margie and he had been in the same graduate-level Russian class at the University of Michigan.

"This is Boris." He was quite eager. "When can we meet?"

"Tonight? She sent you a package and I've—"

"Of course, tonight is good. My wife, Masha, will be home soon."

"How about seven o'clock?" Nick, smugly, had always named his time and a Russian had yet to turn him down.

"*Da, da, da.* Where?"

"By the Leningrad Restaurant?"

"Good. We live very close to it."

"Okay, I'll see you there. At seven," concluded Nick.

"*Da,* okay."

Nick hung up. Margie had been in Kiev for three months the year before, and had asked Nick to deliver a package to Boris and Masha, her best friend in Kiev.

It was 6:30. Checking the street again, he picked up the box and stepped out of the booth. The Leningrad Restaurant was located at the other end of Kreshatik and Nick tried to recall precisely which statue of Lenin it was near. He had seen so many monuments to the revolutionary leader that he couldn't remember if it was the one in marble, steel, or granite, or the one charging, pondering, or lecturing. If he was not mistaken, the one on Shevchenko Boulevard featured a much larger than life red granite Lenin, beckoning to the people as if he were making a dramatic speech.

Several blocks later Nick walked a sloping street downward to the busy Kalinin Square. The dense, mid-rise apartment houses on the street were mainly postwar structures, this central area of Kiev having been nothing more than ankle-deep rubble after the Occupation. Lingering near one of these buildings were four *"droozhniki"*—a "good friends" citizen patrol—who eyed Nick, an obvious foreigner, with caution. Farther down, a couple was snuggled together in the shadows of a tree. The man, in a gray suit and pink shirt, jokingly punched his girl friend, and she laughed, hiding her face in his chest and embracing him. Nick eyed her fashionable miniskirt as it traveled up her thigh.

In front of him a lopsided woman stopped to rest her heavy string bag of cucumbers on the sidewalk. Groaning, she picked up her load and achingly trudged on. She was about to rest again a few short steps later when she spotted a huge line emerging from the square. Seeing the queue, she summoned what energy she could muster and ran forward, yelling, "Who's last?" as she frantically searched for the end. Nick's interest was aroused too. Whatever they were selling had to be good—why else would so many people be lined up?—and as he passed the woman, who was now settled at the end, he heard her shout, "Comrade Citizens, what have I gotten in line for? What is it they have for sale here, hey?"

Dozens upon dozens of people stood in line, their bulging string bags, purses, and backpacks draping from their sides. Yet there was no discord and no shoving. Obviously there was enough of whatever it was, and at the front Nick peered into the center of activity. Alongside a transport truck was a makeshift barrier of crates, behind which stood three matronly women in white hats and robes. On the ground, next to a battered scale, was the prize: two large piles of watermelon. Tempting memories filtered through Nick's mind and his mouth watered.

"Comrade," he asked a woman, her purse full of beets, "how long have you been waiting?"

"Not long," she responded, shrugging her shoulders and not looking at him. "Thirty minutes or so."

Unable to recall the last time he had had fresh fruit other than little green apples, he closed his green eyes and conjured up memories of watermelon.

The woman in the miniskirt, a professional with years of experience, moved slowly, and observed Nick at a distance.

"Where?" whispered the man in the pink shirt, her colleague, overtaking her from behind.

"Just beyond Dairy Store, by Bread Store Number 43." She directed herself toward a display window featuring an enormous pyramid of canned peas. She counted to ten, and then, according to the routine, continued.

The man who had just overtaken her was now in the lead. She was number two. Somewhere behind her was number three, the man with the cropped blond hair. Behind him was number four, the man who had bent over and blown his nose on the sidewalk to prevent Miller from seeing his face. And out there on the street somewhere was the light green taxi, their radio control center, whose only distinguishable feature was its long bouncing antenna.

IV

"Shit."

He had called that woman in line "comrade" and he didn't even know her. He hadn't even seen her before. Comrade. It had slipped out all too easily. Not only that, but he had also been tempted to jump right in line without even knowing what was for sale. How Soviet. He'd definitely add that to the list the guides kept at the exhibit called "How Are You Turning into a Sov?"

He knew he had reached Shevchenko Boulevard when he came to the granite statue of Lenin on its monolithic black base. He rounded the corner and halfway down the block saw a tall, thin man in his twenties pacing in front of the Leningrad Restaurant. Nick readjusted the package under his arm. After all this, it was hard to believe that his box was not full of secret codes and plans, but blue jeans, records, and cigarettes. And now that he could get out and move about freely, he was excited to meet Russians and make friends.

The Russian was anxiously sucking on a pungent Soviet cigarette, frowning as he scrutinized those walking by. A broad grin emerged on the uninviting face, however, when his eyes rested on Nick, the obvious American on the sidewalk.

"Nick!" He threw his cigarette to the ground.

"Boris Lupin?" Nick smiled. Margie had told him not to worry, that he could totally trust Masha and Boris and that they would welcome him into their home like a long-lost brother.

"*Da, da.* Oh, it's very nice to meet you." He eagerly took Nick's hand in his and shook it. "Do you have any news from Margie? How is she? What is she doing? She has not written us for months."

"She's fine and she sends her very best." His arm ached from carrying the package. "Here," he said, shoving it outward, "this is for you. From Margie."

"Oh!" His eyes opened wide, wondering what treasures it contained. Then he caught himself, recoiled and looked about. Only when he was sure there was no one watching did he accept the package. "Thank you. It's very nice. The most important thing you could bring us, though, is news of our Margie. You must come back to our apartment." He took Nick by the arm, "I telephoned Masha at her friend's and she'll be home soon. She'll be furious if she misses a single word."

Nick knew he couldn't refuse, nor did he want to. Russians were given to expressing their friendship and love in terms of food and vodka, and this evening would surely be no exception.

Talking in hushed voices, they walked up Shevchenko, then cut down a side street, Boris glancing over his shoulder. As they entered the courtyard of a four-story building, the only sign of life from the street was just another light green taxi that sped past them.

Boris opened a door in the corner of the courtyard and hastily motioned Nick through. He checked behind them once more before following Nick up the dark and musty smelling staircase to the second floor. And again Boris paused, peering down the stairwell. He then got out a long key and opened two sets of heavy doors. Ushering Nick through, he spoke only when they were in the security of the apartment.

"This is our place—actually Masha's parents'. Please consider it your home, too. Come, sit down."

From the cramped entry they entered a windowless living room. Boris turned on a naked overhead light bulb, and Nick's eyes passed immediately to the familiar glassed cabinet that he had seen in so many middle-class Soviet homes, its reddish wood polished to a cold plasticlike gloss. Boris reached into the cabinet's treasured display of dishes and crystal for an ashtray.

Shaking slightly as he lit the cigarette, Boris said, "Margie, Margie . . . such a wonderful person. Everyone in this family loves her dearly, yet she writes so rarely. Have you ever seen Margie and my Masha together? No, of course not. They're so much alike. All they do is talk, talk, talk. So, you're with the exhibit?"

"Yes, I'm a guide." They were feeble words to Nick but he knew they were impressive to any Russian. People were traveling five hundred kilometers just to see FARMING U.S.A.

There was muddled shuffling at the door and an elderly woman's voice hollered, "Yoo-hoo!"

"Ah," said Boris, "it's Masha's *babushka*."

"Yoo-hoo! I'm here, come to listen to the short wave." An attractive, well-kept woman stepped in, her graying blond hair put up in a bun. She froze when she saw Nick and cautiously looked him over.

"Baba Genya, this is Nick," said Boris proudly. "A friend of Margie's . . . from America."

"Yes," said Nick, grinning. "Margie sent me."

"Margie?" Her eyes glowed with excitement. "How is she? She has such neat handwriting. So nice and small and concise. Are you a tourist?" She bent toward his ear and shouted, "Can you say anything else in R-u-s-s-i-a-n?"

"Yes, Baba Genya. He speaks better than you."

She scowled at Boris.

"I'm a guide on the FARMING U.S.A. exhibit," volunteered Nick.

"Oh, I heard about that on 'The Voice of America'," she said. "What is it? Is it a good exhibit?" Then, as if to test him, "Do you smoke cigarettes?"

Accustomed to being interrogated by *babushkas,* Nick knew how to please her. "Never touch 'em."

"Bravo! Very good! Did you hear, Boris? Boris, you smoke too much!"

Teasing her, Boris said, "Margie smokes, Baba Genya."

"No!"

"She does!" He winked at Nick. "She sat right here and smoked in this very room."

"Well, she has very nice handwriting . . . and you still smoke too much!" She reached over and tried to bat the cigarette out of Boris's mouth.

"Now, now, Baba!" Boris jumped back. The door opened. "Oi, Baba, stop. Masha's home."

She threw up her hands and went into the bedroom. "Young people!"

"Hello!" called out a voice in English. Beaming, Masha stepped into the living room. She was plump and had shoulder-length brown hair. Like many Soviet women, her complexion was smooth and healthy; in the middle of her round face was a small, pointed nose. She spoke with a heavy British accent and her words were slow and precise, as if she had thought of the perfect phrase and memorized it. "Who is it that has come from my dear Margie?" Stretching out both hands and taking Nick's she seemed like an actress from a nineteenth-century English play. "I'm so glad to meet you, Nick."

"It's my pleasure." She was entirely readable and Nick liked her immediately.

To restrain herself within the confines of another language was too difficult and she broke into Russian. "My God, I've forgotten it all . . . all my English. Sit down. Relax. Tell me . . . how is my Margie? Is she well? What is she doing? She isn't sick, is she? Why hasn't she written? Is something wrong? Has she forgotten me? Does she remember her little Masha? Maybe her letters just haven't gotten through. Oi, tell me everything. I want to know all the details . . . every last one of them. But have you eaten? Have you had supper?"

"Feed him! Feed him!" cried Baba Genya from the side room where she sat listening to the BBC evening news on the short wave.

"Yes, come into the kitchen and I'll feed you. Come, but you must tell me everything, you mustn't stop talking. Imagine, from Margie!"

Bustling out, she led the way into the kitchen, a cramped space with a bathtub in one corner and a small window in the other. Boris remained in the living room and smoked another cigarette.

"Sit." She pulled a stool from under the table. Taking two cucumbers and a tomato from the refrigerator, she began chopping them. "Now, what of Margie? I want to hear all about her . . . and about you, too?"

"Well, we were in the same graduate program together and we both finished last year."

"She finished? And now?"

"Well . . ."

Nick was exhilarated not only to be out of his stuffy hotel room and out on his own, but to be so warmly embraced by people he knew he could trust. He told Masha a great deal about himself and everything he knew about Margie, improvising at times to satisfy Masha's relentless curiosity.

"You know," said Masha reflectively, momentarily calmed by the shared news, "everyone in this family loves her so . . . Boris, Mama, Papa, Baba Genya. Papa and Margie talk almost as much as we do—and very openly, too. It seems Americans talk so readily about their country's virtues as well as its problems. Nothing hidden. Bluntly, you know? Americans must be a very honest people because they try to answer so fully and completely—you know, frankly."

Boris came in and sat down at the table with Nick. Masha went over and hugged him.

"All our friends think as we do and see clearly as we do, but we don't talk—certainly not openly—and we don't act." She hesitated, then said, "Don't get me wrong. I love my country, and I will support and defend it forever. I don't want to live anywhere else . . . not even in America." She looked at him adamantly.

"Yes, of course," said Nick, playing with a spoon.

He recognized the fierce nationalism instilled in so many Soviet citizens, nationalism that he had at first admired, but later had come to fear.

She added sour cream to the cucumbers. With a softened tone, she said, "I'm not against my country, really, it's just that things have become so loathsome." She paused in thought. "Boris, get the plates." Then slowly, deliberately, as if it hurt her, she said, "What bothers me is the extent of corruption here." While she was full of pride, it was obvious that she did not let this obstruct her view of reality, no matter how painful.

"You know," said Nick, "I can see why Margie thinks so highly of you."

Eager to return to the subject, she smiled faintly and shrugged off the compliment. "There's so much of this under-the-table stuff. Nick, do you know what *blat* is?"

"Of course. Strings, connections, clout."

"*Blat* is today's U.S.S.R. We are perhaps the most corrupt country in the world because this *blat* controls our daily lives, right down to the food on our table. It is impossible to live without it. It's how we all . . . all function from day to day.

"For instance, no one in this country is starving, but some eat much better than others. Many eat literally nothing more than potatoes and cabbage. Others meat. And why do we eat well? Because Mama is a dentist and she has *blat*. Big *blat*. Officially she makes only eighty rubles a month, but she does work on the side. She earns extra income this way, but not too much because instead of charging her patients a lot, she asks them to tell her when they have meat or cheese or *cosmetiki* . . . whatever she needs. So with *blat* she gets in the back door without lines . . . and before things are sold out. Sometimes people even pay her in the form of caviar or crystal glasses or a book that is in shortage. It's the way the whole country works—by acquaintance with someone who is indebted to you and who is able to get something that you need." Masha sighed as if she had just made an enormous, painful confession. "*Blat* . . . it's how we get produce, meat, clothing, razor blades . . . even toothpaste from Bulgaria!" Suddenly she grew quite angry. "Oh, I can't believe I live in a country where in order to live a decent life you don't have to achieve—you have to connive!"

"*Blat,*" said Boris, soberly, "is the only way I got my job. Masha's father is a Party member."

"But he understands everything, sees everything. Papa is a very good man," she said defensively. Then, ashamed, she added, "Still, it's very difficult to get an apartment anywhere—particularly near the center of Kiev—and the only way we got this one is because Papa is a member of the Party."

"Enough of this," proclaimed Boris. "We have a special guest and we must celebrate. It's time for a toast!"

He got up and took a frosted bottle of vodka from the small freezer. Masha set shot glasses on the table.

"Wait, Borinka. Just one more thing," she said to her husband in all seriousness. She turned to Nick. "The higher rank a person has in our system, the more influential he is, the more *blat* he has. That's why so many people support the government . . . they'll do anything, say anything to keep their position and their *blat.* We don't have many idealists around here anymore. Stalin took care of them. During his 'Cult of Personality' he wiped out everything Lenin had set up, he misinterpreted and misdirected all of Lenin's work." She paused. "Anyway, people will do anything if they'll gain from it. Relations between our two countries are strained right now. On 'The Voice of America' we heard about the two Soviets arrested in New York—of course they're spies—and we read about your guides who were kicked out of the country. Things just aren't good between us now. There are all these rumors about the U.S. wanting to play the 'China Card' and every day your country is blasted in the Soviet press. Read between the lines, Nick. To us it is obvious. You Americans . . . you are open and honest, but very, very naïve. Just be careful, Nick, all right?"

He was touched. "Thank you."

"This is why," said Boris in a somber voice, "I kept looking behind us as we walked here . . . just being careful."

"If you hadn't, I would have."

"So now a toast." Boris raised his glass. "A toast to our new friendship with Nick!"

Nick waited for the part about peace.

"And let there never be war between our two countries. *Mir* . . . peace!"

They clinked their glasses together, solidifying their friendship. As he had been taught, Nick exhaled as much air as he could and then put the beading glass to his lips. With a quick motion he poured the entire glass of ice-cold vodka down his throat. Only when he began to breathe did he taste the traces of vodka lingering in his mouth. His throat burned and his eyes watered as he groped for a chaser.

"Very good," said Masha, gasping and handing Nick a hunk of black bread. "Do like this, Nick." She took relief by holding a piece of bread to her nose and inhaling its powerful aroma. "Our black bread is the best in the world."

In the Russian style, they sat crowded together at the table, eating and drinking and talking for hours. Nick told them about the other cities they had been in and about all the pressure at the exhibit.

"It's so damn tiring not only answering the same questions over and over again," he said, "but wondering who you can trust."

Baba Genya left unnoticed. They drank more. Ate more. The table was covered with serving dishes of sausage, cheese, cucumbers, rice, meat, and bread, and still Masha apologized, saying that if she'd only had more time she would have fixed more and better food. Boris kept their glasses filled with vodka and they washed their meal down with toast after toast of vodka.

"Eat. You can't stop yet, Nick," cried Masha, honestly offended when Nick tried to refuse more food well into their third hour of feasting. "You're our guest and you must eat."

The food and vodka was overwhelming, and Nick succumbed to a deep sense of relaxation that he had not experienced in months. "A toast to you," he exclaimed, raising yet another glass of vodka. "Your warmth, your hospitality . . . This is the best evening I've had in months. It feels so wonderful to get out, to be with people. The exhibit and everything has been so intense . . . thank you for this wonderful escape. A toast to you!"

Boris affectionately squeezed Nick's arm and Masha exclaimed, "Like Margie, you come directly from the sun!"

The effects of the vodka swimming throughout his body, Nick smiled like a schoolboy. He loved the Russian sentimentality that was so outright and unabashed, offered without any pretense of self-consciousness.

"Hey, you haven't opened Margie's present yet!" He got up too fast and stumbled.

"Nick . . . oi . . . careful," said Masha. Then, with reservation, she added, "I don't know. I don't know if we should accept the package."

"What? What do you mean?"

"I don't want Margie to think we love her for the things she gives us. She has already given us so much. All our friends . . . things, that's all they think about. Things. It's so absolutely wonderful to talk with you because you are from Margie, our Margie. You're someone living and breathing who comes to us from her . . . and . . . and I don't want 'things' to spoil it. We love Margie for herself alone and . . . and . . ."

"That's the most noble thing I've heard in weeks," said Nick, drunkenly putting his hand to his heart. "But Margie understands that. She knows why you are so special to one another. She loves you both deeply." He wanted them to have the package more than ever. "She sent the package only because she wanted to, only because . . ." He hurried into the entry and got the package of jeans and things. "Here, she'd be mad as hell if I didn't give it to you. You have to accept it."

"As long as you understand, as long as you make her understand . . ."

"I promise," said Nick, becoming dramatic himself.

"Oh, Nick, when will you come back?" asked Masha latching on to his arm. "Will you come tomorrow? Or better yet, spend the night. Yes, please, Nick, spend the night with us. Please!"

"Yes, stay here tonight," insisted Boris. "You must."

Perhaps if Nick had not been so deeply touched by the depth of their affection he would not have gotten so angry.

Remembering the reality of the situation, he said, "I can't. God-damn-it-all, I can't. I'm a foreigner. It would be illegal for me to stay out of the hotel for a night. It would be against the law for me to stay with you. I'd get in trouble and I'd cause worse problems for you."

Masha's burst of excitement likewise evaporated. She put her hand to her eyes, stood up, and went to the window overlooking the street.

"Sometimes things seem so difficult. . . ." Her voice was choked with emotion. "Margie is my dearest friend. She's so nonjudgmental. I can tell her everything that's wrong with my country as well as everything that is right. I can't be so honest with my other friends here. Besides her and Boris, I have no one else I can speak openly with. But when will I ever see her again? When will we be together? Will there ever be a day when I can go to America—just to visit? It's so difficult to keep in touch, to maintain friendships." Across the street Masha saw a couple sitting on a bench. Even from a distance, the man's pink shirt stood out as he placed a hand on the woman's well-exposed legs. "Friendship, love—what else is there? We're people, you know, all of us. Both Russians and Americans.

And in the end, we both want the same things: friendship and love and peace. It's just that governments get in the way." She turned to Nick. "And now is a hard time. Just mind my warning, Nick, okay?"

"Enough," said Nick, as he poured another round of vodka. "Let's drink a toast and open the package!"

V

She ran to the phone as soon as she opened the apartment door. Bulky parcels balanced in one hand, she anxiously yanked up the receiver. Nothing but a dull tone. She slammed it down.

Frustrated and restraining tears, Masha went into the kitchen. She took a large fish from her purse and set it in the sink. Grayish water leaked from the plastic and ran into the drain. Sighing, Masha took tomatoes and cabbage out of her string bag and set them on the small counter.

The apartment door opened. "Hello!"

"I'm here, Boris."

Entering the kitchen, he slipped off his lightweight jacket. "Been to the store?" He tugged at the waist of his new jeans which were slightly too small.

"Yes, I just now got home," said Masha, taking off her raincoat.

"And how are you?" He came up from behind and kissed her. "Is the phone working yet?"

"Me? I'm okay." She shrugged. "I've been thinking . . . thinking about Margie all day. No. Nothing. Nothing with the phone. It's entirely dead. I called phone repair."

"And?"

"Who knows when they'll get out here." Masha sadly remembered that they had waited two years just to get a phone. "How will Nick call us?"

"Don't worry. We can always go to the exhibit and look him up. You want to go anyway, don't you?"

"Of course," she said, rubbing her pointed nose.

"What is it then? What's the matter? You went to the Institute today, didn't you?"

"No, I told them I was sick." She turned and hugged him. "Hold me, Boris, hold me." She clung to him. "I cried about Margie for hours. I . . . I . . ." Tears came to her eyes. "I miss her so. All I have is you and Margie, no one else I can talk honestly with. And where will I be if something happens to you? Oh, Boris, I'm so frightened. I've already lost her and I'm so afraid of losing you. It's not fair!" She sobbed, burying her face in his chest. "It's just not right."

"Sh-h-h. My Masha, my wonderful Mashinka. And where would I be if something happened to you? You know, when we were married I loved you because I knew you would be a good wife, but now I love you because . . . because you are my best friend. Who else do I have to speak with?"

"I'm sorry, Boris." She pulled away slightly. "You're always so . . . stable, and I'm always up and down. I'm just being a fool today."

"Stop. Don't say that." Taller than she, he bent over and kissed her.

"It's been one thing after another. And to top it off, the phone goes out of order! Oh, it makes me so mad. We live in a city of two million people and it'll probably take more than a month to get it fixed."

"Sh-h-h." He held her.

"I went out and got a fish. I wanted Nick to come for dinner tonight, but . . . but the phone! It's just not fair."

Just as Masha began to relax, someone pounded at the door. They both looked up; Masha unconsciously dug her fingers into Boris's arm.

"Who could that be?" asked Boris, startled.

"It's certainly not Baba Genya," she said, nervously wiping her eyes. "She isn't that strong."

Boris broke away from Masha and, with some hesitation, walked into the front hall. He stopped still and waited a moment before saying, "Who's there?"

"Phone repair," called out a deep voice.

Masha ran out of the kitchen and past Boris. "I can't believe it!" Overjoyed, she threw open the door and there stood a burly, amiable-looking man. "You're here to fix the phone?"

With a simple expression, the sandy-haired man said, "Of course." He wore dark blue work clothes and carried a tool kit in one hand.

"How wonderful!" Masha moved aside. "Come in, the phone's this way, right here. I'm so happy. I'm expecting a phone call and I didn't think we'd get a repairman so soon."

Stepping into the apartment, the worker proudly said, "I've been working very hard because after just a few more service calls I will have won a productivity award for the entire region."

Shaking his head, Boris disappeared into the kitchen. He lit a cigarette. Never before had he heard of such service.

VI

Nick stood at a telephone just off the subway platform and dialed the number. This time he held the phone away from his ear and when the expected high-pitched noise came, he slammed down the receiver. It was the fourth phone he had tried. The fourth time a piercing squeal had blared over the lines.

"*Sovietskoye kachestvo,*" Soviet quality, he scowled.

Like many people who had spent an extended amount of time in the Soviet Union, Nick's attitude had deteriorated to the point that he went out of his way to find the country's faults.

Having taken a circuitous route through the pedestrian tunnels beneath Kalinin Square, Nick was confident that he wasn't being followed. He forgot about not being able to telephone Masha and Boris, and became excited again. He had met freely last night, enjoyed himself, and now, for the second night in a row he didn't have to sit back in the hotel, listening to American music and drinking American whiskey in the hard currency bar reserved for foreigners. He was on his way to meet Olga, carrying a bright red and white plastic Marlboro bag with an *America* magazine in it as a present for her.

Completing this last detour—in one subway entrance then out the other exit—Nick was proud of the methods he had developed to learn if he were tailed. Making his way across the elegant platform with its intricate pilasters and bronze Stalinesque chandeliers, he hugged the side of the wall. Not only did the Marlboro bag, which he tried to conceal under his arm, make him stand out, but so did his corduroy sports coat and blue jeans.

A hand tapped his shoulder from behind. Nick froze.

"Comrade," quietly said a male voice. "Your coat—is it for sale?"

Nick turned. Were they testing him? "No." Corduroy clothes and chrome razor blade necklaces were superseding blue jeans as the latest rage.

Everything the youthful blond wore was of foreign extraction, from his *jeanzie* to his bulky Mexican sweater. Only a steel tooth in his bright smile told Nick that this handsome young man was Soviet and not Californian.

"I'll give you a hundred and fifty rubles," said the Russian.

Not bad, thought Nick. Over two hundred dollars for a Korean jacket Nick had bought at a cheap discount store for twenty.

"Forget it."

The man's blue eyes fixed on Nick's shoes. "How about your Adidas? I'll give you one hundred and twenty."

Several months earlier Nick had heard the rhyming Russian saying, "He who wears Adidas will have all the pussy he can handle."

"Forget it," said Nick. He started to go.

"Hey," said the man, reaching after him. "Are you American? Are you one of the guides on the exhibit?"

In his best Russian slang, Nick cast the man a look of disgust, and said, "Buzz off, buddy. I have an accent because I'm from the Baltics."

"Oh . . . oh . . . excuse me." The Russian was shocked and slightly scared. He melted into the crowd.

Nick laughed out loud. If he were correct in his count, something like sixty-three people had asked to buy his corduroy coat in the last five months.

Hopping on the escalator, Nick saw the little circle of light at the top of the elongated mechanical stairs. A knot formed in his stomach. He was not the most confident of men; once in a relationship he tended to remain there for a number of years rather than take any risks. It had been a long time since he had been alone with a woman, and Karen, his girl friend in Ann Arbor, was becoming a faded memory. He wondered if Olga would even show up.

Minutes later, the escalator had carried him to street level, and she was the first person he saw. She wore the same cotton print dress with a gray sweater over her shoulders, and, waiting patiently, stared out the double doors. My God, thought Nick as he approached her from behind, I feel like I've never been on a date in my life.

He had to clear his throat before he could speak. "Good evening."

She was taken by surprise. "Oh . . ." she said,

turning around. "I didn't expect you from the subway."

Nick was relieved to see that she, too, was nervous. One moment she was pulling the sweater up on her shoulders, the next she was wrapping her arms around her body. She shifted her stance from one foot to another, then back again.

Nick was at a loss of words. "Are we going back down to the trains?"

"No." Olga's voice was muted. "Let's go out."

Nick understood that it was best to postpone any further conversation until they were in a less public space. He followed her out onto the broad, crowded plaza in front of the Metro station. Caught between summer and fall, the evening air was fresh and cool, and there were clusters of people standing around talking, smoking, and clutching bags. Suddenly they were caught between an angry ice cream vendor and a screeching woman who were arguing because neither of them had the proper change.

"This way." Olga's soft hand took Nick firmly by the wrist.

Kreshatik Street. It was Kiev's main thoroughfare. The best supplied stores were here, and thousands of after-work shoppers packed the sidewalks aware that if any milk or eggs or meat remained in the city by nightfall, it would be here. Lining one side of the street was a series of ten-story, postwar buildings with stores below and apartments with balconies above. Farther down on the opposite side of the six-lane street was the Tsentralni Universalni Magazine, the large department store on the corner of Lenin and Kreshatik Streets. In one of the few remaining pre-Revolutionary buildings were two stores, General Cheese Store and Fish Shop.

The sidewalk was broad, its two separate pavements lined with flower beds, benches, and a double row of tall chestnut trees. When there was a break in the heavy pedestrian traffic near the Friendship Cinema, Olga spoke.

"I didn't want to meet outside the Metro station. Did you notice all the people standing around on the square? That's where all the dealing goes on, where all the *farsovchiki* meet. There's always a lot of militsiya, too."

The unsolicited candor of her first remarks surprised him. Russians had placed him in the role of confessor before, expressing to Nick what they dared not to their fellow citizens. He wondered if this would be the case with Olga or, if not, just what her motives were. He did sense, however, that he would not have to wait long to find out.

They passed another group of people, and as Nick and Olga walked on in silence, he found his eyes glancing over at her full-breasted and broad-hipped figure. Aware that middle age came early to Soviet women, Nick realized that Olga clearly would be no exception. He also noticed that she now wore shoes with barely any heel. Consequently, he was slightly taller than she.

When they were out of earshot of a group of parents and children, Olga said, "I enjoyed the exhibit . . . hearing what you and the other guides had to say. Particularly you. Your Russian is good and your knowledge of the world vast. The exhibit—it's so bright and beautiful."

"It is an honor that so many of your people are interested in our country. Unfortunately I doubt that a Soviet exhibit in America would be so well attended.'' If she were going to wax eloquent, so would he.

A fleeting hurt expression crossed her face. ''Really?'' She looked at Nick and smiled, ''But you obviously know so much about our country. Surely Americans must know more about us than we do about you.''

Nick shrugged. ''I'm not so sure about that. . . .'' He noticed how tightly she grasped her purse, and guessed that she was anxious to circumvent the opening niceties and get down to the real issue. She wanted something and silence would force it out.

They passed The Children's Store and there were few people about. Olga took a deep breath of air and spoke.

''I will be blunt.'' Her thick blond hair bounced as she walked. ''I have an uncle who lives in the U.S.A. —in the state of New York.''

''Oh.'' The inevitable request. He tensed, then caught himself, impressed that she was broaching the subject so fast. And in any case, it was still early enough to refuse her appeal.

''I came to the exhibit with the hope of meeting one of the Americans in regard to this.''

He, too, would waste no time. ''Why me?''

Olga looked at him as they walked along. Her words were chosen only carefully enough so that Nick would understand. ''I liked what you said best. I'm sure the others were honest, but you seemed more so.''

Nick shrugged. ''I've always had a hard time keeping my mouth shut.''

Her rather serious approach disappeared and she laughed. ''Such humility is handsome in a man.''

Now he wanted to get off the subject and not be so direct. "Are you from Kiev?"

"Yes." She smiled. "Kiev is my home."

"Are you Ukrainian?" He thought for a moment. "You don't have an accent, do you?"

"Very good. I'm half Ukrainian and half Russian. We spoke Russian at home. And you? Where are you from."

"Michigan."

"That's where they make all the cars. Detroit."

"Exactly." Nick smiled. Detroit was automobiles, Chicago was gangsterland, Dallas was where Kennedy was shot, and . . .

"Are you hungry? There's a café up here." She motioned up a side street. "We could get something to eat, but first . . ." Her mannerisms were confident yet gentle, and she stopped still on the sidewalk. "But first, Nick, I would like to be direct. I only hope that I do not offend you by doing so."

"On the contrary, it's a relief. I'm tired of having to second-guess people." He put his hands in his coat pockets.

"I have an uncle in America—my father's brother. They haven't seen each other since before the war. He was captured by the Germans and then . . . then fled to the West. Papa, my *babushka,* everyone thought he was dead all this time. Even the woman that he was to marry had long ago given up and married someone else. Then several years ago, out of nowhere, a letter arrived from this man everyone thought was dead. He lives in the state of New York. Papa knows that he is not a traitor and does not blame him for leaving. He says that Uncle Vanya just knew he would have been in trouble had he returned."

Nick looked up the street. "I've read about that . . . about men who were captured by the Germans and then imprisoned by their own government when they returned to the Soviet Union."

Nick had heard so many stories about family separations, deaths during the purges, and years spent in Siberian labor camps that he didn't want to hear any more. After all, what could he do? Who was he? All Nick wanted was for these people to speak out amongst themselves instead of confiding in someone, like him, who could do them no harm.

"They were bad years," said Olga, shaking Nick from his thoughts. "Papa and Uncle Vanya's mother is still alive . . . my *babushka.* She thought all this time that her son, her first son, was dead. Now, like a tragic miracle, he returns to the living."

Play it up front, he thought. Play it safe. "I will also be direct: what do you want from me?"

"I apologize for asking." Her deep, Asiatic eyes darted from side to side, and her hands pulled anxiously at the gray sweater draped over her shoulders. "But it's so difficult. Do you have any idea? Do you know how hard it is to arrange these matters? I know my uncle wants very much to see his mother and brother . . . and my *babushka* is very old now and soon she'll die. But my uncle . . . he cannot and will not return. He is afraid of arrest. He was born here and was a Soviet citizen . . . and then the Fascists. The war still lives here, Nick, you must know that."

Rather like an impatient child, Nick shifted his weight from side to side. He scratched behind his ear and swung the Marlboro bag in one hand. He shouldn't have come.

"My uncle—he's afraid he'll be arrested if he returns here or . . . or that he might not be allowed to leave."

"Who am I, Olga?" He said it off into the distance. "I'm just a guide on a lousy exhibit. What can I do?"

They started walking again.

"We received a letter from him and Papa answered it. Then we got one more . . . and then nothing. No letters. No telegrams. Papa tried to phone, but he finally gave up trying to get the number."

There had been so many requests that without even hearing hers, he heard himself say, "We're not supposed to get involved."

She was equally obstinate, not willing to retreat for a moment. "If I could give you a letter to take with you, you could mail it when you returned."

"It's not that simple, Olga. In fact, after all the trouble we've had, we're not supposed to be out alone. No one-on-ones." Trying to give himself time to think, he did not tell her that most of the guides ignored this rule. "We've lost three guides. And . . . and an American businessman has even been arrested in Moscow. The Sovs are saying this guy traded over 9,000 rubles on the black market."

"Papa cannot leave to visit his brother," she said, as if she had not heard Nick. "They wouldn't allow it. But my *babushka* . . . she is old and on a pension. It's expensive, but they'd let her go."

"They're afraid that we'll be compromised."

"An exit visa just to get out of the country costs six hundred dollars. And then there's air fare. But we can do it. I've been saving too. We just need my uncle to invite her officially; then we can start the paperwork here."

"Olga," said Nick, sharply. "I can't." Holding the bag under one arm, he lifted his arms up in a show of helplessness. "It would be dangerous. Two Soviet spies were arrested in New York and we've had—I've had—trouble ever since. They watch me a lot. In fact, I don't understand why I'm not being followed right this very moment." He paused, waiting for this frightening thought to strike her. But it didn't. "A lot of complaints have been written about me—they accused me of spreading propaganda in Dushanbe because I gave some friends a copy of *Time,* an American magazine. I never saw those people again. I don't know what happened to them. These are tough times between our two countries and you could get in serious trouble because of me. They threatened to kick students out of college just for coming to the exhibit and talking with us. My God, Olga, you could lose your job just because we're walking along the street."

Undaunted, she persisted. "I only want you to take a letter—a small present perhaps—just to let my uncle know that he should send an invitation."

"Why, why, why," said Nick, rolling his eyes, "does 'no' only mean the beginning of negotiations here!"

Olga, ashamed, turned her head away from him and was silent. Her thick hair, pulled over her shoulder, fell and blocked her face.

"I'm sorry. . . ." He touched her arm that was both soft and strong. "I'm sorry. It's just hard here at times. We're the only link many people have with the West and that gives us a great deal of power. Sometimes I feel like visiting royalty, and sometimes I think

I'm being exploited to hell. You're not the first to ask such favors."

"No, Nick, I apologize." Her eyes, dark and blue, focused on him directly. "I apologize for pressing this matter so impolitely. But I still ask this favor of you. It's very difficult, you know—to ask, I mean. But when you have so few alternatives you must never leave a stone unturned and, yes, you must exploit every opportunity." Furrows of flesh formed on her forehead. "Papa doesn't know of this plan of mine. He would disapprove of my asking. I am ashamed to stoop so low, but what choice is there? So I only ask that you think about it. Don't tell me now. Let's forget about it and get to know one another. . . . After all, you're the very first American I've ever met. In itself that is a very valuable thing . . . at least for me. Look," she said, a subtle smile brightening her face, "the café."

All he wanted was for her to back off and give him some time to think. Relieved, he said, "Here, this is for you." He handed her the Marlboro bag.

Her cheeks, high and wide, flushed red. "For me? Nick, you shouldn't have. Such a beautiful bag." Accepting it, she opened the bag and saw the *America* magazine inside. "Oh, this is interesting." She leaned forward and kissed him on the side of his face. "Thank you."

Her lips, thought Nick, lingered slightly too long yet not long enough. Her constant straightforwardness from their very introduction at the exhibit convinced him of her sincerity and now, with his guard down, he realized how much he yearned for close contact. He touched her briefly on the waist, feeling the soft cotton dress concealing a small ripple of flesh.

"You're welcome."

She motioned toward the restaurant. "Shall we?"

They descended the chipped steps, opened the door, and were struck by the harsh odor of ammonia.

Inside, Nick frowned and said, "Do you want something?"

"Coffee."

There were few people in the dimly lit café. Behind the counter stood a heavy blond woman with a half-dozen gold teeth and bright red lipstick. In a white smock and tall hat, she was picking her cuticles, not paying attention to anyone. In the cooler was champagne, sold by the gram. Alongside were slabs of cheese on black bread, stacks of hard rolls, meat *cutleti,* and glasses filled with sour cream.

Nick ordered two cups of coffee and a cheese sandwich. The woman grunted, blew on her nails, and poured syrupy sweet coffee into chipped cups. Moaning as if she were straining herself and doing Nick a great favor, she grabbed a dry, brown cheese sandwich and tossed it on a plate. Wrinkling her nose, she shoved it toward him.

"Thanks, sweetheart," said Nick. Disgusted, as always, with Soviet service, in English he added, "You do such nice work and wear such beautiful lipstick."

Though the woman didn't catch a word, rudely expressing himself in English was one of the ways Nick eased his frustrations. He cast the perplexed woman a cheap smile, and sat down with Olga at one of the dinette tables.

"Nick," said Olga, examining what he had purchased, "that's not enough. You must eat more. You don't want to get sick do you?"

Still annoyed by the saleswoman, Nick said, "My God, you sound like a *babushka.*"

"Oh." She blushed, but still looked at his scanty meal with disapproval.

Not wanting to talk much in a public place, they drank their coffee in silence. She pulled out the oversize *America* magazine, half-hid it under the table, and thumbed through it.

Massaging the paper between her fingers, she whispered, "Such high quality paper, such beautiful photographs. Is this typical?"

Nick nodded. "You bet."

She shook her head in disbelief. "This magazine is supposed to be sold openly, but it's very hard to get. I've only seen one or two before. You have to have . . . you have to have—"

"Blat?"

"Shhh." She laughed, surprised that a foreigner would know this facet of Soviet life. *"Da, blat."*

They spoke no more of the letter to Olga's uncle as they rambled slowly along the sidewalk. As the sun set, leaving a purplish sky in its wake, the last of summer's days gave way to the first of autumn's cool nights. Olga looped her arm in Nick's, not a sexual advance in Russia, but a sign of friendship and trust. Nick was flattered.

"So what is your profession?" asked Nick, steering the conversation to comfortable territory.

"I work in a film processing factory." She too was glad to forget about her uncle in New York.

"Do your parents live here, too?"

"No, my father has lived in Lvov for many years now, and . . ."

Nick sensed her arm tense in his.

". . . my mother is dead. I lived with my great-aunt for many years." She volunteered nothing further.

Nick threw his head back and inhaled the cool air. "Really?" He could not restrain a slight grin.

Noticing this, Olga frowned. She was confused and hurt that he was amused. "What . . . what is it?"

So that was what made her different, he thought to himself. He hesitated, and then said, "My mother died, too."

"Seriously?" Suppressing a smile of her own, she asked, "How?"

He coughed and cleared his throat before saying, "From cancer. I was ten." He searched her eyes for her reaction, only to realize that she hadn't been so much listening as looking at him. "How about yours?"

She realized what he was asking, and, turned away at once, and barely audible, said, "She was . . . run over by a streetcar." Quickly, to get it over with, she added, "I was thirteen."

"Olga . . ." He squeezed her arm. "I'm sorry."

She ventured nothing further, and by her reaction Nick guessed that the severance between mother and daughter had been most brutal. Perhaps, he speculated, Olga had even witnessed the accident. He pulled her arm tighter against his side.

They walked on, each of them slipping backward in time. Sensing this and not wanting to lose the present, Nick adopted an almost cheery tone.

"So tell me what you think of Kiev," he said.

"It's clean, green."

His reaction was reflexive. "Olga!" He stepped away. Berating her, he said, "Don't tell me what the Party says, tell me what you think."

She found it funny. "But this is what I think." She squeezed his arm in hers.

"Oh." Nick was confused. Was he developing a knee-jerk reaction to anything positive about the U.S.S.R.?

"Nick," said Olga, interrupting his thoughts, "have you been to the Monastery of the Catacombs?"

"I've had a lot of offers, but not yet."

"Good, let's go now. It's open late tonight. There's a bus that goes directly there from that corner."

"Sure."

He felt her warmth against him and he wanted to help her. How could he go wrong if he insisted on seeing her letter before taking it? He could help them. Who else would? It was just a family reunion, a family reunion that had been waiting thirty-five years. Here was a chance to really do something and to help someone. He should do it. After all, there wasn't any reason not to take the letter if it didn't contain anything troublesome.

"Where do we cross? Here?" asked Nick, his mind on Olga and the letter.

"Da."

Nick, preoccupied, stepped off the curb. She screamed just as he heard the car.

"Nick!"

He threw his head to the left. A light green taxi was heading straight toward him. All that he could focus on was the grill of the car as it raced forward. This is it, he thought, just as he had imagined it. A hood ornament on some fucking Sov car. He stepped back, but tripped as his foot reached for the curb.

"*Bozhe!* My God," screamed Olga.

He'd never guessed how strong she really was. In one forceful movement she latched on to his arm and jerked him up and onto the sidewalk. He fell backward on the concrete, and she lost her balance and fell a few feet beyond him. The taxi whizzed by only inches before them, its hubcaps brushing up against the curb. Sparks flew and there was the cry of screeching metal.

"Jesus!" cried Nick, covering his face from flying debris.

Then it was over, as quickly as it had begun. The taxi didn't stop or even slow. Its engine racing, the automobile disappeared around the next corner and left the odor of burnt rubber to foul the air. Olga was sprawled on the sidewalk gaping at Nick. Her cotton print dress was smudged with dirt and ripped in two places.

"Man, oh, man." Nick shook his head in disbelief. Sitting on the ground, he used his hands to edge himself farther away from the dangerous street.

Olga sat up. "Are you all right?"

"Thanks to you." He tried to shake loose a pebble that was imbedded in the palm of his hand.

Her brow was wrinkled and her eyes open wide. "What about your hand?"

"It's okay. It's just scraped." He glanced at her. "How about you, are you all right?"

She reached out for his hand, took it, and gently brushed away the dirt. "I'm fine."

He inched closer to her as they sat on the sidewalk. Their eyes caught and held. Olga shook a whisp of hair out of her face. Only as he was in the process of bending over did he question his action. And even though it was too late except to pull awkwardly away, he was aware that to stop now was the last thing he wanted. He watched her eyes drift shut and her chin raise slightly, more fully exposing her lips. He closed his eyes. As if they were testing cold water, their mouths met lightly, pulled away, and then came back to one another. Their arms reached out and they embraced. She opened her mouth and he kissed her. They kissed and held on.

"Stop that!" yelled a ratchety old voice.

They split apart. "Fuck," said Nick in English, able to guess the source of their problem.

"That's *ne-koolturni*—not cultured. You young people stop that!" cried a *babushka,* coming toward them and waving her flabby arms. "I won't have any of that on my street. *Ne-koolturni!* And get up off the sidewalk. How disgusting, sitting on the ground! You'll get sick. Up, up, up! Girl, don't you know you'll hurt your ovaries by sitting on cement?"

"Come on," said Nick. He reached out and helped Olga to her feet. "Let's go."

"Are you sure you're all right?"

"I'm fine. What about you?" They stood up and brushed themselves off. "Thanks again."

"Ne-koolturni! Ne-koolturni!" cried the *babushka.*

They walked for almost an hour, saying little and putting off the visit to the Monastery of the Catacombs. His arm around her, they made a large circle and covered many quiet blocks. Nick took in the night air and felt very distant from the exhibit, the United States, and even the Soviet Union.

Then, abruptly, he sensed something wrong even before Olga spoke. Her tranquil air slipped away, and he felt the stiffness, the tenseness, mount in her. She pulled away from him.

"Kreshatik is right down there." She was more nervous than he had seen her and she acted as if she had forgotten something. "You know the way back from there, I'm sure."

Not yet, he thought. "Wouldn't you like to get something to drink? Maybe we could find a bar or . . . or . . ." Nick was bewildered.

"I must be going, really. I . . . I . . ." She took his hand and pressed it to her cheek, then kissed it. "Nick, please don't feel obligated to . . . you know, take the letter to my uncle."

Her words were full of guilt. She had never said whether she was married or involved.

"I want to see you again, Olga. Soon."

She cast her eyes to the ground. "I must go now, but in several days I will come to the exhibit. Perhaps we can see each other . . ." She failed to finish the sentence.

"When, Olga, when?" He reached out for her.

"As soon as I can." She kissed him on the cheek, hesitated and then turned and started off.

"Good-bye!" he called out despondently.

"Yes," she cried without looking back, her pace quickening. "Until our next meeting!"

She slipped her arms into the gray sweater as she ran, and Nick watched confused and hurt. He watched until her blond hair and white dress were but a light blur in the dark night. Then she disappeared around the corner, and he clung to the fading sounds of her shoes as they clattered on the sidewalk.

Shoving his hands in his pockets, he turned in the direction of the Dniepro Hotel. If only she hadn't left so abruptly, he would have told her. Yes, he'd take the letter. Gladly. He'd even take a package and telephone her uncle if she wanted him to. Now, however, he'd have to wait . . . wait for Olga to come back to the exhibit. But when would that be?

A breeze picked up and Nick heard the fluttering sound of material. He glanced upward. Hung boldly across the street was a large red banner secured at its four corners to the apartment buildings on either side of the street.

The banner's crisp white lettering against its pure red background announced: LENIN IS ALWAYS WITH US.

VII

The chauffeur-driven black Volga sedan sped along carrying KGB Colonel Mayakovsky from Kiev's Borispil Airport to the evening meeting he had summoned. The car heaved upward as it hit a buckle in the pavement and crossed onto the bridge spanning the Dneiper River. Alone in the rear seat, Mayakovsky reached out with his gloved hand and braced himself.

Leaving the loamy plains behind, across the broad river he saw the right bank, its green rolling hills rising high above the water's edge. Breaking through the tree tops and silhouetted by the last of the day's light were the churches and cathedrals of the Monastery of the Catacombs. It was a scene fit for a postcard: the sky a lustrous orange, the sun too bright a yellow to behold, and the onion domes and towers of the monastery well-defined black images in contrast. Shielding his eyes from the light, Mayakovsky remarked that this same view had welcomed visitors to Kiev for hundreds upon hundreds of years.

Mayakovsky was not, however, a visitor to Kiev. Born and raised in the city, he was in the midst of a prodigious career in the Committee for State Security—the KGB—and was returning that night from a Kremlin meeting in Moscow. He had been in conference there since the moment he had flown in that morning. The topic was both urgent and irritating: retaliation against the United States for the incarceration of two Soviets in a Connecticut jail. It was of the most pressing relevance to Mayakovsky's current assignment—surveillance of the American guides during their stay in Kiev—and he was quite pleased with himself. The June arrest in Moscow of Frank Korman, the American businessman, had brought no results. The expulsion as personae non gratae several months ago of two of the exhibit guides had likewise not produced the desired effect. And neither had the seductive approaches of a handsome KGB agent toward the third guide; the CIA had caught on and spirited the woman out of the U.S.S.R. Mayakovsky had convinced the Kremlin, however, that his strategy would secure freedom for his two colleagues held in the U.S., and the Kremlin had given its approval to conclude the operation already underway.

The sedan heaved again as it flew off the other end of the bridge, causing Mayakovsky's hat to fall off the seat and onto the floor. The chauffeur deftly maneuvered the vehicle around several corners, and then accelerated to nearly twice the lawful speed. He paid no attention as they sped past a yellow police jeep, aware of the privileges provided by the colonel's stark license plate.

"Chauffeur, not so rough on the corners." Mayakovsky picked up his hat by its black plastic visor and dusted it off.

The driver nodded rigidly. "Does the Comrade Colonel wish to bypass the Dneipro Hotel?"

"No."

Mayakovsky straightened his olive green uniform and smoothed his light brown hair. On each shoulder of his jacket was a single metal Soviet star, and on the left side of his chest were six medals, pinned carefully there this morning for his trip to the Kremlin. In his mid-forties, his face was decidedly boyish, though in the last few years he had aged much; in another ten years his youthful appearance would be totally gone and he would look old for his time. Aloof by nature, Mayakovsky had a permanent crease in his forehead left by his persistent, critical scowl.

As they neared the Hotel Dneipro, Colonel Mayakovsky rubbed this crease with his fingertips, thereby obscuring his face. Though he doubted any of the American guides could spot him in the speeding Volga, it would be foolish to be any more lax. His reason was simple: his temporary office, which he visited every day dressed in ordinary street clothes, was not far from the site of the American exhibition. It was from there that he supervised the surveillance of both the American guides and the Soviet citizens who visited FARMING U.S.A. From the outside, the small tan building appeared to be nothing more than an ordinary place of work. Inside however, Mayakovsky directed the Soviet floor controller and the undercover agents who roamed freely through the exhibit. Ordinary Soviet citizens who misbehaved at the exhibition were brought to this place, also, for identification and interrogation purposes. And in the small room next to Mayakovsky's office was the monitoring equipment that recorded the transmissions from the bugs located in such places as the exhibit director's office, the guide lounge, and Nick Miller's irrigation stand.

The black sedan made a sweeping arc around the ring of larger-than-life portraits of Party officials. Leaving them, the Hotel Dneipro, and Komsomol Square in its wake, the chauffeured Volga drove Mayakovsky on to the special evening meeting.

Crowned with an abundance of needlelike antennae, the massive gray granite building rose abruptly from the street. Thick, stark columns lined the facade of the structure, the only edifice in the area that rose above the treetops, and the entrance was disproportionately small, as if to allow few in and even fewer out.

Instructing his chauffeur to wait, Mayakovsky proceeded directly to the sixth floor. The slapping of his black leather boots announced his arrival, and although he was late, the others would be there. The meeting, specifically regarding the American exhibition, was urgent.

A door at the end of the empty corridor popped open and Mayakovsky's longtime aide, Vishnyak, stepped out. He had a thin mustache and a diminutive frame, and he bowed his head only slightly.

"Good evening, Comrade Colonel," said the aide. "I trust you had a pleasant trip."

"Everyone is here?" Mayakovsky handed him his hat.

"Yes."

Hearing muffled voices emerging from the conference room, Mayakovsky paused in the antechamber. He coughed, once, twice, and when there was silence, the colonel nodded to his aide. Vishnyak took hold of the doorknob, turned it slowly, and then in a quick movement swung open the door. The five who had been waiting sprang to attention. The colonel entered briskly.

"Be seated, comrades."

He took his place at the head of the rectangular table, and his aide brought in a short stack of papers and placed them in front of him. Vishnyak left, gently shutting the door behind him.

Before Mayakovsky sat five men. On the right side of the table were the two in charge of plainclothes surveillance at the exhibit. Next to them sat their colleague in charge of surveillance of the guides at the Dneipro Hotel and of the electronic monitoring of their rooms. To Mayakovsky's left were two more; Police Chief Alekzander Alekzandrovich Petrovsky, who openly patrolled the area around the exhibit, and Lt. Viktor Yezhov, one of the Soviet crowd controllers.

"I called this meeting because a decision has been reached." Mayakovsky paused. "Those of you sitting here will play an important role in the execution of this vital plan." He looked at Petrovsky. Having once served beneath him and having now risen far above, the colonel knew Petrovsky to be efficient and dedicated. "The Korman trial will proceed." His eyes ran over the two plainclothesmen and the hotel operative. Good, unquestioning workers. "He will be found guilty of illegal currency exchange and speculation, and sentenced appropriately." It was obvious they approved. "We have struck once. And like a great, benevolent bear, we have struck kindly. The American government does not understand this, however, and their failure to heed our warning will be their demise.

Yes. We will strike again. And again. With precision. With bold regularity. You need not question. Our success will be most satisfying."

There was silence in the room, stillness from the street. He stared at Lieutenant Yezhov, whom he had chosen with reservation to work at the exhibit. As far as Colonel Mayakovsky was concerned, the lieutenant was too ambitious and too independent. Yezhov's impressive command of the English language had swayed the decision, though, and Mayakovsky, to appease himself, made a determined effort to keep a concerted eye on the young officer. It was the colonel's firm conviction that the only way to assure success was to take complete control of all the variables.

"We will strike closely this time. The target, you will be pleased to know, will be one of the insolent guides at the American exhibition." He scrutinized them all. They were satisfied. "The target: Nicholas Miller." Yes, satiated. Miller had caused more problems than all the other guides.

"He will be charged with a number of illegal acts of aggression against the Soviet people. A most pleasing aspect, of course, is that Miller is both an employee of the American government and without diplomatic immunity. This, of course, will enable us to put him on trial as a CIA agent . . . for illicit acts against the Soviet people." There was no need to say that he would be found guilty. "He will, accordingly, receive the proper sentence as an enemy of the State." Mayakovsky examined each of them. "We will strike and strike again until we are successful. This will be the beauty of our success. Korman, Miller . . . there will be others, if need be."

"We will not arrest Miller tonight," he said, continuing. "We will not arrest him tomorrow." Yezhov frowned, and the colonel disapproved of this independent display. "No, we will make no moves until the closing of the exhibit." Mayakovsky took great satisfaction in relaying this aspect, which he had personally formulated. "We do not wish to take action while the exhibit is still open, and the guides have a forum in which to speak." They had discussed this point at length in Moscow and Mayakovsky had forcefully stressed patience. If they were to arrest Miller now, there would be a large and vocal outcry from those "blundering and babbling idiotic guides." No, he had argued, it was wiser to wait until the guides had disbanded and packed up the exhibit and were on their random and ridiculously individualistic ways out of the U.S.S.R. Let the group split up. Make the arrest then, when there would be no support. The guides would have broken up and would be traveling through various parts of Europe. They would be, to the Soviet Union's benefit, unavailable for comment to the American government or to the Western press. "The arrest will come later. You will receive your orders at a future date." Mayakovsky never divulged more than necessary. By relying on no one, by trusting no one, he had always delivered complete success.

"For various reasons," he went on, "it was decided that in the other cities Miller should be aware of the fact that he was under observation. And he was aware of this. He knew, to his credit, almost the instant each time he was followed. However, it will not be so in Kiev. It is necessary for Miller to believe that he is now able to roam the city freely." His face taut, he wanted to be certain that they understood this point. "As you are aware, I have brought in one of Moscow's finest teams. Observation of Miller is totally restricted to them, and you are to do anything they—one woman, three men on foot, two by car—ask of you." Mayakovsky felt no need to explain anything further, not even that he had had Miller's friends' apartment bugged and that they would be forced to testify against Miller after his arrest. The dispersal of information and authority would only jeopardize the coordination of the operation. One director with complete control was the best alternative. "Therefore, until further notice you are not to take any action of any kind . . . absolutely none!" He emphasized this to Yezhov by catching his eye and holding it. "All of you are to continue your work . . . to continue observation of the Americans at the exhibit and at the hotel. But you will not act otherwise unless under my personal and direct orders. Is that clear?"

Silence.

"Good. You are to report any peculiarities you or your subordinates notice directly to me. The plan is solid. It is good. Let the Americans relax so that they expect nothing. This is when we will strike. Questions?"

Silence.

"Good. Dismissed."

The five men rose, saluted, and filed out of the room. Colonel Mayakovsky leaned back in his chair. It had been a long day, a victorious day.

"Vodka!" he commanded.

His aide brought in a glass of chilled vodka. He took the glass.

"Shut the door, Vishnyak, as you leave."

"Yes, Comrade Colonel," said the aide backing out.

Mayakovsky held the glass up to the light. Pure. Powerful. He was confident. Very confident. He had won the first battle by delaying Miller's arrest until his departure through Moscow. The events of Kiev were totally in his control, free of interference, and now he was able to get things underway as he saw fit. And that's the way it should be, he thought. After all, how could the vast and disorganized Moscow machinery pull off as stunning a victory as he could?

He put the glass to his lips and drank the refreshing liquid. It was sure to work. Besides, the best agent—his prodigy whom he had imbued with all of his beliefs and tactics—was working for him. Quite the willing student, she was as unique a person in her aptitude and sense of purpose as any he had ever seen.

Olga. Unknown to his subordinates here in Kiev and even to the Kremlin, he had great faith in her and the documents she was obtaining from the old woman. Planted on Miller, they would be most persuasive.

VIII

Just as he did every day after the exhibit, Lt. Viktor Yezhov took the trolley bus to the main subway station on Kreshatik. Dressed as a civilian, he carried his uniform and pistol packed neatly away in his briefcase; and, tall with a narrow frame, he walked with an air of superiority. From Kreshatik he took the Metro to the end of the line, got out in the new "microregion," and walked to his former wife's apartment, a small one-bedroom place in a featureless building surrounded by identical high rises containing identical apartments.

He was tired. After the meeting with Colonel Mayakovsky the night before, he had stayed up late thinking, and today the crowds had been heavy at the exhibit. Now he sat on a wobbly stool at the kitchen table, his briefcase at his feet, while his ex-wife, Sonia, and her parents entertained their guests in the living room.

Laughter and loud talk filtered into the small kitchen. They had prepared a sumptuous meal; Sonia had waited in line for two hours to get a slab of beef and her mother had used all the *blat* she could muster to obtain a tin of caviar. Already they had been at the table for nearly two hours and there was no end in sight. The occasion was a joyous one: Sonia and Mixhail, the guest, had announced their engagement.

Sonia's father, a handsome man of medium stature whose bald head was rimmed with a band of white hair, came into the kitchen humming the song "Moscow, My Capital." He half-danced toward the refrigerator, frolicking as one usually does only in complete privacy. He hated Yezhov and delighted in pretending that his former son-in-law was not and had not been sitting there for close to an hour. He flippantly took the freezer door handle by two fingers, clicked his tongue, and swung open the door. The older man, squinting impishly, snatched another bottle of chilled vodka and, happy that Yezhov would soon no longer be living with them, could restrain himself no more. He burst into song.

"*Moskva, stolitsa maya!*" Moscow, my capital.

"Andrei Pavlovich," said Yezhov with disgust. He lifted his steel-frame glasses and rubbed his face. "I beg you!"

But this caused his former father-in-law to sing louder, and Yezhov looked out the window in disgust. This was one of the new suburbs of the city, occupying the site of a former village and its surrounding sandy fields, and the twenty or so look-alike apartment buildings were packed around a worn, treeless courtyard. Yezhov neither hated nor liked the nine-story buildings, identical copies of which could be found in microregions outside of Moscow and Leningrad. Such a residence merely offered a private apartment in which to live, which was precisely why he had married Sonia three years earlier: with Sonia came her parents, with her parents came the apartment. It was simple: she was his ticket out of the cramped KGB dormitory and into a private dwelling.

Sonia's parents were not at all pleased when she and Yezhov married. Originally from a small Ukrainian village, he was a natural student of the English language and had been awarded a position within Kiev's KGB some years earlier. Always seeking a way to advance, he had rapidly risen to the rank of lieutenant by, at first, doing fine translations of tape-recorded conversations amongst foreigners, and, later, successfully associating with tourists: an Australian woman, whom he had taught to drink vodka the Russian way, was now raising his bastard son in Sydney. For too many years, however, he had lived in a men's dormitory, and when he had not been able to stand it any more, he had started hunting for a local bride. That is when he spotted Sonia at the bar above the Metro station on Kreshatik, and brought her a couple of vodka, champagne, and cognac cocktails. They announced their engagement a few days later—"The sooner the better," Yezhov had said, kissing her neck. "I just don't want to lose you"—and were married within two weeks.

Her parents recognized the opportunist in Yezhov. He was no worse than the others, however, and rather than see their only child move into the woman's dormitory adjoining Yezhov's they insisted that Yezhov and she live with them. Which is exactly what Yezhov had expected. He and Sonia, whom he had never loved and grown to loathe, readily welcomed the chance to reside in the living room.

The marriage had, in one simple stroke, solved the complex problem of housing for Yezhov. For single men from the countryside, a bed in one of Kiev's dormitories was viewed as an incredible opportunity; the likely prospect of waiting ten to fifteen years for a room in a communal apartment or, if later married, one's own apartment, was ignored. Yet for Yezhov, who had been raised in a single-family dwelling in the country and who was accustomed to home cooking, that was not good enough. He was able to overlook the fact that his family's log house did not have indoor plumbing, yet he could not forget the relative privacy it provided. He simply could not tolerate living in a room with five other men, the extraneous commotion, or the barely palatable food cooked on a kerosene burner. For Yezhov, the marriage had therefore made the first trying years of city life bearable enough so that he would not have to retreat to his backwater village. There, where his ancestors had been serfs, later rich peasants, and after the Revolution, bound, again landless, to the earth as workers on a collective farm, the outlook was bleak.

At first everyone was happy. Sonia's parents who, like all Soviet parents, had expected to support the newlyweds, were pleasantly surprised with the *blat* their new son-in-law acquired; they never had to spend another kopeck on their daughter again. Sonia, too, was thrilled with her husband's career and all the *kosmetiki* and *jeanzie* he was able to obtain; the years ahead, she knew, would be more and more full of such material luxuries as her husband continued his rise. And Yezhov was glad to be away from his village and in Kiev, where he was getting his foot further and further in the door of the KGB.

The bliss lasted eight months. They tolerated the situation for another year. And when Yezhov assumed that he had amassed enough influence to be given an apartment of his own, he divorced Sonia. Yezhov, however, had poorly judged his status at work and just how much *blat* a KGB lieutenant really had. While his work was commendable, his position was by no means important enough to secure an apartment of his own. He was quite coolly received when he applied for housing.

"*Nyet.* No apartments!" snapped the harsh-faced woman in charge of distribution. "For single men, either a dormitory or, if you're lucky, a room in a communal apartment."

Shocked, he refused both. After all, what had he come to the city for? The solution, of course, was the typical one: he would continue living with his ex-wife and her parents until he was given an apartment of his own. He gave Sonia the entire living-room couch and took the farthest corner for himself. Her parents balked at first, swallowing their pride and accepting only when Yezhov offered rent not in the form of rubles, but *blat.* They plainly did not want to go back to potatoes, cabbage, and long lines.

That, however, was a year ago and now Sonia was getting remarried.

"To your health, Mixhail Ilyich, and a long and fruitful marriage to my beautiful daughter!"

Yezhov heard joyous laughter and the clinking of glasses. They were all happy. For Mixhail it meant that he would be moving out of his parents' crowded one-bedroom apartment where his sister, her husband, and their baby also lived. For Sonia it meant that she would no longer have to sleep only a few feet from her detested ex-husband and that she would no longer have to tolerate his occasional mounting of her in the middle of the night. And for her parents, it meant that they would be rid of Yezhov without losing any of the luxuries to which they had become so accustomed. Mixhail, a staunch member of the Party, was a factory worker with a two hundred and fifty-ruble per month income and a sure future in management.

Everyone was happy, that is, except Yezhov. Sonia and Mixhail's marriage was to everyone's advantage excluding his. He was being forced to move out, yet he had nowhere to go. He flatly refused a dormitory or communal apartment.

He recognized Sonia's lithe step coming toward the kitchen and lit another cigarette. As if to spite him, she too hummed.

"You're a filthy whore," said Yezhov, a cigarette perched on his large lower lip. He inhaled the cigarette smoke and admired its flavor.

A brunette with heavy make-up and a waist that grew year by year, she came in laughing. "Perhaps. But that never stopped you, now did it?" With rapture and exaggeration, she continued her melody—the theme song from "The Godfather"—and reached into the refrigerator for a long, thick roll of prized salami.

"We both know why you're doing this."

Sonia stood up and, with one hand on her pronounced hip and the other pointing the salami at him, spoke matter-of-factly. "Yes, I suppose we do." She crossed through the tiny square kitchen and checked the hallway. When she was sure no one was coming, she leaned toward Yezhov. "But my darling Viktor, it was the only realistic way I could think of getting rid of you. I didn't want Mama and Papa to suffer for my errors. After all, you don't bite the hand that feeds you unless, of course, you have another choice. And Misha's a good man. I like him. He doesn't drink too much, he'll be a good father, and he'll always take good care of me. Oh," she said, laughing to herself, "and he's a better lover than you, too, and I must admit that has influenced me." Just then she spotted the briefcase at his feet and, her hands clenching, she tried not to express her true emotions. Inside the case was the gun, neatly packed away, that her husband always carried. The worst evening she had spent with Yezhov—and the one that made it clear she had to get rid of him—was three months ago. Her parents out for the evening, he had held that gun to her head, pinned her down, and, his body swelling with vodka, forced himself sexually upon her.

Now, determined not to be intimidated, Sonia slowly lifted up the meaty salami, admired it and to Yezhov said, "Yes, he's much better . . . much, much better." Proud of herself, she turned and sauntered down the hallway to rejoin the others.

Yezhov, the blood racing to his face, slammed his fist on the table. "Bitch!" He puffed madly on the cigarette, a Marlboro given to him by one of the guides.

There had been a time when he was quite good to her. That, of course, was in the beginning. Few were more considerate, loving, or generous. She had been the focal point of his future and of his career. Yezhov had turned to her in as kindly a way as he now turned to the guides at the American exhibition, his new hope for the future.

He filled his lungs with smoke. Held it. Then let it

slowly trickle out of his mouth. Here and there he saw lights pop on in the other buildings. From across the way came sounds of another drunken celebration, those of a birthday party, he guessed. From an apartment below blared the music of the rock group "Deep Purple." The record was scratched, the stereo of inferior quality.

Mixhail stomped in. Though he was as tall as Yezhov, his frame was larger and much more muscular. He had a pale Ukrainian baby face darkened with the shadows of a heavy, well-shaved beard. His hair was in disarray and his bulging eyelids were red.

"Cognac! I brought a bottle of cognac!" His intoxicated movements were quite erratic. "Where is it?"

Yezhov delighted in his cigarette and paid no attention.

"You! Where's my cognac?"

Gloating, Yezhov looked out the window. "I drank it."

"You what?" Mixhail frantically searched the counter, the top of the narrow gas stove, and the kitchen's single cabinet. "Hah. You did not. It's right here, right on the stool where I left it."

"She's a real bitch, you know." He took a drag on the cigarette. "And her parents are about as greedy as they come." Just in case Mixhail posed any problems, Yezhov let his hand drift down to his briefcase.

Putting both of his swollen hands on the table, Mixhail leaned forward. His voice lowered, smirking, he said, "You should hear what they say about you!" He burst into forced laughter, spraying saliva as he did so, scooped up the cognac, and headed back to the little engagement party.

Yezhov eyed his replacement with disdain, then

wiped up the few droplets of spit that Mixhail had projected onto the table top. He had to get out of there, out of that apartment. Soon. But under no circumstance would he return to the dormitory. That meant, naturally, that he would have to find some means of distinguishing his work and himself.

The American guides, thought Yezhov. Somewhere in the assignment lay the opportunity to excel, and the premium for Nicholas Miller would undoubtedly be the largest.

IX

Nick ground his teeth. Rather like a squirrel, he scratched his hair above his ear with quick, short movements. Then he rubbed his tired eyes. Two days. Would she come to the exhibit today? He shook his head. He had to stop thinking about Olga.

In front of him, on the modular wall of the guide lounge, was the scribbled list entitled "How are you turning into a Soviet?" Nick ran his finger down the list:

1. Seeing things and buying them in large quantities (I bought four jars of mayonnaise yesterday—who knows when they'll have it again)
2. Strutting in blue jeans
3. Drinking entire glasses of vodka without blinking
4. Being nasty to everyone except children
5. Getting in line without knowing what they're selling at the other end
6. Carrying around bags just in case I find something to buy

7. Asking people their nationality
8. Getting off on gold teeth

Nick took out a pen and added:

9. Calling someone comrade

"Not bad, Nick," said Linda, peering over his shoulder. She was one of the few guides he was close to; the months of huge crowds and long hours had put a strain on all the guides' relationships. "It's kind of creepy, isn't it? I mean the longer we're here, the less it's like looking in at the Soviet Union and the more it's like looking out at the rest of the world."

A few of the other guides seated in the guide lounge sipped their morning coffee and grunted in agreement.

She headed for the coffee percolater. "Can I pour you a cup?" she asked, getting one for herself.

Nick yawned. "You bet. It takes at least two cups to give me the energy to convince Sovs that rich American kids aren't the only ones who can afford college."

He liked her. Tall and thin and attractive, he found this young woman from southern California refreshing for her ability not to get mired in the U.S.A. versus U.S.S.R. rut. Her biggest complaint about the Soviet Union was that, either from the tension or the diet, the tight ringlets in her hair had vanished and her hair had become droopy. She was also rather creative: for escape she scoured the city in her free time looking for Soviet sunglasses. Thus far she had almost two dozen varieties, ranging from a pair with bright green lenses to ones with a silvery pointed frame.

Nick accepted the cup of coffee, took a sip and rolled his eyes in delight.

"God, this tastes good," he moaned, leaning on the

large percolator.

Back home he frequently took his first cup into the shower, letting the hot water rush over his back as he tried to prepare for the onslaught of a new day.

"Wow, you guys, listen to this," said John Kornichuk, a first generation American of Ukrainian extraction. He tugged on his right earlobe as he read a day-old *International Herald Tribune,* just arrived from the embassy. "A big Russian Orthodox Church official from Moscow died when he was in Rome. The Metropolitan of Leningrad and Novgorod."

"Was it natural," asked Nick, concentrating on his coffee, "or did someone do him in?"

"Huh?" Kornichuk, who spoke Russian, Ukrainian, German, Farsi, and a bit of Japanese, sometimes had trouble speaking plain English. "Oh, natural. Natural but weird. It says here that he was in Rome to congratulate the new Pope." He raised his head, puzzled. "Which pope? I've lost count—there's been a whole slug this year. Anyway, it says he was in audience with the Pope and he dropped dead, just like that." He tried to snap his fat fingers but couldn't. "He buckled over right in front of the Pope. A heart attack or something. And look at this," he said, reading further down the page, "there's a big technology fair coming up in Vienna. All sorts of computers, seminars, and so on. I wonder if they need any guides. . . ."

"Forget it, Kornichuk," said Mr. Thomas, the stocky, cigar-smoking exhibit director, coming in. "No technology fairs for you until we're finished here." He looked around and shouted. "Everyone in the guide lounge. On the double!" He had served in the army for a number of years. "Now . . . the doors don't open for another half hour but there's already a huge line out there. It's going to be hectic today at best, perhaps our busiest day yet. There are a good three thousand people in line already and more coming every minute. So I want you all to go out a bit early and clean up your stands. Do a good job and get ready for a mob. Make sure everything is nailed down good and tight. We don't need any more stuff stolen."

"I thought there wasn't any crime in the Soviet Union," said Nick in a taunting tone.

Mr. Thomas cleared his throat. "Excuse me, Nick. I mean we don't need to have any souvenir hunters take anything else."

Under his breath, to Linda, Nick whispered, "Like my windbreaker, your umbrella, or Randy's dictionary."

Mr. Thomas continued. "And make sure the exits aren't blocked. Do a good job. Watch what you say." He glared at Nick. "We don't need anyone spouting off. It's going to be crazy out there today. We'll do what we can for you. Good luck."

"It's showtime," groaned Linda as she got up.

Nick gulped his coffee too fast and it burned his tongue. "Shit." He fumbled with his cup, spilling some coffee on the floor. "Damn-it. This is probably some sort of sign that the KGB is after me."

Linda laughed. "Honestly, Nick. You and your 'Cagey Beasties.' You're so paranoid sometimes."

He mulled over her words and shrugged. "You never know. This might be the day they start gunnin' for me."

* * *

Almost fourteen thousand Soviet visitors had passed through the exhibit by one o'clock. Dreading the afternoon crowds, Nick wondered how many more they could possibly handle before the five o'clock closing. And he wondered how much longer he could take being cramped and pinned in by so many people. Sometimes it was almost like being buried alive. He shivered. It was enough to bring out the claustrophobic in him.

Nick crossed through the large, permanent Soviet building that housed the American exhibit, and hesitated at the door of the exhibit itself. He took a deep breath, opened it, and a thick cloud of stale, moist air—trapped by the tentlike canopies suspended over the entire exhibit—rolled out. Inside, like cattle on a truck packed tightly to prevent independent movement, Russians filled the room dangerously beyond capacity.

Anything but eager to enter the confining environment, he looked for a hole, a way in, and finally in Russian said, "Excuse me, I must get through." Nothing happened. In English: "Hey, you guys, I gotta get through to my fucking stand. Will you get the hell out of the way? Really now, move it!"

Upon hearing a foreign language, people turned and smiled. Several nodded and greeted him.

"You must get through?" asked one woman, smiling. "You are an American? *A-m-e-r-k-a-n-e-t-s?*"

Nick nodded and the woman, without further question, took him by the arm. She forced the way open for him.

"Out of the way!" she shrieked. "Move so this foreigner can get through!" She clenched her fist and pounded on those who wouldn't move. Then she turned to Nick. "There, *molodoi chelovek.* You go do what you have to—you can get through now. And thank you for coming to visit us."

Speaking English when necessary to clear a passage, Nick made it through the sea of visitors to the country music stand. As always, there was an enormous crowd straining to acquire as much information as possible about the institution that, for every age group, surpassed *jeanzie* in popularity: American music.

Over the heads of the visitors, Nick called out to the guide whom he was relieving. "Okay, Randy, you're off. I'm on."

Randy was the tallest of the guides, and his lanky body swayed as he rose. Beads of sweat dotted his forehead and trickled down into his blondish hair.

"Thank God." He leaned against the wall for support. "I'll bet you in the last hour at least fifty people have asked me how difficult it is to get a record in America. And at least twenty people have asked me how many meters are on each of these damned eight-track tapes. Fuck, what do they want to know that for?" Randy moved aside as Nick stepped up onto the stand. "Take it away. God, do I need to lie down."

Nick pulled out the chair and sat down. On the wall behind him were posters of country music stars, sequin-studded singers with dazzling white smiles. On the counter in front of him was an eight-track carousel tape player, the kind used in American restaurants to provide hours of nonstop music. And on the other side of the white formica counter, pushing and straining to get closer, were well over a hundred Russians and Ukrainians. Only the luckiest had managed to wedge themselves right against the counter and they guarded their positions adamantly.

Separated a few feet by the table top, Nick scanned the people in front and those, standing on their toes, who peered in from behind. Each person's eyes were constantly shifting from side to side, and up and down. Drinking in all the information they could, the visitors were making precise mental lists of the clothes the singers in the posters were wearing, the type of watch Nick had, his blue jeans, and anything at all about the mysterious tape player, including its two speakers.

Their faces, however, were blank. Some bit their lips, others clenched their jaws, but nothing more. It was a strong Russian characteristic to take note of things visually but to keep verbal public expression to a bare minimum. And this they did. Only the eyes darting from Nick to the tape machine to the posters betrayed their intense curiosity. Nick knew that all he had to do was cast them the faintest signal—an apathetic smile, a weak hello—and, like water from a burst dam, he would be inundated with questions.

Nick turned up the music. Like the counter, it was another barrier. A Western singer blared away to the accompaniment of a steel guitar, and Nick prayed that the imposingly loud music would stifle the chance of being queried. How much, thought Nick, could he give them? He could tell them everything he knew, describe his life in minute detail, give every fact and statistic about America he'd ever heard, and still it would not be enough. More, more, more, they would demand.

Then it happened. The icebreaker. One tape finished, popped up, and the entire carousel rotated until it gobbled up the next tape. Astonished gasps arose from the audience.

"Oi!"

"What was that?"

"My God, Sasha, did you see?"

Someone daringly called out: "Again! Make it do it again!"

"Da, da!" came the approving echo. "Again, again!"

"Oh, shit," said Nick, smiling to himself. "Why not?"

He pressed the reject button and the tape machine repeated its magic: one tape popped up, the carousel spun to the next, and another tape was pulled down into the play position.

"Amazing!"

"Marvelous."

"Incredible. Now that . . . that's technology."

"Okay," said Nick, conquered by their innocent charm. "What can I tell you?"

An embarrassed hush fell over the crowd; the spontaneity was gone and it seemed that no one would speak up. But then one man coughed, and it was all the prompting they needed. The questions came rapid-fire, one overlapping the other.

"What groups are popular in America?"

"How much does a record cost in the United States? Are they in shortage?"

"Yes, tell us how hard records are to get."

"Are stereos terribly expensive? Thousands and thousands of dollars? Are they hard to get too?"

"What concerts have you been to? Can only the rich, important people get tickets, or can anyone get them?"

"Do Americans like Russian rock music as much as we like yours?"

"What's the latest from Ella Fitzgerald?"

"Yes, tell us all about Ella!"

Without a pause, the questions went on until a sharp, stern-looking woman quieted the others, and said, "Don't you get tired of answering all these questions?" She had orangish-blond hair and a dab of green iodine on her cheek.

"That's an understatement if I've ever heard one," said Nick, stretching. "This is our third city and going on 700,000 Soviet citizens have visited the exhibit. What's hardest is answering the same questions over and over again." Nick thought for a moment. Most of all he like being candid to the point of blunt with the visitors. "There's a great deal written about my country here, but most of it is one-sided. Countering that with any credibility is very frustrating because, it seems, most people automatically class me as an agent of the U.S. government and of the CIA."

Eyebrows were raised. The Russians were taken by surprise that Nick so freely spoke of the feared American agency, which, for them, carried the same reputation that the KGB did for Americans. No one countered Nick's self-incriminating statement, however, and feeling awkward, Nick turned to the woman.

"So how about an original question?" he asked, trying to get out of the limelight.

The woman, flattered by the attention, wet her lips. "Oh, me?" She shed her harsh expression, cast herself into deep thought, and then said, "You . . . you stand up and get some fresh air. Let me think. You take a little break and let me think. You're working too hard with all these questions."

Nick had never been so mothered, either by friends or complete strangers, as he had been in the Soviet

Union. He stood up, and from his vantage point looked out over a mass of people so dense that none of the displays themselves were visible. Before him was virtually nothing but a solid assemblage of bobbing heads: some bald, some not; some natural blonds, some terribly dyed rust-colored ones; many kerchief-covered, a few without. Every inch of floor was occupied by people clamoring to get a glimpse of something, anything, that would give them a clue of the outer world.

To the left Nick caught sight of someone jerking his head. It was Boris, obviously afraid to wave or shout, but trying very hard to get his attention. A moment later Nick saw Masha and Baba Genya briefly appear in a gap in the crowd, and they too signaled an eager, yet subdued, greeting. Nick had telephoned them the night before, and they had mentioned their plans to come to the exhibit as well as their wish to take Nick sightseeing. He nodded in return, and they understood the signal and melted back into the crowd. They would meet as soon as Nick was able to get away from the stand.

Nick sat down. The woman was still there, with a finger to her mouth and thinking hard.

"So, do you have a question?" asked Nick.

As if the woman had shed her protective outer shell, she now let show her warm, friendly inner feelings. "Well." She blushed. "I have many questions, though I do not know how original they are."

"Ask me anything."

"All right." She cocked her head to the side and, with deep curiosity, said, "What's your nationality?"

Though it was by no means original—the most original question had been when someone had asked Nick in front of two hundred people, if he were circumcised—it was his favorite of the standard questions. Forgetting what he should and should not say, he couldn't resist manipulating this simple conversation into a provocative one.

"My nationality is American." He was fully aware that this was not what the woman had in mind.

"Yes . . . but what is your real nationality?"

"American." Nick took a deep breath. Once tapped, this conversation, like a loose thread being pulled and pulled without ever ending, would lead from one topic to the next.

"No, you don't understand me." She bit her chipped fingernail as she thought how to rephrase the question. "Your nationality . . . English, German, French?"

"I'm American, but my ancestors were from Europe." He was ready to make his point.

"Da, da," she said, eager to break through the language barrier. "What is the nationality written on your documents?"

Bull's-eye.

"Documents?" said Nick, feigning confusion. "We have no documents."

It was such a foreign concept that it was impossible for her to grasp it. "What?" she was incredulous. "No . . . no internal passports?"

"None. My government doesn't by law require identification."

"Nothing?" she was speechless. "But, but—"

"Nothing."

She burst into a nervous laugh and searched the people to her side for help. "But how do Americans get by?

How do people know who you are?''

''I tell them who I am.'' Nick felt a tinge of guilt for playing with her. She was fascinated, though, as was everyone else who could overhear the conversation. ''We have no work books either, where we are required to record every place of employment. I am a citizen of the United States and therefore my nationality is American. My ethnic background is another matter and only of personal interest—it has never been and, I hope, never will be noted by my government.''

Half-talking to herself, trying to make sense of it all, she explained, ''But we have internal passports and we must record our citizenship—Soviet—and our nationality. I am Ukrainian. I thought every country was like that, but . . .'' In all sincerity, she looked up at Nick. ''But without an internal passport here we will not be given a residency permit to live in a city, we will not be given an apartment, and we will not be given a job. Are you absolutely sure you have no documents, no passports?''

''Wait,'' said Nick, lifting his finger. ''I said we have no internal passports,'' For full effect, he pronounced his next words with great care. ''We do, however, have to have passports when we . . . travel abroad.''

The crowd was stunned. Finally a young man spoke up.

''Travel?'' he asked, suspiciously. ''Can Americans travel out of their country? Freely, I mean.''

Nick smiled to himself. Even though this was precisely the type of thing that angered the Soviet authorities—they wanted him to stick more to agriculture and less to such inflammatory issues—he couldn't resist. And for the next half-hour he was bombarded with questions about travel abroad. Who can get a passport to go outside the country? Can only the rich and influential? Whose permission must you get to leave the country? How many hundreds of dollars does an exit visa cost? Must you tour with government-sponsored and approved groups? How many dollars are you allowed to take out of the country? Where are you permitted to go and how long does your government permit you to stay out of the country?

Nick was besieged by an uninterrupted flow of questions about identification and travel until another guide relieved him at the end of his shift.

"Thank God," said Nick as he stood. He stretched and as he searched the exhibit for Boris and Masha, his eyes met Olga's.

Nick stepped off the guide stand and pushed through the overwhelming crowd. Without the slightest facial expression, their eyes caught once, lingered momentarily, and he knew it was enough. Nick went to the side wall covered with the enlarged photograph of a tomato harvester, confident that she was only a few paces behind. At the wall, he pressed his shaking finger on the picture as if he were pointing something out. It seemed forever before she was standing by his side.

"I apologize for leaving so quickly the other night," she said, facing the photograph.

People swarmed around them. Someone bumped into Nick and he looked at the man distrustfully.

"Is everything all right, Olga?" He was both relieved and excited that she had come back to the exhibit. "I don't want to make any problems, but

I'd . . ."

Olga reached out, hesitated, and then touched the photograph with the tip of her long finger. She moved it slowly as if she were tracing the outline of the pictured tractor. When she reached the tractor's front wheels, her hand brushed Nick's. He wanted to touch her, to talk freely with her, but he knew he couldn't. Not here at the exhibit, anyway.

"Will you meet with me again?" asked Olga.

"Of course." He detected something melancholic in her. "When?"

"Tonight. Same place, same time?" She had a sad air about her, and her deep blue eyes stole a glance at him. Resting her hand momentarily on his arm, almost as if she were pleading, she said, "Will you?"

"Sure." If it hadn't been so stuffy, Nick would have sworn he was blushing.

Olga set off without further word. Almost as if she were ducking underwater, she dove into the crowd and disappeared. Uplifted and hopeful, though of what he wasn't sure, Nick started off in the opposite direction toward the irrigation stand.

Whether they cared to or not, people were barely moving through the exhibit, carried along in a solid mass from the moment they stepped into the hall until they were dumped out the exit. If the masses for some reason panicked now, it was clear to Nick that he would be trampled to death on the spot.

Someone latched onto his shirt and pulled.

"Hello." The voice was muffled.

It was Boris, Masha at his side, struggling not to be carried away. They both wore the jeans Margie had sent.

"Over there." Nick motioned toward an overlooked corner that was like the tranquil area behind a rock in a stream.

Huddled in this obscure part of the exhibit, Boris said, "When can we meet again?" His eyes rested only briefly on Nick. Otherwise they constantly scanned the room for fear of someone watching.

"How about tomorrow?"

"Good," said Masha, eagerly taking him by the wrist. "Come for dinner. We'll go sightseeing first."

Nick checked about. "I'll look forward to it." If Boris were worried, maybe he should be, too.

"Tomorrow evening," said Boris, "at 6:30. Same place."

"I'll be there."

"So many people, Nick." said Masha, gazing at the great magnitude of people. "It must be difficult work. So, so many people. We had to wait four hours in line just to get in."

Nick looked around. "I thought I saw Baba Genya."

"She went out," said Boris. "Not enough air."

"I've got to get to my next stand. Besides . . ."

"Yes," agreed Boris. "It's best not to stand here too long."

"Until our meeting " Masha smiled with excitement.

Viktor Yezhov watched from the other side as the guide, Nick Miller, spoke with two young Russians. He couldn't see their faces until they turned, and even then his view was obscured by the other visitors passing by. Pushing aside a *babushka,* he leaned to the left and got a good look: a tall, thin man with dark hair, and a short pudgy woman with a clean, wide face and pointed nose. Yezhov closed his eyes in concentration. He would remember the two faces, just as he would be sure to remember the woman with the thick blond hair who had spoken with Miller a few minutes earlier.

Quickly, Yezhov worked his way through the crowd to a predetermined spot near the irrigation stand. Near the spinning lawn sprinkler display, he leaned up against the wall, and tried to appear bored. He was quite pleased with himself. His estimation was correct: Miller passed by moments later.

By design, none of the guides knew he spoke fluent English, so in Russian, Yezhov cried, "Nick, so busy!" He laughed and slapped the American on the back in a jovial manner.

Miller was distressed, and his words were sharp. "What do you want?"

"You must be very tired by now," said Yezhov sympathetically.

Above the din of thousands of people, a woman's voice cried out in English. "Jesus Christ, Nick, would you get the hell over here?" It was Martha, the guide on the irrigation stand Nick was to replace. "I'm about to collapse."

In English he shouted back: "I'm trying to, Martha, but this yo-yo just latched on to me."

Yezhov had gotten everything—though he didn't know the precise meaning of the derogatory word, it was obvious that it wasn't complimentary—yet as if he hadn't understood a word, in Russian he asked, "What's the probelm?" He opened his eyes innocently and pulled Nick aside. "You're the only guide I like.

The others have no spunk.'' He took off his steel-frame glasses and cleaned them. He leaned toward Nick and intimately said, ''Can we meet sometime? I'll show you beautiful, green Kiev.''

''Listen,''—Nick's impatience was showing—''I'm supposed to relieve the guide at the irrigation stand and I'm already late.''

When Miller started to walk away, Yezhov again took him by the arm. ''Just tell me when we can meet. I'll get a bottle of vodka and the two of us will have a good heart-to-heart talk.'' Yezhov checked around like a conspirator, and in a whisper said, ''I want to hear all about America.''

Nick was openly irritated. He broke loose. ''We'll see.''

''Good, good,'' called out Yezhov as Miller walked away.

Yezhov had to suppress his satisfaction. One of the other controllers had just reported a Jew who had made an anti-Soviet statement. Yezhov, however, wasn't goint to tell Mayakovsky about the young Russian couple or the blond he had seen talking with Miller. He wouldn't report his own possibility of meeting with Miller, either. Not yet, anyway. The compensation wouldn't be big enough.

No. He would wait until he had definite information that could be used more conclusively against Miller. And somehow, just somehow, Yezhov was sure he'd be able to get something substantial. Patience. That's all that was required.

X

The electric trolley bus hummed along as it carried the last stragglers from the American exhibit to the center of Kiev. Some sat thumbing through the colorful brochure they had been given, *Agriculture in the United States,* with its patchwork cover; the article inside on private land was as foreign to them as the one on fast-food restaurants, complete with glossy photos. Other passengers on the trolley were content to blankly stare out the window into the darkening night. There was much to digest, much to contemplate. Undoubtedly, the American exhibit presented much propaganda—it was, after all, a government exhibit—but it also contained startling information that could not be ignored.

The new and already deteriorating high rises of Kiev's outskirts gave way to the older, denser, and shorter buildings of its center. It was almost seven o'clock when the trolley crossed the end of the Red Army Street, passed the large granite statue of Lenin on Shevchenko, and eased onto the broad, bustling head of Kreshatik Street. Evening shoppers, hoping to find the last of the day's goods, wearily searched the city's main stores. They emerged hollow-faced on the swarming sidewalks, carrying in worn string bags what groceries and merchandise they had been able to find.

With the briefcase containing his uniform on his lap, Yezhov was on this trolley bus, returning late from the exhibit. Occasionally he was called on to translate something found at the exhibit—a book, magazine, or letter. Tonight he had worked past his regular hours translating a recorded conversation, from English into Russian, that had been picked up by a microphone planted near the tractor display. Concerning nothing more than hockey in the United States, the conversation had taken place between a guide and a visitor who had wanted to practice his English.

The trolley's electric motor wound down as it slowed in front of the large, enclosed farmers' market on Bessarabskaya Square, the first stop on Kreshatik, and Yezhov considered getting off. He wanted to buy some hard sausage, and one of Kiev's largest stores, Central Gastronom, was nearby. He abandoned the idea, however, when he recalled his experience of the previous week.

"Sausage?" the white-smocked saleswoman had shrieked in disbelief. "Sausage—*nyet!* Meat—*nyet!* Eggs—*nyet!* We sell out before ten in the morning, every morning. Haven't you ever shopped before?"

It was true. He hadn't. He had hardly ever gone to the store for food. He had supplied Sonia and her parents with a good deal of meat, butter, and, occasionally, corn oil or fruit. But all of that he had acquired through *blat.* Sonia and her mother had always done the rest of the shopping. And all of the cooking.

But now things had changed. Sonia and her parents had stopped inviting him to the table, and tonight they were sure to have eaten long ago. Yezhov even suspected that Sonia would have made sure that there were no leftovers in the house except a few onions, garlic, and, if he were lucky, some stale black bread.

"Just be thankful," Sonia had said a few days earlier, "that we haven't thrown you out already. But you'll be sleeping on a bench at the train station soon enough, that's for sure."

Time was running out. Yezhov knew that only too well and he cringed. He'd heard of a room for rent in a widowed *babushka's* apartment, but other than that, he had no leads. He hated even the thought of a dormitory or communal apartment, and he'd get a room in a hotel before he'd sleep at the railway station. So what was he to do? Wait. Wait until the American exhibition was over.

Yezhov, briefcase in hand, got up from his seat as the trolley approached the main Metro station, the second stop on Kreshatik. This was where he transferred every night to the subway, which he rode the rest of the way to Sonia's. Stepping forward as the bus rolled to a stop, he glanced out the window and onto the busy plaza in front of the station. At that instant a woman on the sidewalk caught his eye. He couldn't see her face, but he knew she was familiar. Important even. It was her hair.

"Are you getting out?" Yezhov pushed past a boy.

He took hold of one of the chrome poles and bent his tall body over. Looking out the fingerprint-covered glass of the trolley, he still couldn't see her face. He licked his large lower lip. Why was this woman familiar? He hurried to the front of the bus, knocking an old woman off balance.

"Molodoi chelovek!" Young man, cried the *babushka,* striking him with her purse. *"Ne-koolturni!"* Uncultured.

The woman on the sidewalk turned and climbed up the steps to the plaza. She was heading toward the Metro when Yezhov remembered. Yes, he knew her. Exiting from the front, he shoved aside a man with a knapsack, jumped off, and raced after her. She was ahead, up on the plaza, weaving in and out of small, tight groups of people trading cigarettes and jeans. Then he lost sight of her. He bounded up the steps and dodged around an ice cream stand. Where was she? He had yet to see her face directly, but he was sure it was her. It had to be. The cascading blond hair. Where was she?

There. Swinging open one of the big glass doors to the Metro. Yezhov ran ahead. He would lose the woman if she hurried down the escalator and jumped on a train before he had time to catch up.

He threw open the door with one hand as he crammed his other into his pocket for a five-kopeck piece. But no sooner had he crossed the station's threshold than he came to an abrupt stop. He spun to the side, head down and one hand fidgeting with his glasses. There she was, the blond woman, standing by the turnstyles at the top of the escalators. She was leaning over the railing, apparently searching for someone coming up from the train.

Yezhov caught his breath and glanced over his shoulder as he walked to a bank of change machines on the opposite wall. He deposited a coin in one of the machines and then banged it with the heel of his hand. He put more money in and hit the metal box again. He was unsure of what to do next, not wanting to lose her yet fearful that she would notice him. It was her, though, of that Yezhov was positive. It had just taken him a few minutes to place her.

A continual stream of evening shoppers entered the subway building, pushed through the turnstyles, and rode the long escalators down to the trains. Even more emerged from below, on their way to Kreshatik's stores. Only the blond woman, a nearby buxom stationmistress in a tight, prim, black uniform, and Yezhov remained constant in the building. Yezhov, out of frustration, hit the machine one time too many.

"Comrade citizen," called out the stationmistress in a stern voice, "is there a problem?"

Realizing his error, Yezhov shook his head and froze. He dared not face the stationmistress, for the blond woman might be looking at him, too. Through the large sheets of glass, he spotted a row of gray telephone booths outside. He gathered his change and hurried out.

Yezhov chose the booth that allowed him the best view of the Metro entrance. Stepping into the booth, he closed the door behind him, picked up the receiver and placed it to his ear as if her were making a call. He leaned against the back wall and through the Metro's glass doors watched the blond woman. One moment she was straining to see down the escalator, the next she was peering out the doors and onto the plaza. From his vantage, he had a clear view of her, and now Yezhov needed to decide his next move and just how far he should go. Telephone in hand, it occured to him that he should call Colonel Mayakovsky. But what was there to report? As of yet, nothing. The woman was obviously meeting someone—she seemed not to know from which direction to expect her guest—but who would it be? Her husband, boyfriend, or mother? And where would they go?

The frown on the blond woman's face disappeared, replaced by a welcoming smile. She stepped away from the escalator, pulled her hair back behind her head, and straightened the beige skirt she wore. Her eyes fixed on the stairs, Yezhov saw the woman mouth a greeting to someone coming up. Then the man she was waiting for rose into view on the mechanical stairs. First the light brown hair. Then the eyes, the green eyes, of that Yezhov was sure. The American clothing—a plaid shirt and corduroy coat—confirmed it all. Of course. How stupid of him. Why hadn't he realized it sooner? She had been waiting for Nick Miller.

Miller greeted the Russian woman with a brief kiss on the cheek, to which she responded by blushing. A discussion of some sort ensued. There appeared to be a disagreement on Miller's part. He was hesitant, she encouraging. They did not go back down to the trains. Finally the blond woman went to the exit and subtly motioned him after her. Miller, at first clearly perplexed, gave in with a smile that showed many of his white American teeth. Together he and the woman started across the plaza.

Yezhov remained in the telephone booth studying the Metro station. He observed each person who came out, yet even his trained eye could not detect what he was looking for. Next he scrutinized the plaza, wondering if perhaps someone could be dodging in and out of the clusters of people. Or maybe it was one of the ice cream vendors? His attention focused on a side alley; would anyone appear? Finally, unable to discern if another agent were following Miller, Yezhov started out. Miller and the woman had already reached the street and Yezhov had no intention of losing them.

He found them up ahead on Kreshatik's upper walk, which ran along the storefronts. Separated by a band of grass and a row of linden trees, Yezhov stuck to the lower sidewalk, keeping an eye on them and examining Volgas, Moskviches, light green taxis, and all other vehicles. Seated in tempting positions along the benches was a row of prostitutes, and Yezhov checked over each one of them; they, however, misinterpreted his interest and cast him seductive glances. Farther along he observed a couple admiring shoes in the window of Shoe Store Kiev. Next he suspected the woman carrying the tattered, plastic Finnish shopping bag with a naked frozen chicken poking out. Even the man with the son wearing a red Pioneer scarf did not escape Yezhov's scrutiny. And several blocks later, when Miller and the woman passed the store, Modern Woman, and turned left off Kreshatik, Yezhov was forced to admit it. To his amazement, Miller was out alone, meeting with a Soviet woman, and there was no agent following him.

He couldn't make any sense of it. He considered contacting Colonel Mayakovsky and he might have had there been more time. Sensing that this might be the opportunity he had been waiting for, however, Yezhov was not about to give it up so readily. At least not until there was something substantial to report. If any problems did develop, Yezhov knew that he could always claim that he had not called in because he did not wish to lose Miller and the woman.

Yezhov was equally surprised that they were so easy to follow. At one point he even overheard them laughing. Only Miller glanced back once as they led a clear trail to their destination. They turned left at the farmers' market, cut up a small side street, and briskly walked up the steep hill above Kiev's main street. They continued for three more blocks, turned right, then left, and arrived at Number 14 Revolutsiya Street.

Yezhov waited several minutes before cautiously entering the old five-story building and did so only when he could hear their footsteps on the staircase several floors above. The foyer was dark, in disrepair, and reeked of urine, some drunk having relieved himself in a corner the week before. Yezhov edged forward. The staircase was open in the center, and the chalky walls glowed with the light of a naked bulb. Above, as Miller and the woman climbed, he could make out their hands sliding upward on the banister. With the only sound that of their shoes slipping into the wells worn in the staircase, they went to the very top floor. Yezhov was disturbed by the ensuing silence until the soft sound of a door opening and gently closing filtered down. Next came a coarser noise; a whole string of grunts and groans tied together with heavy breathing. On the banister Yezhov saw the shriveled hand of a *babushka* laboriously working downward. He backed away.

Near the front door Yezhov searched for a name. With the light faint, and the white walls having turned to a sepia brown, he was unable to see much and ran his hand along the wall. A mailbox. There had to be a mailbox. Above his blind fumbling he heard deeply strained, asthmatic breathing. He froze.

"I'm looking for my friend." Yezhov could barely make out the *babushka's* jowly face in the dim light. To make it worse, the woman was dressed entirely in black, including her kerchief. He wondered how she got down so fast. "Ivanov. Ivanov, Yakov. Do you know him? I'm lost. Is this his building?"

With a look of distrust on her waxen face, the *babushka* shook her head. Her globular double chin quivered.

"Oh. It must be the next street over."

The old woman stared at him in the dark. Though perhaps heavier than he, she was much shorter. She was not intimidated, however, and as if she were frightening a crow away from her garden, she jerked up her arms.

"Yes," said Yezhov, backing out. "I remember now. The next street over."

He hastened up the street, sure that the *babushka* was checking on him. He turned once, and she was there, a hand cupped over her eyes, guarding her building. He went around a darkened corner, then peered back. The old woman had given up and was hobbling off in the other direction.

Yezhov crossed the street and resting his briefcase at his feet, positioned himself beneath a large chestnut tree. He had an unobstructed view of Number 14 Revolutsiya Street, a pre-Revolutionary building whose ancient yellow plaster was falling off like great scabs. On the top floor there was only one light on and it came from the room with the balcony.

Yezhov had forgotten about his hunger and did not feel the weariness in his bones. On the contrary, he was excited and encouraged. Leaning against the thick tree as the last of the day's light faded, he was determined to wait and see how long Miller stayed and to obtain any other information he could—information, absolute and incriminating, that Yezhov could then use to make an impressive report.

Five minutes later, as if to make things blatant, Miller and the blond woman stepped out on the balcony.

XI

Motioning outward and hoping that Nick appreciated it, Olga said, "It's a good view, don't you think?"

Over the treetops, past the pitched red metal roof, and down the hill was Kreshatik and Kiev's center. Silhouettes of pre-Revolutionary and Stalinist buildings, both classical in form and severity, filled the rolling horizon. A flurry of lights popped on as the last of the day's light slipped away.

"It's not bad," said Nick, wanting to like it for Olga's sake. "But that sign's got to go." He pointed to a neon GLORY TO THE COMMUNIST PARTY OF THE SOVIET UNION sign that glowed red in the distance. "In the States we use neon to push hamburgers and fried chicken, not doctrine."

She laughed and fell silent.

Alternately rubbing his hands together and snapping his fingers, Nick hadn't stood still for a moment. By all rules he was not supposed to be out alone with a Soviet, particularly with one of the opposite sex, and here he was in her apartment, lured there by the promise of "good Russian cooking."

He took a deep breath. "You know, it's nice to be here, away from the exhibit and the hotel."

She smiled, yet did not look at him. "Good. That's why I asked you."

Nick leaned on the rusted wrought-iron railing.

"No!" Olga grabbed him, sinking her fingers into his forearm. "The view's nice but the railing is awful. It's old." She pulled Nick back and shook the railing. Bits of rusty metal and crumbled brick cascaded to the street below, landing on the pavement with dull thumps.

Olga took a step away from him. She raised her eyebrows, and said, "Relax. Don't be so nervous." But gone was her self-confidence and she too trembled. "Let's go in," she said, not wanting him to notice. "I'm . . . cold." She wrapped her arms around herself to ward off the evening chill.

Olga had a narrow room in a communal apartment. On each side of the room were two plain desks, two small closets, and two plain single beds. Olga seated herself facing him on the other bed, an awkward empty space now between them.

Nick was disturbed when he realized that he didn't know if Olga was married. Maybe she even had a kid.

"Olga," said Nick, masking his concern with a disarming smile. "Are you married?"

She reddened. "No." She sat stiffly on the bed. "I have a roommate. She's away on vacation now."

"I see." He figured there was no sense in stopping now. "Are you involved with someone . . . a man, I mean?"

"Nick." She winced, unaccustomed to such directness. "No." she said, as if she were ashamed. "No, there's no one."

"Oh."

Before he could ask why she had so abruptly left the other night, she interrupted the lull in their conversation.

"This was my roommate's parent's apartment and she grew up here with them—all three in this room. They waited in line fifteen years for a new apartment, and finally they were given one in a new high rise on the edge of town. It has a bedroom, their own living room, and a kitchen and a bath too. Nadya—that's my roommate—got married just before her parents moved. She was tired of living with them. She's never said so, but I think she got married just so she could keep this room." Olga reached over to the desk and took a brush. "Anyway, she got divorced last year and I moved in. You know what a communal apartment is, don't you?"

"Sure." Nick guessed she was elaborating on the subject to avoid any more personal questions.

Olga ran the brush through her thick and somewhat tangled hair. "This is a nice one. There are five families here and everyone gets along cordially. There's a big kitchen that we share. The bath is good, too, and everything's clean. You know the old *babushka* we passed going down the stairs? Her room is next to the kitchen and she lives to clean the halls."

Nick unobtrusively dried his somewhat sweaty palms on his pants and looked around the room. "Was this always a communal apartment?"

"Oh, no. Before the Revolution it was for just one

family. This was probably the living room, you know" —she motioned with the brush—"because of the balcony. The family next door undoubtedly lives in the old dining room. The others live in the old bedrooms and we share everything else—the kitchen, the bathroom. There were some that were built as communal apartments, but, no, this used to belong to just one family. A merchant perhaps."

"Olga . . ." The warnings of what could happen kept nagging at him and he stood and wandered over to the balcony door. Shaking his head, he said, "God, I hate it. I hate having to distrust someone from the start. I mean, the guilty-until-proven-innocent approach is just disgusting."

"I . . . I . . ." Her voice was feeble.

Gazing out the door, Nick said, "I'm sorry, Olga. I don't mean to offend you. It's just that they've pumped us up with all these fears of what could happen to us. You know, in Dushanbe and Tselinograd they followed me all the time. It scared the hell out of me and I was sure they were going to arrest me and accuse me of selling drugs or being a spy." He laughed. "My God, I got so paranoid that I imagined all sorts of things—like being sent to Siberia . . . and worse."

"Nick," said Olga, uncomfortable with the subject.

He turned toward her, a grin on his face. "It all seems pretty funny now." He took a deep breath and sighed. "Olga, tell me once and that's all. I can trust you, can't I?" he asked, almost pleading.

She glanced away, thought better of it, and then looked directly at him. "Nick, I . . ." She hesitated for perhaps a moment too long. "Yes. Of course you can." She brushed her hair with quick strokes.

The tension ebbed from Nick. He returned to the bed opposite her and sat down. "Good. All I want is to believe what I see."

Relieved that he demanded nothing further and questioned nothing more, she regained her composure. "You must be starved. Let's eat."

They sat at a small table pulled into the middle of the room. Olga was intent on being a good Russian hostess, and the table was cluttered with more platters of food than they could possibly eat. She poured them each a shot of vodka.

"Mir i droozhba." Olga raised her glass.

"Yes, peace and friendship." His voice lacked sincerity. To Nick the phrase had been repeated so many times that it had sunk to the same level and was as removed from reality as the maxim "Have a nice day" was in America.

Olga swallowed her vodka like cough syrup. Nick threw his down as fast as possible to get it over with.

"Very good," gasped Olga, patting her chest. She was breathless and her eyes watered. "Not many foreigners can drink good Russian vodka like that."

"I've had a lot of practice." It was one of his many standard lines. Reaching for the black bread, he wanted to get past this barrier of being a foreigner in the U.S.S.R. and return to the one area that he and Olga had in common. "Olga . . ." he began slowly, "what's it like losing a parent here?"

She was startled. Pulling her hair back, she said, "I've . . . never really talked about it before."

"I'm sorry. I don't mean to be . . . crass." He raised his shoulders. "It's just that, well, I don't know you very well, but you seem very strong and very stable. As if you had a purpose. A direction. I envy that in you. My mother died, too, and sometimes I think that was the most determining factor in my life. Determining in the sense of interruption and . . . well, to be frank . . . I've never really been sure what to do. I guess I'm talking about direction . . . I . . . I don't know."

Withdrawing into a series of painful memories, Olga arranged *zakuski*—hors d'oeuvres—of smoked fish, sliced onions, tomatoes, and cucumbers on Nick's plate almost as if he were not there.

"It's kind of like going through a war . . . an internal war," continued Nick. "And while others might sympathize, unless you've been at the front, you really don't know what it's like. After all, cameras can't get there and there's no way to put it on television. You know, without knowing anything about them, I've been automatically attracted to a lot of people . . . a lot . . . who have also lost a parent." As a guise to lessen the intensity, he picked up his fork. Looking at her out of the corner of his eye, he said, "I feel the same way toward you, Olga."

Her hands in her lap, her deep blue eyes cold, she didn't hear him. Trancelike, she said, "I thought I'd die too." To use a cliche was safer and less threatening than expressing the depth of her real emotion. "Mama was killed, Papa turned to vodka, and I . . . I moved in with my great-aunt." She shook her head, chasing away the memories, and addressed Nick. "I'm sorry. You must eat." She picked up her fork. "Eat, Nick. You are my guest," she said, dismissing the subject.

He cut a slice of tomato in half, but he would not be so easily pushed away. "Where's your dad now?"

"Lvov."

He began to eat, and strained to sound as if they were talking about quite a normal subject. "Do you ever think of moving there?"

She laughed, perhaps more than necessary and glad for the release. "Kiev is my home. This is where I belong. Papa was born in Lvov and so he returned. His mother is there too. I see him once or twice a year, but this is where I belong."

The onion was strong; he quickly ate a thick slice of black bread covered with butter. "That's such a foreign concept to me. I can't imagine feeling so strongly attached to one place." He put his fork down and scratched his head.

She was confused. "I thought you said you were from Michigan."

"Now I'm from Michigan, but before . . ." He shrugged. "Dad's a journalist, and after Mom died we moved all over the place. The East coast, the West coast, Houston, Chicago. I call Michigan home because . . . because in the past few years that's where I've been the longest. You see, mobility is the password of the United States."

She barely heard him, though. Realizing that he had spoken, she reached out and touched his arm, "I'm sorry, I was . . . was just thinking about my mother. I . . . I . . . Yes, you were talking about Michigan." She wiped her mouth. "What can I say? Kiev is my home. I can't imagine leaving."

"I envy that," said Nick. "When I go back to the States I don't know what I'm going to do and I . . . I don't know where I'm going to live. Christ, I worked part-time in a bookstore for three years and I sure don't want to go back there.''

Wanting to forget her own thoughts, she concentrated on his words. She did not, however, understand. ''But doesn't your government give you a job in your field when you graduate?''

''No,'' he snapped in response to one of the most frequently asked questions. Defensively, he added, ''No, and I don't want anyone to give me a job. I just want to figure out what I want do with my life. That's how my mother's death interrupted my life—it stunted me.''

''Oh.'' She served him the rest of the smoked fish. Seizing the opportunity to get away from any more personal questions, she stood and said, ''You finish this, and I'll be right back. I have some borscht on the stove.''

Nick admired her as she stepped away from the table. Without any trace of weakness, she was very feminine. Attracted to her wide face and thick blond hair that were both beautiful and graceful, Nick also realized that, yes, she was a survivor. Probably more so than he was. He could as easily imagine her in a brocaded gown attending a ball right out of *War and Peace* as fighting in the trenches of World War II.

A few minutes later, rather matronlike with the sleeves of her white blouse pushed up and beads of perspiration on her brow, Olga returned with a steaming pot of borscht. Putting a hot pad down first, she set the pot on the table. From the desk she took two large bowls and ladled beet red borscht into them.

''Now I know why everyone wants to meet people from abroad,'' said Olga, calmed and sure of herself again. She rapidly stirred a small glass jar of sour cream and then spooned a large puddle into the middle of his bowl. "It's interesting. So much information."

"Versus disinformation," said Nick, referring to the Soviet method of reporting half the truth according to their needs.

She handed him his bowl. "Yes, disinformation." She shook her head. There was, after all, nothing she could do about it. "I have a question for you. About food. I heard one of the guides at the exhibit say that you have no lines for food in America. Is that really true?"

"If he lied, why shouldn't I?" He stirred his soup and its sour cream, and the borscht turned pink. "Why should you believe me any more than the other guide at the exhibit?"

"Oi, Nick, I . . ." She enjoyed being forced to be specific about something not personal. "I believe you because you are here, an individual. I believe you because your words seem to come from deep within you. But at the exhibit, well, it's from your government, and . . ."

"That's just it, Olga." Nick relished having an audience that would at least seriously weigh his words rather than automatically assume he was spewing propaganda. "That's the difference between us. My government has done a lot of things I don't agree with—from Viet Nam all the way down to the interstate highway system—but I still cling to the hope that people come before government. In fact, every American wants desperately to believe that even if it is no longer true: we want to believe that our government works for the people. Whereas here . . . well, would I be wrong in saying that the people work for the government?" Before she had a chance to comment, he said, "What it means, Olga, is that what any of the guides say—including myself—is what we believe. You've got to make an attempt to understand, though.''

She would not be backed down by theory. ''But I want to know,'' she said, firmly. ''Do you have food lines?''

Nick took a large spoonful of soup and swallowed it. ''No.''

''Do you really have all that fruit, too?'' Olga wanted no doubt left in her mind. ''I saw at the exhibit that most of your fruit and vegetables are grown in California and then shipped all over the country.''

He was slightly irritated. Russians seemed to think that the existence and availability of a substance signified the quality of life in a country. He hoped for more from Olga.

''Yes,'' he said. ''Apples, oranges, strawberries, pineapple, every type of fresh vegetable . . . yes, we have it all. And most of our produce is from California.''

Amused, she clapped her hands in astonishment. ''Last year we had oranges for a while from Morocco. But none so far this year. And I've only seen photographs of pineapple. As far as things like strawberries, they're a treat a parent buys once a year for his child. And bananas . . . I haven't the faintest idea what they taste like.'' A thought seized her and she turned to Nick like a mischievous schoolgirl. ''Nick, have you ever eaten a banana?''

How could he ever tell her that his father used to make him eat corn flakes topped with bananas day after day? ''Yes,'' he said, firmly. Suddenly he wanted to be very close to her or very far away; he wanted to tell her everything about the rest of the world or to leave her in peace. He spotted a large chunk of gristly meat floating by some chopped beets. "I get frustrated here. I'm from the West, yet I know a fair amount about your country. Take this piece of beef, for example." He touched it with his spoon. "It bothers me not only that you had to wait in line or bribe someone or use *blat* to get it, but that you wasted time to get something that should have been there automatically. And this is Kiev—a major city. Do you know what it was like in Tselinograd? They hadn't had any meat in that city for six months before we came. And when we, the Americans, arrived a city of over a quarter of a million people finally got meat. Only it was crap like cow hoofs, tails, and pig ears."

Knowing that he spoke the truth, Olga, disgraced, turned away. Nick could not restrain himself and continued his lecture.

"It doesn't have to be that way," insisted Nick. He leaned forward, bracing himself on the table. "It just doesn't. For the same reason, there doesn't have to be a paper shortage in a country with more forests than any other in the whole god-damned world. That's what I can't stand. In America we waste a lot of natural resources and material goods, but here, God, it's the waste of humanity that burns me."

She covered her mouth and stared down at the floor.

"Olga," said Nick, scratching his eyebrows. "I'm sorry. I got a little carried away."

"You're right." Her voice was sullen. "It's just a little painful."

Without thinking, Nick said, "Next time I come I'll bring you some canned pineapple from Hawaii. I can get it from our embassy."

Accepting his clumsy apology, she turned to him. "Really?"

Then he felt ashamed. He felt as if he were recklessly entering her world and turning it upside down. He'd go home and everything would be fine. But what about her? "Olga." What could he honestly do for her besides hurt her with all this information, all these dreams that for her could never be? "I decided the other night, well . . ." The power to make someone dissatisfied with life frightened him. "I decided I'd very much like to take that letter to your uncle."

"Nick . . ." Her cheeks flushed.

"I was going to tell you the other night but then you ran away."

"How wonderful." Her eyes glowed with dampened success.

"I'll take a letter and I'll call. Maybe I could . . ." —he felt ashamed that he was asking this of her— "maybe I could see the letter before."

She was momentarily taken aback. "What about a package?" she asked with trepidation. "A package. Would that be too much of an inconvenience?"

"I'll . . . I'll . . ." He stalled as he stared into her hopeful face. "Sure. I can take a package." He smiled.

"Oh, Nick, thank you!"

"You're welcome."

She got up from her seat and came around the table. Brushing her hair back out of her face, Olga leaned forward to Nick, who was still sitting. And only at this last moment did she hesitate. He reached out, however, and nudged her closer and gladly accepted her shy kiss on the side of his face. Not letting Olga pull away, he returned her kiss more directly.

"Nick . . ." It was not a reprimand.

Suddenly, with his bowl of borscht before him, he felt ridiculous. "Shit." He dropped his soup spoon and napkin to the floor, pushed his chair back, and stood.

"Olga," he said, facing her.

Nick reached out and took her hand. Olga withdrew. He put his hand on her waist. She inched forward with a small step, a small movement. Closer. Nick wrapped his other hand around her back. Afraid to let go, afraid to hold on, she shook with fear.

"It's okay," he said, understanding.

Olga needed no further enticing. She embraced Nick in a quick, compulsive movement. He knew at once, however, that it was not sexual. She burrowed her face into the nook between his neck and shoulder, and he understood that she wanted something much more than passionate kisses and sensual touches.

"Oh, God, Nick . . ." she moaned with pain.

His green eyes large and confused, Nick said, "Olga . . . what is it?" He thought she sounded guilty, and he held her tightly, not letting go.

Suddenly she became angry. "You hit a raw nerve, Nick." She wanted to hit him. Instead she clung to him desperately.

Nick ran his hand through her hair. "What are you talking about?"

"I thought I could cover it up with other talk, I thought I could get past it, ignore it. But . . . I can't!" She stopped breathing for a moment. "I . . . thought I could ignore it, but now that someone, now that you're holding me . . ."

"What . . . is it?"

At first Nick wasn't sure. Then he felt a second and a third, and then a whole series of spasms. Just as he realized that she had cut off her breathing again, he felt her fingers digging deeper and deeper into his back. She was trying to hold something in and her body, fighting this thing, shook violently. Then she ran out of air and when she took a breath, it came rushing out. Tears came in a sudden torrent and Olga, her body racked with sobs, cried uncontrollably.

"Olga . . . Olga . . ." At a loss, not knowing what to do or how to help her, all that Nick could do was pull her as close to him as he could. "What is it, Olga? What's the matter?"

Her speech garbled, she sounded like an animal in great pain. Moaning inhumanly, she clenched Nick with all her strength. She threw her head back and tried to speak.

"I . . . I saw . . . it, Nick!" She cried, her face twisted into a spasmodic contortion. "I saw!"

"Olga, what? I'm here. What did you see?"

"I . . . I . . ." she said in rhythmic, heaving sobs. "I . . . I . . ." And then, tortured, she blurted it out: "My mother. I . . . I saw her murdered!"

Overcome with agony, the strength she had relied on all these years rushed from her body. At last, after so much time, she had finally told someone that her mother had not fallen under the steel wheels of that streetcar, but that she had been pushed.

Hours later Olga lay in bed and listened as Nick closed the outer door of her communal apartment. Motionless, her eyes were fixed on the ceiling until, a few minutes later, she wrapped the sheet around her naked body and hurried to the balcony. As she opened the doors the cool night air rushed over her and chilled her. She stepped out and, hearing footsteps, searched the street five stories below. She spotted the figure of a man walking in the direction Nick would have gone, but it was not him. Nick did not carry a briefcase nor was he that tall.

It had taken her over an hour to calm down, to stop the flow of tears. Nick had lowered her to the bed and held and rocked her. He had been kind and responsive and as understanding as he could have been without any information. She had clung to him silently, like a child, not telling him anything. She couldn't. Already he knew far too much and she, because of this, was weaker. And when, after she had finally stopped crying, he had asked a few simple questions, she had quieted him with a kiss and a touch. Though responsive to her sexual advances, at first Nick had been reluctant. To avoid having to explain, Olga had been persistent, however, and together they had become lost in their desires. From now until this operation was completed, Olga was sadly aware that it would be a great struggle for her to maintain self-control.

Nick had wanted to meet tomorrow night and she lied and told him she had to work. The truth was that Mayakovsky had ordered her not to meet with Nick for several days; via the monitoring system in the Russian couple's apartment, Mayakovsky had learned that they had arranged an evening with Miller. "The more normal, the more well-rounded Comrade Miller's life is here," Mayakovsky had advised Olga, "the better off we will be in the long run. Let him settle into a comfortable pattern—nothing too intense. After all, we don't want to arouse suspicion."

Besides, her Aunt Elizaveta had asked to be escorted to church the next night. There was a special service at Saint Vladimir's Cathedral for the Metropolitan who had died in Rome, and the old woman, who rarely ventured out, wanted Olga to accompany her. Though Olga strongly disliked going to the Cathedral, her aunt's requests were few. It was the least Olga could do.

A slight breeze came up, lifting the sheet around her and causing it to billow out. Shivering, Olga went in. As she closed the balcony doors behind her, she glanced around the room and realized that it was a fairly nice room and a decent communal apartment. In fact, she decided, she wouldn't mind living there permanently instead of just until the American exhibition left Kiev.

Drained of emotion and physically worn out, Olga wanted to cry and run away from it all, but she knew she could not. She regretted having told Nick about her mother's murder, but sadly, she realized she had told him because she trusted him. She trusted him in the sense that he would always call a black object black, and a white object white. She was curious whether this was an American characteristic or if this was simply how Nick differed from the average Russian.

Though she wanted to, Olga did not get back into bed. She let the cotton sheet drop to the floor and slowly began to pull on her beige skirt and blouse. When she was dressed, she went to great lengths to smooth her clothing, brush her hair, and put on fresh lipstick. She wondered, too, who they had moved out so that she could temporarily move in. She shrugged. It really didn't make any difference.

Olga gathered her purse and the key and left to make her report. Resolved to recount only as much as Colonel Mayakovsky needed to know, she had to be strong again. Just as long as it didn't interfere with the operation involving Miller, her personal life was her own affair. If she even hinted to Mayakovsky of what had happened between Nick and her, question would lead to question, and Olga doubted she could withstand having her own beliefs and loyalties challenged any more that night.

Her large brown purse in one hand, she pulled back her thick blond hair with the other, and then opened the door. It would all be over soon.

XII

In the small building which housed his temporary office near the American exhibition, Colonel Mayakovsky, furious, stood with his back to Lieutenant Yezhov. The colonel's large metal desk separated them.

"You what?" Mayakovsky slammed his fist against the office wall and a nearby photograph of Lenin tilted to the side.

"I followed them." Yezhov, in civilian clothes, shifted in his seat. He was to begin his workday at FARMING USA within a few minutes.

"Who instructed you to do so? Under whose orders were you acting?" Mayakovsky turned around and leaned on his desk with both hands. His face was red with anger.

"No one, Comrade Colonel." Lieutenant Yezhov had expected anything but a reprimand. He still failed to see his error. "I can assure you that they did not notice me."

"I should hope not!" bellowed the large man. "Besides, that is not the issue. The issue is that you were given clear instructions not to act without my orders. And what did you do? You did the exact opposite!''

''Yes, but . . .'' began Yezhov, resentfully. He had always disliked Mayakovsky's totalitarian approach to his subordinates.

''But? But what? Do you think I am unaware of what I am doing? Do you perhaps think,'' said Mayakovsky with a sarcastic expression on his boyish though wrinkled face, ''that I am shirking my duties?'' He had no tolerance for such unnecessary and potentially dangerous interference.

''Of course not, Colonel Mayakovsky.'' Yezhov raised his thin arms from his lap. ''It was obvious, though, that Miller and the woman were not followed, so . . . so . . .''

''Comrade Yezhov, let me remind you of the importance of this operation. Due to its serious nature, it is justifiably complex. You are only one member of my large staff and I find absolutely no need to keep you posted of everyone's comings and goings.'' Mayakovsky, in street clothes—a baggy gray shirt and dark pants—had no intention of informing Yezhov that he had called off Miller's usual tail so that Olga could work unhampered. ''You were brought in for your language skills and for no other reason. Your job is to monitor the guides' conversations at the exhibit and anything any Soviet citizen may say in English. Let me make it perfectly clear that your actions of last night far exceed your duties.''

Yezhov was dumfounded, and Mayakovsky stepped across the room and gazed out the window. Past the park area of flower beds and benches, on the other side of the Exhibition Park of the Economic Achievements of the Ukrainian Soviet Socialist Republics—the VDNX—the colonel could see the faint outline of the low pavilion housing the FARMING U.S.A. exhibit. The grounds were vast, full of ornate one-story Stalinesque exhibition halls, and Mayakovsky's temporary office was well secluded from the Americans.

The colonel rubbed his forehead and exhaled. "Go on," he ordered, his eyes out the window. "Tell me the rest."

In a deep, defensive voice, Yezhov related the entire sequence of events; how he had recognized the blond woman from the exhibit, watched her as she met Miller, and then followed them to number 14 Revolutsiya Street. He had even observed Miller and the woman on the balcony of her apartment. Almost an hour later the lights were extinguished.

Mayakovsky interrupted, lifting his broad hand and saying, "What?" Upset, he twisted around. "The lights? Out? How long were they off?" There had to be a mistake.

"The remainder of the evening."

"You're sure of this?" This was new information and Mayakovsky was disturbed. "You're sure the lights stayed off?"

"Yes," said Yezhov, looking coldly through his East German glasses. "Positive."

The many fine lines on Mayakovsky's face grew deeper. "When did Miller leave the woman's apartment?"

"Shortly after midnight." Yezhov considered how much was best to divulge before adding, "I followed him at a distance only as long as it took to ascertain that he was returning to the Hotel Dneipro."

"And the woman?" Mayakovsky thought he knew the entire events of the previous evening. Evidently he did not, and he tried to mask his concern. "Did the woman go anywhere?" he demanded. "Did she?"

"As I said, Comrade Colonel, I followed Miller. I assumed that the woman remained in her apartment."

Mayakovsky placed his hand on the window sill and leaned back. "Yes, of course." Surmising the situation, it seemed that no damage had been done and that Yezhov, after all, had brought some valuable information. "Her name?" he said, trying to read the lieutenant's face. "Do you know this woman's name?"

"No, but I can find . . ."

"That will not be necessary." Mayakovsky put his hand to his face and massaged his eyes. He became lost in thought: what did this imply? Had he placed too much faith in Olga? Realizing that he was forgetting about Yezhov, Mayakovsky looked up and sternly said, "Your actions were out of line. You are not to interfere any further."

Yezhov bit his lower lip and sat back in the chair.

Full of disdain, Mayakovsky said, "What is it?"

"It's just that I . . . I didn't expect to be reprimanded."

"Oh, no?" said Mayakovsky, lifting his eyebrows in mockery. "Just what did you expect?"

"I . . . I . . ." Yezhov decided against any further confrontation with his superior. "Please accept my apologies, Colonel. It won't happen again."

Mayakovsky went to the edge of his desk. "Good. Now let me give you a piece of advice, Lieutenant. You are a language specialist. A very good one. And apparently you have a good eye for faces, too. However, just stick to your job and let others do theirs."

"Yes." Accepting the reproach, Yezhov nodded his head.

"In order for this operation to succeed it must continue smoothly. It is of the utmost importance that Miller does not suspect anything . . . particularly that he is being followed." Mayakovsky paused. "Questions?"

"No, Comrade Colonel."

"Under no circumstances are you to undertake such independent ventures without my knowledge and approval." In a louder voice, he said, "Should you act without my orders again, you will be discharged. Clear?"

"Yes."

"Dismissed!"

Mayakovsky turned to the window and with the back of his hand, waved Yezhov away. He heard the lieutenant's footsteps and the opening and closing of the office door. Interference. He hated it.

"Damn!" He pounded his fist on the edge of the window.

Looking out, Mayakovsky watched as Yezhov headed for the American exhibit, which would soon open. What was he, a colonel, supposed to do? Make everything public information, disclose all aspects of the operation? Of course not. The delegation of authority, the possibility of more such independent action, the likelihood of questions—these could foul all the plans.

Yezhov, carrying his briefcase, walked by a hall which contained government demonstrations of the latest construction practices and how they were implemented to give the Soviet people new housing units. Then, as Mayakovsky continued to stare at him, he passed a hall displaying modern home appliances—four burner gas stoves, kitchen cabinets, sinks, washing machines—that were promised for every future Soviet home.

"If it weren't for people like you, Comrade Yezhov," said Mayakovsky to himself, "all that and more would be ours already."

As he turned to his desk, Mayakovsky noticed that the official black and white photograph of Lenin hung crookedly on the wall. He made no attempt to straighten it before sitting down.

Lieutenant Yezhov was most eager in his work. Too eager, thought Mayakovsky with contempt. He was just another of those without principles, without commitments, trying to get ahead, trying to attain recognition for the material wealth it would bring him. Yet Mayakovsky could not dismiss him. Not yet, anyway, for now it was best to have Yezhov directly under his supervision where a careful watch could be kept. Besides, as long as Miller didn't suspect anything, the operation continued to progress.

Mayakovsky tapped a pen on the top of his desk and contemplated Yezhov's account of the previous evening. He was most disturbed. How did this reflect upon Olga? He shook his head. More than anything else, Mayakovsky was disappointed in her. She had come close to one o'clock last night and supposedly made a full report. Obviously it wasn't. According to Yezhov, the lights had been turned out and stayed out until Miller had left after midnight.

Olga, however, had stated in her usual straightforward manner that she and Miller had enjoyed a leisurely meal, gotten along quite well, and then taken an evening stroll. She had mentioned nothing at all of their apparent intimacy.

XIII

Wearing running shoes, jeans, a fresh blue shirt, and his corduroy coat, Nick walked briskly down the street. On his way to meet Boris and Masha, he thought of Olga and was happy. Silly happy. At the same time, he was disturbed about her mother—who could have killed her and why?—and he found it difficult to accept that something so terrible had actually happened to someone he had been so intimate with.

A slight breeze blew across his angular face and through his brown hair, and his small mouth formed a tender smile. Simply, it had felt good to be close to someone. Nick was the type who was attracted to women he could talk intimately with; he had never considered picking a woman up at a bar and—though he'd never admit it—found even the idea unpleasant. And thus Olga's story had for Nick subconsciously bridged that gap and created a link. His major disappointment of the day was that he would not see Olga and be with her and touch her tonight.

Nick broke into a carefree whistle, albeit not a beautiful one. His head tilted slightly back, he noticed signs of autumn: a faint yellow and red glimmer on the tops of a few green trees. His stride was vigorous. Though not as meticulous, he had performed the ritual stops and checks, and found, as he had expected, no tail.

A haggard middle-aged woman in a red flowered dress was making her way down the sidewalk toward him. Her lips dryly pursed and her small eyes withdrawn, she was loaded down with bread and cheese in one hand and a string bag of loose eggs in the other.

"Why, oh, why," muttered Nick to himself, "can't they get their shit together enough to make egg cartons?" As they passed he waved to the woman and said, "Hi, there!"

Greeted by a person she had never seen before, the woman froze, her mouth agape. Soviet street etiquette required that there be no loud talking, bold gestures, singing, whistling, or even smiling. While home life was as emotional as possible, anything that made a person stand out from the masses on the street was considered in the worst taste.

"Ne-koolturni!" she said, accusingly.

The woman grumbled to herself, stormed away, and Nick shook his head. What would she have done had he dared to play frisbee on the street? In Tselinograd he and another guide had played too close to the grotesquely enormous—Nick had been only as big as the nose—statue of Lenin. The police had gone berserk.

Puckering his lips, Nick went on and whistled with relief. Now there were new experiences which would become good memories. Sure, it was tough dealing with thousands of Sovs everyday simply because their knowledge of America was so twisted; they knew, for example, the precise percentage of unemployed workers in the U.S., but had never heard of unemployment insurance or welfare, or that the average length of unemployment was six weeks. It was exacting and tedious countering these "half-truths" and accurately portraying the U.S. with its great strengths and shameful weaknesses. But it was also a challenge, for they yearned to know and Nick had to give them credit for that. After all, how much did Americans know about the U.S.S.R. and how many Americans would wait for hours and upon hours in line to see a Soviet exhibit?

Nick turned left when he reached Shevchenko Street, and in the distance spotted Boris and Masha waiting for him in front of the Leningrad Restaurant. Boris, puffing on a cigarette and pacing back and forth, was the first to see Nick, and he discreetly nodded his head in greeting. They briskly approached one another.

"Good evening." Boris countered his subdued words by tightly grasping Nick's hand in both of his.

Nick forced himself not to smile. "Hello." These were people he cared about, and without realizing it, he restrained himself lest they attract too much attention.

"Nick!" Only Masha could not hold back, and she planted a big kiss on each of his cheeks. "How are you?"

He thought of them—was it really only the second time they had met?—and of Olga. "Everything's good. Very good. Better than it has been in months."

"I missed you so," said Masha, taking his arm. "The phone was out of order and even though it was quickly fixed, I feel that we lost precious minutes of our friendship together. How was your work today? Oh, and I liked the exhibit so much. Baba Genya did, too. But so many people! You guides are remarkable. What a lot of work you have."

"We had 25,000 people yesterday." Nick shook his head and rolled his eyes. "Can you imagine?"

"Oi." Masha, pulling on his arm, looked at him with exaggerated sympathy. "Are you tired? You poor thing, you must be."

"I feel great right now, but . . ." The strenuous day yesterday, the late night with Olga, and another full working day today could catch up with him at any moment.

They began to walk up the tree-lined boulevard away from Kreshatik and the statue of Lenin, and toward their apartment. Masha pulled up the collar of her rain coat to ward off the chilly air. It was growing dark and heavy bells began to chime in the distance.

"We thought we might show you a few things," said Boris between puffs on his cigarette. "That is, if you like."

"Absolutely." Nick was only beginning to realize how much he had not taken advantage of.

Her small nose twitching, Masha said, "There's lots to do when you have more time. Perhaps when you have a free day we could go to the zoo or for a boat ride on the Dneiper or to the Monastery of the Catacombs —it's a museum now." She pointed to the somber bells in the distance. "But tonight we thought we'd take you to Saint Vladimir's Cathedral. It's not a display, it's something living. A living part of Old Russia. I'm sure you'll like it. The choir is famous and the icons are beautiful. There are only several working churches left in Kiev, and Saint Vladimir's is the largest and the main one." The bells tolled mournfully. "It's very close. Just up the street."

"A *babushka* told us there's a special service tonight," said Boris. "This would be an excellent time to see a traditional Russian church service. It'd be very interesting—so dark and ancient."

"Did you hear?" Masha turned to Nick so sharply that she was walking sideways. "The Metropolitan of Leningrad and Novgorod died in Rome. Can you imagine? He was speaking with the new pope and he just toppled right over." She let her head flop on her chest. "Dead on the spot."

"Yeah," said Nick, recalling how John Kornichuk had told him about that and the technology fair in Vienna. "One of the guides read about it in the foreign newspaper we get."

Boris winked and, so that no one on the street could hear, said, "We heard about it on 'The Voice of America.' "

"So we'll go?" pleaded Masha.

"Sure." The night air was invigorating.

"Good. Then afterward we'll go to our apartment for some good Russian food," said Masha. "I made blini."

"And I have some questions about the exhibit." Boris threw his cigarette to the ground.

Their arms looped together, the three of them walked in a row; Boris, tall and thin, Masha, much shorter and quite pudgy, and Nick, of medium height and slightly overweight. Even though he had only recently met them, Nick felt inside that he had known them for a long time. He knew he could show up at any time of night and they would take him in. He believed he could ask them for thousands of rubles and they would loan it to him. And he was sure he could ask for any Soviet product and they would search it out, wait in line, and present it gladly to him. Already it was a relationship as dependable as it was dependent; a relationship proven as much by love and affection as the things they could do for one another. Already it was a friendship in the Russian sense.

The seven cupolas of Saint Vladimir's stretched high into the darkening sky. It dominated the vicinity, protruding well above the surrounding apartment buildings and occupying its own half-block area. A nineteenth-century imitation of the Russian Byzantine style, it was a massive stone structure with plain outer walls and arched, ornamented windows and doors. A thick band of grass and trees encircled the cathedral and paths of fine gravel led up to its intimidating arched entrance.

"It was built a hundred years ago to commemorate the 900th anniversary of Kiev's conversion to Christianity," said Masha as they headed off Shevchenko and up the path.

An ever increasing number of old people, bent and weary, hobbled out of the night toward Saint Vladimir's. The vast majority of them were old women, the men of their generation having long ago perished in the First World War, the Revolution, the Civil War, Stalin's purges, or World War II. The air was still and all that could be heard was the scuffling of old shoes on the gravel walkway. The cathedral's bells, powerful and almighty, began again and broke the morose silence.

As if into a great funnel, the people were drawn toward the heavy oak doors. On patrol was a large *babushka,* inspecting all who wished to enter this place of worship. Nick, Boris, and Masha were obvious because of their youth, and the old woman singled out Masha with fury.

"Young girl!" came the shrill voice. "Put something on your head. You have to have something on your head in church or you can't go in, can't go in!"

Frightened, Masha quickly grabbed the scarf from her pocket. "Oi, I almost forgot."

On the worn stone steps sat a decrepit old blind woman. She held a cup in one shaking hand and a worn and cracked cane in the other. Nick reached into his jeans and threw a few kopecks into the cup.

"God bless you," said the feeble woman.

Above her was an obese *babushka* whose sagging flesh was puffed out around her toothless mouth. She shoved her flabby arm at Nick and rattled the few coins in her dented tin cup. And behind her was a frail old woman leaning against the stone wall for support. Apparently unable to hold her cup, she had set it on the step beside her. Rotting clothes hung from all their aged bodies and Nick was hit by their thick odor, heavy in the air.

Typical of all public places, only one of the massive doors was open and people pushed through it as if it might close any minute. The elderly gathered more strength than imaginable, and Nick felt arthritic hands and boney arms swarm over him and shove him. Pandemonium was rampant as people jammed up against one another like frightened cattle. Forward. Forward. If they forced themselves harder then certainly they'd go forward. An acidic voice cried out in pain.

Masha led the way, taking Nick by the arm, and Boris protectively took the rear. Passage was again hampered in the foyer due to an interior door that was also only partially opened. The pushing became more intense, the groaning more widespread, and Nick was pressed into the rear of a grandmother so hard that his hands sunk through her fat and to her ribs. Another *babushka* was stationed at the threshold of the cathedral itself, searching for *hooligani* and others who had no church business.

When they came under intense scrutiny, Masha compulsively said, "We have a foreign guest." Because it was a church, she felt safe in confiding the magic word: *"Amerikanets."*

The woman's suspicious frown vanished and she opened her toothless mouth and beamed. "Welcome, my children. Be at home. Welcome to Saint Vladimir's Cathedral."

They left the outer world with its last traces of daylight and in a single step entered the earthly heaven of Eastern Orthodoxy. Thousands of slender beeswax candles, dedicated to the deceased Metropolitan, cast their soft yellow glow outward and upward. Mounted in pyramidal clusters on brilliant brass stands, the candles provided the only light and cast deep, shifting shadows throughout the cavernous cathedral. Thick clouds of musty incense swirled sensually about the congregation, filling the lungs with delight and stinging the eyes. High overhead, through the smokey haze, an enormous fresco of the Madonna and Child seemed to float on the domed ceiling.

The ever-dramatic Masha placed her hand on her ample bosom. "I could die from such beauty."

The drawn, haunting faces of ancient icons in muted browns, deep reds, and dark greens—their gold leaf backgrounds capturing the candlelight and sparkling with life—covered every wall and filled every niche. These stark images of the Holy Mother, Christ, saints, and martyrs beckoned mysteriously down to the Believers as their link to the Kingdom of God. The paintings were simultaneously somber and stiff, frightening and lifeless, weightless and inspiring. Throughout the cathedral bronze, enamel, marble, and gilt were used in every possible place and combination. Portraits of ancient Russian princes adorned the thick pillars that rose like thousand-year-old trees. Separating the sanctuary from the rest of the cathedral, the profusely gilded iconostasis—its rows of icons depicting church hierarchy from local saints on the bottom to the Old Testament Patriarchs on top—was elaborate and resplendent, beautiful and overbearing.

The bearded deacon in his long flowing robe sang out in his baritone voice. *"Gospodi pomiliu!"* Lord have mercy! His voice was pure and domineering.

Instantaneously came the mournful response of the choir: *"Gospodi pomilui!"*

Unseen in the rear balcony, the choir sang unaccompanied and carried the Gregorian chants to emotional highs and desperate lows. The devoted congregation repeated the chant in an unhurried manner. People crossed themselves once, twice, three times, and bowed their heads. *Babushkas* wept openly, their tears glistening on their weathered faces.

A strong beautiful voice sang out at Nick's side. Drawn to it, he turned. Pushed by another nun from behind, a legless nun sat perched in a baby carriage that had been converted into a crude wheel chair. The heavy black material of her habit hung from a crown on her head, wrapped around the edge of her face, flowed down into a pile on her lap, and fell over and onto the carriage wheels.

"Gospodi pomilui! Gospodi pomilui! Gospodi pomilui!" Her operatic voice, clear and rapid, carried the song far.

There were no pews. The entire floor was open, filled with a vast sea of continually moving Believers. While many members of the congregation had stood clumped for hours around the deacon at the front, others came and went as they chose. A few prayed in front of their favorite icon, lighting yet another candle, crossing themselves, and kissing the venerated object three times. Other devout women drifted about the cathedral comfortable and unnoticed, stopping now and again to answer the deacon's song and cross themselves. Still others, stoicism and patience etched in their faces, knelt and kissed the floor. Sporadic sobbing floated through the air.

The deacon continued the service of the Burial for the Dead. A bald priest with a cherry red nose and a long gray beard swung the heavy gold incense burner over the celebrants. Smoke billowed out, magically embracing the congregation, and they bowed submissively, murmured a prayer, and crossed themselves with fervor.

"Gospodi pomilui!" sang the deacon.

"Gospodi pomilui!" echoed the choir.

A younger priest in a black robe took the incense burner and removed it to the rear. The congregation, recognizing the signal, seethed forward.

"Let's get a closer look," said Boris.

Nick, Masha, and Boris moved to the front of the cathedral where they became lost in a throng of Believers. A long fenced-off area jutted out into the main body of the church, and a line formed through the end of it and up to the bearded deacon. Wearing a red- and gold-brocaded robe and a circular black hat that was flat on top, he held a large gold Russian Orthodox cross—a slanted bar at its base—and one by one Believers stepped forward, reached upward with their lips, and kissed it.

While their clothing was plain and baggy, the deep aged eyes of hundreds of *babushkas* stared out from beneath colorful scarves. Looking like dried apple dolls, their faces were pudgy and wrinkled, their mouths sunken and toothless, and their walks crooked and irregular. Overcome with grief, these were the same women—perhaps comprising the strongest institution in the U.S.S.R.—who kept order on the street as they saw fit; theirs was the only publicly critical and tolerated voice heard in the U.S.S.R. Mixed amongst them were several elderly men and a handful of younger women. On the other side of the fenced area, the figure of an obviously much younger woman stood out and caught Nick's attention. Tall and graceful in her movements, she appeared to be in her twenties and, her back to Nick, was turned talking to a *babushka.* He felt a rush of excitement. Her blond hair, not quite successfully controlled by the flowered scarf on her head, reminded him of Olga's.

Clothes rustled, priests mumbled, and beeswax candles crackled. The choir, their voices filled with suffering, renewed its song. Slow and methodical, the voices sadly split, rejoined, repeated their refrain, then faded away.

"Well," said Masha, leaning against him. "What do you think?"

"Fascinating. So sensual." He couldn't take his eyes off the young woman.

"Shhh!" hushed an old woman, impatiently.

Even more quietly, Masha said, "Let's go back and look at some of the icons and frescoes."

Nick was paralyzed. The thick blond hair. It was amazingly familiar. If she hadn't been wearing a scarf, Nick would have sworn it was she. And even though she was some thirty feet away on the other side of the brass fence, the smooth curve of her neck, the gentle shape of her back . . . Nick had caressed such a similar body just the night before. Then the young woman stopped talking to the short *babushka,* stood upright, and brushed her hair out of her face. She further shifted her position, standing on one foot, the other. She turned toward the front, directing her attention toward the deacon and exposing in the candlelight the clear, healthy complexion of her broad face. Her deep-set eyes remained dark.

Filled with happiness, he spoke too loud. "Olga!" How wonderful.

The deacon heard Nick and, pulling on his long beard, scowled in his direction. Hearing her name, Olga shifted. Confused, she gasped when she saw Nick and covered her mouth with her hand. As best he could, Nick waved, excited to see her. He motioned for her to join him in the rear. She seemed puzzled though, even shocked, as she struggled to make sense of the situation. Her eyebrows pinched together in a furrow over her nose, she apparently did not know what to do. At a complete loss, she could not and did not return Nick's warm greeting. Clearly, she couldn't believe he was there, too, in Saint Vladimir's Cathedral. Was she scared, was that it? Nick waved again. Frozen, she didn't respond, didn't even acknowledge Nick except with a look of . . . fright. That was it. She was not confused. She was afraid. She shook her head and spun away. Away from Nick. Olga bent down to the *babushka* at her side, grabbed her by the arm, and began forcing their way out of the crowd.

Nick put his hand to his head and inched forward. There had to be a mistake. All he wanted was to see her, talk with her, be with her. But she was moving away. Rapidly. Christ, Olga was running away from him, escaping from him. Nick lunged forward, only to collide with the brass fence.

"Shit." He started pushing his way back out of the crowd.

A hand grabbed him. "Nick?" It was Masha, unable to hide her concern. "What's the matter? Where are you going?"

"I'll be right back."

What in the hell would make her want to get away from him? What had happened? What could have changed in the last twenty-four hours? Had someone found them out; could the KGB have come and harassed her? What would make her flee so terrified?

Nick jumped up, his corduroy coat flying open, and tried to spot her. Nothing. Only a mass of scarf-covered gray heads, flickering tapers, and the drawn, Byzantine faces of the icons. He cut through a lingering cloud of incense and choked on the smoke.

"Hooligan!" cursed a *babushka* as he pushed past.

Women groaned, heads turned. Nick hurried to the thick pillar on the other side. Standing beneath a haunting icon of the Praying Virgin, he frantically searched. Olga. Where was she? What could have happened? The light was dim and he could not see far. In the distance he heard the beautiful voice of the legless nun, her chant reverberating throughout the cathedral. Someone reached out and struck him.

"Molodoi chelovek!" Young man. *"Skandal, skandal!"*

Frantic, he looked all around, spinning, searching. Where could she be? He broke into a run. Out of the dense crowd, he ran to where he had seen her. He lunged through a small clump of women, shoving them aside. Women cried out, some thinking that Nick was militsiya, others that he was KGB. Frail people tried to scurry out of his way. He jumped again. Olga had disappeared. Nowhere to be seen. His head pounding, Nick didn't know where to go, what to do. Was this it? Was it over so fast between them?

He spotted their covered heads furtively bobbing through the congregation like animals running in fright through a deep wheat field. They were not heading to the main entrance at the rear of the cathedral, but to an obscure chapel on the side. They were trying to get away from him. It didn't make any sense. He had to find out. He tore after them.

She ripped the flowered scarf from her head and her liberated blond hair seemingly exploded and fell onto her shoulders. The old woman, limping, struggled to keep up. And as the two of them reached the threshold of the chapel, Olga, like a fleeing convict about to be captured, spun around. Her eyes, wide and white, met and locked with Nick's for a frenzied moment. Almost dragging the *babushka* behind her, Olga ducked into the darkness of this side chapel and disappeared from sight.

Wasting no time, Nick burst into the chapel. Only a handful of shimmering candles filled this neglected room, and it took several moments for Nick's eyes to adjust to the darkness. Filled with smoke-covered icons and a multitude of black corners and niches, it was an overbearing room, a room which a child would never enter without a parent. There were paintings of suffering saints, grotesquely carved wood crucifixes whose gold leaf was faded and dusty, and icons with eyes of jewels which glowed like embers. Nick stepped forward, trembling. This was a place lost between the divine and the inhuman, satanic in its mysticism.

Olga was not to be seen.

And then, as Nick's eyes became accustomed to the darkness, he saw the old woman. She was precariously perched upon a step in front of a gold-sheathed, emerald-studded icon of the Virgin Mary. A handful of *babushkas,* toughened by a revolution and two world wars, surrounded her like tough old cows protecting one of their sick.

Nick took a step forward and approached this gathering. At first they would not move aside. Refusing intimidation, Nick cut through them. The old woman, small and portly and white-haired, was leaning against the icon, panting as if she would collapse any second. Exhausted, she glanced to the side and saw Nick. A frightened, though loving smile came to her weary face and, with her twisted hand, she crossed herself.

"Do not worry, my child." Her voice was weak and she struggled for air. "She will come to you."

The old woman kissed the icon with her parched lips, and then the other *babushkas* drove Nick away.

XIV

With the luminous white stone of Saint Vladimir's Cathedral soaring upward behind them, Masha said, "Poor Nick, you look so tired all of a sudden."

The mournful though muffled wail of the choir filled the undisturbed night air. The unaccompanied voices then faded away, their Gregorian chants evaporating into the atmosphere, and only the hoarse snoring of a beggar *babushka* asleep on the cathedral steps could be heard.

"But I could have sworn . . ." In shock, his words trailed off. Dazed and confused, he shuffled along, scraping his shoes against the fine gravel. "I was so sure."

"You need something to eat." Masha was certain this was the remedy. "You need to eat and relax. You've been working too hard. We'll go right back to our place. It's not very far." Masha took him by the arm. "Don't worry, Nick. Boris and I will take care of you."

He shook his head. "I'm sorry." He raised his eyes and looked at them. They were clearly distressed. He had to tell them something. "I thought it was a friend." Everything and everyone seemed suspect and distrustful. "A friend from Michigan." Once he got going, he found it easy to lie. "I haven't seen her for years and I could have sworn it was her." He saw their puzzled expressions and added, "We studied Russian together. Her grandfather was from Saint Petersburg and she has a Russian name too . . . Olga." The intensity of the incident had burned up what little energy he had had. His mind was foggy, his limbs heavy. The exhaustion of his months in the Soviet Union, which he had tried to keep at bay, came crashing down upon him.

Concern on his face, Boris was taking a cigarette from his shirt pocket when he motioned toward the street. "What luck." He started off. "There's a taxi. I'll grab it." He jogged ahead.

"Relax, Nick," soothed Masha, taking charge. "We'll be at our place in no time." She patted him on the shoulder. "Look, Boris got the taxi. What wonderful luck. One cab on the whole street and it's ours. We'll be at our place in just a few minutes and I'll give you some good Russian food."

Feeling quite distant, Nick said, "I wonder if I'm getting sick." He dragged his feat.

She led him along. "You've just been in a hotel too long. You need to relax in a good Russian home." As they neared the cab, Masha, in a hushed tone, said, "Nick, it would be better if you let us do the talking."

It took him a moment to understand. "Oh, sure." Of course. She didn't want the driver to know they were taking a foreigner home with them.

Boris, an unlit cigarette in his mouth, stood on the edge of the street, proudly holding open the rear cab door. He helped Nick in, Masha followed, and Boris climbed in front, slamming his door.

The driver grinned, a dark two-day beard on his face. "Where to, comrades?"

Boris spoke quickly and tersely. "To the corner of Victory and Gorky Streets."

That, thought Nick, really sucks. They don't want the driver to know the exact address of their house, either. Slumping in the rear seat and resting his aching head on the back ledge, however, he knew they were right.

No one spoke as the light green taxi pulled away from the curb, leaving Saint Vladimir's Cathedral in their wake.

"Isn't it funny how much Americans and Russians are alike?" said Masha, serving boiled potatoes. "I mean not only in looks, but in character, too. There's something very similar about us. We're both rather childlike, I suppose. Perhaps it's that neither of us is pretentious by nature. I've met people from France and Germany before, but I automatically feel closer to Americans. Others say so too. Maybe it's because both Americans and Russians want others to like them, want others to approve of them." She heaped potatoes onto her guest's plate.

"The world is small." Nick really wasn't paying any attention to her. Suddenly he noticed the growing pile of potatoes before him. Irritated, he stuck his hand out.

"Hey, that's plenty."

"Just a few more . . . they're garden fresh and you look so tired." She sat down between Boris and him. "Take some sour cream. Mama gets it at a store in the country—Mama and Papa are still out there, out at their dacha—and it's the best in the whole wide world." She picked up the small jar and automatically began telling Nick the whole story. "Mama has big *blat* at the store—she does all the teeth for the manager's entire family—and that's how we get this sour cream. Country fresh." She ladled spoonful after spoonful over Nick's pile of hot, steaming, buttered potatoes.

Nick stared at his plate and grimaced. He didn't want to eat potatoes with "big *blat*" sour cream oozing all over them. He was sick of it. Sick of it all. How could people do it? How could they sacrifice so much of themselves? In a country based solely on a visionary theory, there were no more dreamers. Just realists whose only goal was to get ahead, to survive, without changing the things that were wrong.

"Nick," said Masha, tenderly nudging him. "Eat. We saved the sour cream just for you."

He made an unpleasant face. Not as naïve about the Soviet Union as a simple tourist nor as hardened to their way of life as a Russian, he was lost somewhere in between. He looked at his plate. Could he even stomach the sour cream?

"Work's getting to me." said Nick, his hands in his lap and wishing he were back in his hotel room. "There has been so much pressure." He cast his eyes aside. "I have trouble letting things that bother me slip by."

"Eat, Nick. Food will do you good. Of course you've been working too hard. Eat the potatoes." So concerned was she about Nick's appetite, that she could not eat her own food. "We'll have some blini next."

Boris poured them all a glass of vodka. "But first a toast. A toast to your health, Nick, and to our friendship!"

"*Da,*" feebly responded Nick.

He raised his glass, clinked it with theirs, and gulped down the vodka with ease.

What did it all mean? Why had Olga run away? Why had she been so overcome with fear? What could have changed in the last twenty-four hours? The whole scene flashed through his mind. Again he saw Olga's dark blue eyes open in fear. Again he saw Olga and the old woman force their way through the crowded cathedral. And again he saw the dark, forgotten chapel.

Perhaps it was best not to know. That would be the easiest. The safest. She had left abruptly the first time they met and now she had actually run away from him. They had bumped into one another by chance at the cathedral and she reacted by fleeing. So how was he supposed to judge her? The Russian way was guilty until proven innocent, the American way innocent until proven guilty. So what was he, an American in Russia, supposed to do?

Cooly, he looked up at Masha and Boris. "As a matter of fact, all of the guides are having a bit of trouble."

Boris nodded and poured another glass of vodka lest their glasses be empty.

"Another toast?" said Nick, seizing the chance. "How about one for Margie?"

"Yes, a toast for Margie!" exclaimed Masha.

They brought their glasses together, then, like kids running into frigid waters, they drank the vodka all at the same time in one stiff shot. Masha, gasping, ate a potato while Boris tried to remain calm. Nick's eyes reddened.

"As I was about to say," began Nick, finding it easier, "one of the guides came to me the other day with a problem." He supposed it would be better to use a name. "It was one of my friends, Linda. Perhaps you could give me some advice for her."

"Certainly." Boris poured yet another glass of vodka.

"We'll help," said Masha, leaning forward onto the table. "And bring her with you next time you come."

"Many of us are struggling with the question of friendship." Even though indirectly speaking of Olga and their relationship, it gave Nick new energy. "The people here are extremely friendly, but sometimes it's hard to tell whom to trust. I mean, how is a foreigner supposed to know who is sincere or who is just after something?"

"You mean a black marketeer?" said Boris, leaning back in his chair and reserving judgement.

"That too." Nick speared a potato and thought for a moment. "I knew I could trust you right from the very start because of Margie's assurances. But Linda, well, she has some serious doubts about a relationship."

"I'm a specialist in matters of the heart." Masha put her hand to her chest.

Nick took a bite. "She met this Russian man and liked him right away. But she really wasn't—how do I put it?—sure what he wanted. Well, it turned out this guy was direct enough. He wants Linda to take a letter and maybe a package to a relative—a long-lost uncle —in New York."

Boris and Masha were clearly skeptical.

"Go on," said Boris, scrutinizing Nick's words.

"They've met twice. Alone. He told her about the letter the first meeting they had. They had a good time together, actually, but then this guy got jumpy, you know, and left abruptly. They met a second time and . . . well, they had an intimate evening together. Very intimate."

Scratching the back of her head, her eyes on the table, Masha was disturbed.

"And then Linda ran into this Russian in a . . ." Nick hesitated. He was shocked at himself. Lying had never been easy for him, yet here he was doing it compulsively and out of control. "She ran into him in a store quite by accident. Only when he saw her, he got scared and ran away. You know, at first he was startled to see her and then without saying anything—as fast as he could—he just cleared out." Nick's hand drifted over to his glass of vodka. He ran a finger around its rim. "Well?"

The situation was serious and the two of them thought about it carefully.

Boris sat up, his mind decided, "It's not good."

"No, not at all." With heartfelt sympathy, Masha said, "A real friend wouldn't act like that. A real friend is someone you can always count on."

"That's right. A true friend wouldn't be so skittish."

"Oh . . ." He'd wanted to hear anything but that. Dejected, Nick pushed at the potatoes on his plate with his fork. "So . . . so what should I tell Linda? What's your advice?"

Boris left no room for question. "Not to take the letter, of course, and not to have anything to do with this man."

"There's something offbalance about it all," added Masha. "I'd distrust this man and only, only take the letter if he could explain everything in absolute detail."

"I see," muttered Nick. Depression seeped slowly through him. They knew their country, their system, and they knew what was best to do. But he didn't want to forget about her. He didn't want to let go. He ran his hand over his head, pulling at his hair.

Something occurred to Boris. "I suppose the picture could change," he said, softening his tone, "if your friend were acquainted with this Russian in the full context of his life. If your friend, Linda, has only met this man and none of his circle of friends, then stay away. Stay far away."

Nick looked up and searched both Boris and Masha's faces. There was hope after all. "In other words, if this American were introduced to some of the Russian's friends or family you think it might be all right?"

Boris lifted his hands in a gesture of helplessness. "Who knows? Perhaps it might be. Only not on the street. If he invited this guide home to meet his family, his inner life, then I think maybe everything would be all right."

"I see." Nick's mind was working fast. Friends. Did she have friends? What about family? There was her father and wasn't there an old aunt somewhere, the one she had lived with?

The phone rang.

"Excuse me." As Masha got up, she noticed Nick's plate. "Nick, eat your potatoes before they get cold. Blini are next." She went into the small front hall and picked up the phone, saying, *"Da?"*

"Now I have a question for you." Boris motioned toward Nick's glass. "But first let's you and I have a little toast."

"Another?" he moaned, not able to believe it. Aching with exhaustion, Nick knew he couldn't handle much more.

"Yes, a man's toast." He reached over and filled Nick's glass until vodka spilled over onto the table. "We must toast our meeting."

Nick shook his head. "Boris, I can't. Really."

"Come on, Nick. A toast, and then I want to ask you about the exhibit."

At the mention of the exhibit, Nick picked up his glass. He knocked it against Boris's and, vodka dripping into his lap, gulped down the crystal clear liquid. He lost his breath, swooned, and flushed with a warm glow. A nauseous sensation rose in his stomach and he doubted whether he could focus on Boris's question.

"At the end of the exhibit, just before the exit," he began, "there is a film about food and food distribution in the United States. We watched it three times."

He took several deep breaths and the urge to be sick passed. "Hell, Boris, everyone watches it three times. And when I'm hungry, I watch it five times myself."

Nick knew the film by heart, as did every guide. It began with a digital clock sounding its electronic alarm. A young boy gets up and goes downstairs. He eats breakfast—cereal, milk, bacon, and orange juice. Then the deep-voiced narrator asks: "Where does all this food come from and how does it get to the boy's house?" The film progresses from farm to food warehouse to supermarket. In the suburban store there are nice but ordinary shots of the produce section, the meat counter, and people dressed in polyester calmly picking their goods from aisles and aisles of shelves as Muzak plays in the background.

"Are there really stores like that in America?" asked Boris, twisting his head to the side and a bit intoxicated. "Isn't it even just a bit propagandistic? So much food! Such a choice and no lines! My God, all that meat!" He poured Nick more vodka. "Drink up and tell me the truth."

Nick bowed his head and sat there trying to suppress his disappointment and anger. He shut his eyes, only to have his head spin.

"Shit, Boris. It is the truth," said Nick, losing his patience. "Why are the predominant questions always about material goods—whether there's a shortage of something or enough to go around, and how much this or that costs? You know, I have to incite discussions about freedom of movement and freedom of information. Don't you care that I can read *Pravda* at home but you can't read the *New York Times* here? Really, sometimes I think people here are more materialistic than we are."

In a soothing voice, Boris said, "We'll talk politics later, Nick. Just tell me, is the film honest?"

Nick raised his head. Boris was innocently waiting for him to answer. Nick grabbed the bottle and poured more vodka for the two of them.

"A toast to blue jeans, Boris!" After he had emptied his glass and gotten his breath back, with a vengeance Nick said, "We've got those fucking supermarkets on every God damned corner in America. You can wear your corduroy coat, get in your big car, smoke a cigar, and go there anytime. Hell, they're even open all night long, twenty-four hours a day."

Masha stepped around the corner, phone in hand. "Boris, this new phone! It's just awful. That was Larissa calling but I couldn't hear her at all and there was this humming noise the whole time." She slammed down the receiver and came into the kitchen pouting. "It makes me so mad."

Nick felt the vodka pumping through him and knew what had to be done. Guilty, he thought. Until proven innocent.

XV

" 'And then Linda ran into this Russian in a . . . she ran into him in a store quite by accident. Only when he saw her, he got scared and ran away. You know, at first he was shocked to see her and then without saying anything—as fast as he could—he just cleared out.' "

With his large hand, Mayakovsky reached over and stopped the cassette tape player. Birds chirped, leaves rustled, and the early morning sun seeped through the trees. It had the makings of an exceptional, even hot day. Sitting on a rusting bench in the Hydropark, he braced the tape player with one hand and turned the control to fast forward. He had listened to it a dozen times since the tape had been brought to him in the middle of the night, and he knew just where to stop it.

" '. . . should I tell Linda? What's your advice?' "

Mayakovsky turned the machine off and stifled a yawn. "I didn't get much sleep last night. Need you hear more?"

"No." Olga, preoccupied, sat on the opposite end of the bench. Hollow-faced, she sorted over and over the events of the previous night and their ramifications.

"It's pleasant out here, isn't it? An island park in the middle of the Dneiper River. No cars. Nice and quiet." Shifting his large-framed body, he checked about, searching the shrubbery with his youthful but wrinkled eyes. "Some of the guides go out running in the morning, but I doubt they'd come this far. Still, you never know where they're going to show up. You don't object to meeting here, do you? The exhibit grounds would have been unsuitable. Our Mr. Miller is just the type to wander around where he shouldn't."

Olga was silent, still unable to believe how fouled things had become.

"The tape continues. As I said, in the end they advise Miller to never fully trust a Russian unless he invites you into his circle of family and friends." He raised his shoulders indifferently. "Perhaps. Then the phone rings and the woman has some nonsense conversation with a friend by the name of . . ."—Mayakovsky massaged his sleepy face,—"Larissa. The equipment, however, did a rather poor job of monitoring both the phone call and the rest of the conversation between Miller and the fellow. There was this incessant humming. Didn't anyone test it before installation?" He made a tight fist. "Damn, I can't rely on anyone." He shook his head in disgust. "It's quite clear, isn't it?"

"Yes." Olga was ashamed. She felt both beaten and defeated. Her superior's concilliatory tone further humiliated her, even though she tried not to express this.

Mayakovsky stared at her, this attractive blonde in

whom he had taken a personal interest and whom he had tried to teach so much. "I placed great faith in you. More than in any of the others. Evidently that was my error." Though he was running his finger along a crack in the bench and appearing very relaxed, Mayakovsky was waiting, curious whether she would volunteer further information of her evening with Miller.

Olga did not defend herself. She wore her white cotton print dress—now mended and washed after her fall on the sidewalk with Nick—and smoothed a crease in it, as if that might somehow take the attention and pressure off her.

"It changes the entire operation quite considerably. Oh"—Mayakovsky waved his hand as if shooing away flies—"the staff doesn't know a blessed thing. Fortunately Miller feebly disguised his question—the last thing I want right now is interference. I was phoned late last night and told that one of the guides, Linda Swanson, had been meeting with one of our citizens and that possibly she would be taking some papers out of the country. Which is fine. Just fine. A handful of agents are out after her now. Our hotel personnel are searching her room again, putting in more monitoring equipment, and so on. I've even gotten rid of a few of my most troublesome people by sending them to the exhibit. I'm sure they'll make our Comrade Swanson's day most interesting."

Olga was not paying attention.

"The plan must change, but the fewer involved the better. I still maintain that position. It allows me a little more freedom as well as more reliability and flexibility. More space in which to operate. Wouldn't you agree, Olga Mixhailovna?" he said condescendingly.

"Yes." But she really wasn't listening.

"A large staff reassures Moscow, too. They think the more agents involved, the larger the operation, the better the chance is for success. The fools. You'd think they hadn't learned a thing in the war." Mayakovsky paused and became quite serious. "It was a large mistake to run out like that."

The words burst out of Olga: "I shouldn't have let my aunt persuade me into going with her to church in the first place."

Like a judgmental father, Mayakovsky said, "Of course not."

She ground her teeth. Bending over, she rested her head in one hand. "I've never panicked before. Never."

"But you did." He inhaled, then let the air trickle out in tiny amounts. Olga had still not divulged further information about her contact with Miller. "And now our little plan has developed a few kinks. It won't be so easy as just dropping a few documents into Miller's hands. No, not so easy. But we can still manage. Wouldn't you agree?"

"Yes, I'm sure of it." Olga's response was flat.

"Is there anything else?" asked Mayakovsky, testing her. He examined her closely for any reaction. "Anything more about Miller, perhaps?"

Olga sat upright and turned to him. Her face blank, she said, "No."

That she so easily failed his small test took even him by surprise. Disconcerted—could so much rely on one so uncertain?—he was forced to recoup his thoughts. Frowning and pulling on the tip of his chin, he realized what had to be done and regretted the steps which would have to be taken. He forced himself to ignore the tinge of sadness he felt within himself.

Finally, Mayakovsky said, "So . . . you know what to do? Everything's clear?"

As she had earlier agreed, Olga said, "I will arrange for Miller to meet my aunt."

"Yes," said Mayakovsky, almost coaching it out of her. "Your family here in Kiev. And?"

She shut her eyes and with difficulty said, "She will pass the documents to . . . to him."

"Exactly. First you must regain Miller's confidence. And if a relative is what it takes, then that's what we'll provide. There's nothing else to it. Second, well, who wouldn't trust such a sweet old *babushka* like your aunt?"

"But you're sure?" said Olga, abruptly, losing control of herself. Almost begging, she continued. "You're sure that there will be no danger for her . . ." She cut herself off, regretting her outburst and fearful what Mayakovsky would think. She pulled her hair behind her head with one hand and cast her eyes to the side. She became quite serious. "If at all possible, I just don't want her dragged into it."

"Please, Olga Mixhailovna." Mayakovsky touched his heart in feigned sincerity.

They sat a while longer in silence and then Mayakovsky checked his watch.

"I've got to get to the exhibit site," he said, gathering up the tape recorder. "As a colonel, I have a chauffeur at my disposal. But as a mere office worker in a nondescript building near the American exhibition, all I have is the Metro and the buses." He laughed. "It just wouldn't do to have one of the Americans see me climbing out of a limousine—it might arouse unnecessary suspicion." Getting up, he added, "Today, though, I might cheat and take a cab from Kreshatik."

Mayakovsky rose and stretched; and, towering over Olga, he seemed more imposing than ever. Out of uniform and in lightweight civilian clothes, he appeared a bit too heavy and, his shirt not completely tucked in, slightly pedestrian. With military precision, he sucked in the morning air, admired the day, and, saying nothing further to Olga, departed. With long, casual steps, he made his way along a narrow dirt path cut between wild grass and overgrown bushes. Sure of himself and what needed to be done, he headed for the Metro station in the center of the island, the Hydropark's only major intrusion from the outside world.

Lost in thought and staring blankly at a trail of ants on the ground, Olga sat frozen until he was gone. When she could no longer hear his feet stomping the earth or his hands pulling aside the branches, she leaned forward on the bench and slipped off her Hungarian sandals. Rubbing the naked soles of her feet into the ground, loamy soil refreshingly squirmed up between her toes. She sighed with relief and, with her sandals dangling from one hand, began strolling through the woods toward the Dneiper River.

Besides the other night, Olga could not remember the last time she had cried. Even though she thought of her mother every day, she was as shocked by her outburst as Nick must have been. Repeatedly, too, she saw the face of her mother's assailant—sharp features, dark eyes, a mole on his left cheek—seared into her memory. As a child she had told no one about the man because she feared that he would kill her, too. Later she did not speak of it because, sadly, there was no one to share it with. That was why, she supposed, it had come gushing out the other night. Not only did she trust Nick, but he had asked the right questions, pushed the right buttons, and there was no holding back this thing within her. It scared her to have such an explosive memory ticking away deep inside her.

Though unvoiced, Olga had always prided herself on a clear-cut vision. For the first time that she could remember, however, things were not as plain as she preferred. When her mother had died, she mourned. When her father had turned to drink, she left. When she had finished school, she went to work. Work that she did not necessarily respect, but which held a future.

She followed a meandering sandy path down to the beach along the river's edge. Bright and sunny, it was quiet that morning, not a ripple on the water's surface. And there, across the broad Dneiper, perched in the forests of the high right bank, was the sprawling Monastery of the Catacombs. The sign of Kiev for almost a millenium—first as the religious soul, now as both an historical and, operating only as a museum, political statement—its white towers shot upward and over the green trees of the rolling hills. The gold onion domes of these towers seemed to catch and magnify the sun's rays.

Aunt Elizaveta. Nick Miller. Where did they fit in with her duties and commitments? Two individuals juxtaposed against an entire cause.

Confused, Olga kicked at the sand. Missing was the clarity she had always clung to for guidance.

XVI

Without a doubt, he could no longer trust her.

A true agent, thought Colonel Mayakovsky as he sat in his office that afternoon waiting for the call from Moscow, allowed his profession to permeate every pore. The inner personality core was replaced with duty, and one's character only served as the perfect mask. In this way, when confronted with an unexpected circumstance with no time for rational thinking, one's reflexive response was as an agent. Not as an individual. That was the true agent, and a true agent Olga was not.

It had become so obvious. Mayakovsky knew it the moment he had seen her walking toward him in the Hydropark. She didn't even have to speak, though her words only further confirmed it all. He had seen it before in other agents. That schism when personal belief and sense of duty have become disjointed. Perhaps it was only just beginning in Olga, that withdrawn look that signifies "What should I do?" and "What must I do?'' are no longer wed. He was aware, too, that now the gap was opened, he could not risk being vulnerable to its widening.

It had been another busy day at the exhibit. How many visitors? Fifteen, twenty thousand? He didn't care. Just the usual, there had been no crises. The dozen or so provocateurs had filtered in and out of the exhibit, discrediting the American guides' propaganda as well as keeping a damper on the atmosphere. And the plainclothesmen had reported the inappropriate activity on the part of the Soviet visitors. Three people had been brought in today for questioning; a man who had traveled three hundred kilometers from his village to ask one of the Americans for a Bible, a black marketeer, and a man who had too eagerly pointed out the shortfalls of the Soviet system.

In his temporary office on the grounds of the VDNX and only a short walk from FARMING U.S.A., Mayakovsky placed his elbows on his desk. He pressed the tips of his fingers to his temples and gingerly massaged his scalp in small, tight circles. His thinning hair, which had matured to a bland brown, seemed to creak under the pressure. A bit of his inherent tension dissipated. He hadn't sat still for quite some time, but waiting for the phone call from Moscow, which was already five minutes late, he was forced to do so.

It had been his policy never to depend on anyone. In the early years of his career Mayakovsky had learned not to rely on those who outranked or those who served him. It was a strategy that had served him well and benefited his career. He had broken this cardinal rule, however, by allowing too much—virtually the entire contact with Miller—to depend on Olga. A great deal was now jeopardized because of this, and he blamed himself as much as Olga.

The fact that she had not fully and accurately reported her evening with Miller was crucial. Never mind that she had probably slept with him, for that too could have served its purpose. What was detrimental was that she was withholding information, no matter how irrelevant. The incident at Saint Vladimir's Cathedral only confirmed what Mayakovsky had begun to surmise: Olga, for an unknown reason, had become personally involved. She could no longer be relied upon to act solely as an agent. A shame. At their meeting in the Hydropark, Mayakovsky had patiently waited, inwardly hoping that she would more precisely recount the evening. She did not, however, and had it not been for the overly ambitious actions of Lieutenant Yezhov, Mayakovsky would never have found out. Now he would have to use her in other ways, in some new strategy. There was too much at stake and Olga was in far too valuable a position. Besides, even if he did want to replace her there was not enough time. So . . . he'd take full advantage of her as he saw fit.

There was a quick rap on the door. He recognized the knock of Vishnyak, his aide, who had followed him up the ranks of the KGB.

"*Da.*"

Vishnyak stepped in with a respectful manner that would have pleased a tsar's general. "Your call from Moscow, Comrade Colonel."

He picked up the receiver of the red plastic phone. "*Da.*"

"Kutofkin here."

He recognized his elderly commander in Moscow.

"Mayakovsky."

"Of course." The line crackled. "Top concern at the Kremlin continues to be expressed for our two men being held in Connecticut. I merely wish to know, Colonel Mayakovsky, the present status of the operation under your direction. How may I report the progress there in Kiev?"

The static on the line hissed into Mayakovsky's ear; a better telephone line did not exist so far from Kiev's center. "Let me assure you that nothing has ever received my greater devotion. The situation . . ."—he caught himself wanting to hesitate—"is well under control. Everything is satisfactory. Our target, by the way, has been most cooperative."

The old man, now on the periphery of the Moscow oligarchy, was one of the few original Bolsheviks to survive Stalin. He was pleased. "Good. Good."

"And surveillance of the other Americans continues to turn up the most interesting information."

"Really?" This type of affair was Kutofkin's favorite and he could not conceal his curiosity. "Such as . . . something for immediate use?" He looked forward to his conversations with Mayakovsky.

"Perhaps. You can expect an updated report soon," said the Colonel with professional conciseness. "And may I inquire as to the status of things in the capital?"

"Everything's set here in Moscow. Nothing has changed in the least since you were here. In fact, there is even more impatience to see this affair successfully executed and Comrade Miller in prison. For a long stay. As you know, this whole business has been of great concern. You have full backing, though; you needn't worry about that. Therefore, if you should be in need, do not hesitate."

"My thanks, but you have already seen to everything."

"Well, then . . ." Kutofkin broke into a cough. "Naturally this means so much to so many people, not to mention the distraught families of the men the American government has—how shall I put it?—kidnapped. We have great confidence in you, however. All of us here in Moscow are most pleased with the typical authority and efficiency with which you are handling this matter. Indeed, your outstanding service to the Soviet state has been recently noted."

Mayakovsky could not restrain his pleasure. "My gratitude, comrade."

"I just wanted to check personally. I will report that all is in competent hands. Please contact me should you require anything further." Again the elderly Kutofkin coughed painfully. "I say . . ." He pulled the receiver away until the consuming fit had passed. "Excuse me. A cold of sorts. Now, as I was saying. This whole business. They want to put our men on trial. Cheap. Very cheap. The poor Americans . . . they change leaders so often and this new president is just a farm boy from the South. Rather naïve. He just doesn't know how these matters are handled. Why, just last spring we apprehended one of their CIA people right here in Moscow. I personally saw to it that she was on the first flight out of the country. But we shall teach them a new lesson, don't you agree? They've got two of ours, we have one of theirs, but soon . . ." The old man laughed.

"Let me assure you that we will deliver nothing short of a full and satisfying success." Mayakovsky tensed, his hand wrapping tightly around the receiver.

"Very good, Colonel. Get on with it."

The line clicked dead. The dial tone blared into Mayakovsky's ear for several moments before he took the phone from his ear and then dropped it into its cradle.

Yes, he thought. They have two of ours and we have only one unimportant American businessman. For now, anyway. And with Olga's help, though he would not inform her of her new role, success was imminent.

XVII

The yellow Icarus bus was packed. Each and every seat was filled, and the passengers in the aisle were crammed chest against shoulder, shoulder against face, face against back. There was no space to even raise one's arm or, for that matter, to lower it; one staunch woman had dropped her purse, felt it sliding down her leg, but could not reach it. Those standing counted on the sheer pressure of the people around them to keep them from toppling over as the loaded bus zoomed along Kirov Street.

A man much shorter than Olga said, "Pass this up."

Olga took the four kopeks for the purchase of a ticket, inched her upright hand forward, repeated the phrase, and the person smashed against her similarly took the money. A few minutes later a soiled ticket of flimsy paper was passed back, followed by another, then another. The tickets went unclaimed, however, and continued circulating until an old man yelled that they were just passing the same two around and around.

The air aboard the bus was thick with the coarse odor of Russian *papirosi* cigarettes and the sweet, pungent smell of Red Moscow perfume. The windows were steamy and Olga struggled to see out. They were just passing the Dneipro Hotel, and she could barely make out a group of foreign tourists casually getting into their specially appointed tour bus. Although she had hoped to catch a glimpse of Nick, she did not spot any of the exhibit guides.

The bus barreled past Komsomol Square because it could take on no more passengers; the cries of those who missed their stop went unheeded. Suddenly the bus shot off the square and over the crest of a hill. An excited and unorchestrated clamor arose from the otherwise silent passengers as they felt their dinners heave in their stomachs. Some young people laughed. A few others charged the driver with hooliganism. Yet the driver failed to slow the vehicle and it sped down the steeply inclined road that led into the lower town, Podol, along the very banks of the Dneiper.

Olga squeezed off the bus at the first stop in Podol, Krasnaya Square, in front of the old Kontraktovy House. Hesitating, she dreaded where she was going, what she had to do. Filled with remorse, she could not think of anything else. If only she hadn't panicked when she had seen Miller. Then Aunt Elizaveta wouldn't have had to be involved.

Wearing her light gray sweater and cotton dress, Olga walked along, her head hung in sadness. Barely paying any attention to her surroundings, she crossed through Podol's decrepit and historical neighborhoods, which were among Kiev's oldest. Lost in thought, she passed two- and three-story eighteenth and nineteenth-century buildings with peeling yellow plaster and baroque detail in severe disrepair; there were remnants of cornices, decapitated cherubs, and walls permanently stained with grime. In a secluded corner of Podol she passed the walls of Kiev's last nunnery where the women in the heavy black habits, forbidden to teach or recruit, were one by one dying away.

She recalled his face—that angular face with the small mouth, green eyes, and light brown hair—so receptive and charming, so open and happy, when she had seen him at Saint Vladimir's. He had cried, "Olga!" not with malice, but with joy. And how had she responded? With fright.

It had all been in vain, too. In spite of her desperate efforts, the incident resulted in exactly what Olga was trying to prevent: Elizaveta's involvement. She had heard Nick call out her name, been paralyzed with stupor, and then, assuming that he had been followed, had run.

She feared the group assigned to follow Miller. Mayakovsky had called them off whenever she had met with Nick, but she was positive they had tailed him that night. Rotating and using radio-equipped taxis, they had surely followed him into the cathedral. The instant Olga had seen Nick, she knew that somewhere in the church at least one of them was watching and noting with whom the American was making contact.

No, Olga was not afraid for herself. She had no reason to be. It made no difference if they had seen her speaking with Nick. They were not aware of her part in the operation, but Mayakovsky would have taken care of that. In fact, he probably would have reprimanded them for potentially fouling the entire scheme.

Instead it was Olga who had placed everything in jeopardy. She had fled, fearing a link—even the slightest—that could be used to trace the documents from Nick to Olga and from Olga to Elizaveta, their source. When the papers were planted on Miller, Olga wanted absolutely no trace of their origin. She had to protect Elizaveta. She owed her no less.

Olga left the main road and paused at the base of the dirt path. Above, perched on the hillside separating Podol from the main part of Kiev, was Elizaveta's ancient two-room house. Unpainted and bearing traditional decorative woodwork along its eaves and around its windows, the house was, like Elizaveta, from a different century. Olga started up the path.

Mayakovsky was well acquainted with the documents. The plan to involve Miller was, after all, his idea. Recognizing their historical significance and potential impact when he had learned of the papers two years earlier, Mayakovsky had advised against action until the perfect time.

"They're not hurting anything down there in your aunt's catacomb," he had said in his typical authoritative manner. "We could bring them out now. But why? They're safe down there—that's where they survived the Nazi occupation. The old woman's not going to do anything with them, anyway. No. It is wiser to wait for that special moment when we can exploit them for their fullest effect. Those documents—those telegrams—are very significant and we could gain a great deal by exposing them . . . at the proper time."

That time came after the two Soviet agents were imprisoned in Connecticut and after the American businessman was arrested in Moscow. When the Kremlin decided that their next target would be one of the American exhibit guides, Mayakovsky was convinced.

"Now!" he proclaimed, pacing back and forth with enthusiasm. "Now is the time."

Olga consented, having come to the conclusion that it was safest for Elizaveta, once and for all, to be rid of the documents. Olga realized, too, that her own direct involvement would further assure that no harm would come to the old woman. Her only stipulation for obtaining the documents from her aunt and placing them on Miller had been that Elizaveta in no way be implicated.

"Olga Mixhailovna," Mayakovsky had condescendingly said. "Just so long as you are able to get the telegrams from your aunt, I don't care what you tell her or what she knows. She'll be left in peace. Besides, what good would it do to involve an old woman in this? It would only complicate things. Another factor to deal with. No, I agree with you. Let's just carry on as if she never existed."

Short of breath, Olga arrived at the house. The unpainted exterior walls were gray and splintered with age, while the intricate carving around the windows, looking like wooden lacework, was a faint, faded white. Olga knocked on the cracked door and worn wood tore into her knuckles.

"Aunt Elizaveta?" she called. "I'm here. It's me. Olga."

Olga surveyed the house. Most such private dwellings in the city had been destroyed, replaced with featureless high rises. This house and a few others nearby had survived because of their precarious hillside location.

"Aunt Elizaveta?" Worried, Olga rapped harder.

"Yoo-hoo!" cried a voice that, like the house, betrayed its age. "Over here!"

Walking on two boards laid on the damp earth, Olga went around the side. The house, built right into the hillside, had neither an indoor toilet nor running water, and her aunt stood in the mud next to a decrepit pump.

"Why, Olga." Elizaveta let the last of the water dribble into the second bucket and embraced her niece. "My darling, is everything all right?"

"Of course," said Olga defensively. "But you shouldn't be doing this—getting two full buckets of water. It's too strenuous. You'll hurt yourself."

Elizaveta was undaunted. "It's my exercise."

"Can we talk?" Olga stepped through the mud, splattering dirt on her dress, and picked up the buckets. "I have news."

Elizaveta's face became a mass of tight tiny wrinkles. "News? I hope nothing happened because of the other night. I still don't know why you had to leave like that . . . so fast and all. Have you spoken with Bishop Tikhon? Everything will be all right, won't it?"

Olga struggled to conceal her misgivings. "Yes . . . everything will be fine." Mayakovsky's final instructions were to have Elizaveta meet Nick. Bowing her head, she said, "Let's go in. I'll explain everything."

They trod silently back to the front of the house. Inside, Olga set the pails of water near the tin sink. Elizaveta took off her dirty shoes and put on her *tapochki*—slippers. Olga's pair was by the door, as always, ready for any hoped-for visit.

"Here are your *tapochki*, Olga," said Elizaveta, handing the felt slippers to her. "Will you have some cabbage soup and black bread?''

''No.''

''Some tea? I'm going to have some.''

''Thank you, no.'' Her blond hair hanging down as she leaned on the counter, Olga took off her shoes. She hated what she had to do and hated herself for doing it. She just wanted it to be over.

Elizaveta went ahead and lit the kerosene burner for tea. ''That poor young man.'' She shook her head, clicking her tongue. ''He was so confused. I wanted to explain, to tell him everything. I wanted to . . .''

''Did you?'' Olga looked up sharply. ''Tell him anything, I mean?''

Elizaveta shook her head and her double chin wiggled. ''My dear Olga. Trust me, believe me, I didn't. I only told him not to worry and that you'd come to him.'' Grinning, hers was a face, softened by time, of love, and compassion. ''He seems a nice boy, though. I wish I could get to know him, talk with him. I wonder what the rest of the world is like without communism, if young people in the West believe in God. But I suppose, as you said, it's best not to meet him.''

Her back to her aunt, Olga gripped the counter and closed her eyes. This was her chance. ''Actually, he . . . he wants . . .''

Elizaveta came over, stood on her toes and kissed Olga's neck. ''Wants what, dear?''

Olga pulled away. ''Nothing.'' She couldn't do it.

She went to the large window, its thick, old glass deformed by bubbles and curves and ripples. As a child she had spent hours looking out this window trying both to remember and to forget. Down the hill and to the right, Olga could see the very edge of the nunnery.

"Your father," began Olga, "was my great-grandfather. My grandfather was your older brother. My mother . . . your niece." She rested her hands on the window ledge, which was so worn and bleached from the sun that it resembled driftwood.

Elizaveta sat at the table, the focal point of the room. "Yes . . ." She became lost in remembrance of those now dead.

"After you took me in and I came to live here, I used to touch the house like this. Look." Olga sensually ran the palms of her open hands in opposite directions along the window sill and, spreading her arms, up each side of the frame. Her hands rejoined at the latch in the middle. "I used to touch the house and the furniture like this and . . ."

"For hours on end," said Elizaveta, nodding her head. "I know. I watched."

"Really?" Olga raised her brow in surprise. Had her pain been that obvious? "I'd think of my great-grandfather, my grandfather, and my mother. I imagined them touching these things in the same places I did and sometimes I even felt them touching back . . . touching me."

Starry-eyed, Elizaveta said, "I can remember your mother standing right where you are. My brother would bring his little girl—your mother . . . oh, she was so cute!—for a visit and she would throw open those windows and breath in the fresh air and say, 'Oh, Aunt Elizaveta, isn't it a gorgeous day!' "

The imagery was too strong. "Mama . . ." said Olga, her head falling against the glass. She couldn't cry, not now, not again. She turned and took several steps forward. "Aunt Elizaveta?"

"Yes, dear. What is it?"

"Have I . . ." Olga put her hand to her mouth and caught her breath. "Have I ever thanked you?"

The old woman was confused. "What on earth for?"

She closed her eyes and lowered her head. "For . . . everything."

"My little Olga." Seated, Elizaveta reached out with open arms. "My darling one, come here."

At first hesitant but then glad, Olga came forward. Troubled, she lowered herself to her knees and let her head fall on her aunt's lap. "Aunt Elizaveta, I . . ."

"Shhh." She held her niece's head in one hand and patted her on the back with the other. "Shhh." She just wanted to ease the young woman's pain.

"I . . . I . . ." began Olga. How could she go through with it all? "Sometimes I feel so . . . so tortured."

"Shhh." Elizaveta shook her head. "When you get to the other end, you realize that life is too short to trouble yourself so."

Olga's eyes filled with tears. She constricted her face into an ugly, tight mass in an attempt to restrain herself. What was happening to her? But she couldn't hold back, she couldn't suck the tears back in. She let loose and sobbed. She let herself drift away.

"Hmmm . . . hmmm . . . ahhh . . . ahhh . . . ohhh." Completely unself-conscious, Elizaveta hummed loudly as she rocked back and forth.

"I . . ." Olga's voice was strained and filled with emotion.

"Hush, my dear. Just let go and realx."

Whenever she had had a problem, Elizaveta had always held her like this, rocking and humming quite out of pitch. And again now it was cathartic to let go, to let the tension flow out. To regress.

"I love you, Aunt Elizaveta." Olga wrapped her arms around her aunt's legs and hugged her.

"Oh, not so hard!" said Elizaveta, laughing and sitting forward. "That tickles!"

"Sorry." Olga smiled and wiped her eyes.

Elizaveta took Olga by the shoulders and held her at arm's length. Looking down at her, she was direct and firm. Without fear Elizaveta accepted as natural that any day could be her last. Olga, however, had many more, and she wanted her niece not to have any doubt, any question. She wanted to be absolutely sure that Olga understood.

Quite lucidly, Elizaveta said, "I love you. I love you, too. More than anything. And I love you for all that you do for me now, if you understand. I mean for all the attention and help you give an old *babushka*. What on earth would I do without you? You've filled my life with so much happiness, dear Olga."

Her aunt couldn't have said anything worse. Olga's eyes swelled red with tears and guilt. "I'm sorry, Aunt Elizaveta, I'm sorry!" There was no way she could go through with it. "I must . . ."

Spitting and spattering onto the stove, the water began to boil over with manic energy. Startled, Elizaveta put her hand over her heart and jumped in her seat.

"Oi!"

Elizaveta raised herself, groaning, from the chair, and hobbled to the burner. She turned off the flame and then stood, dismayed, staring at the kettle of steaming water. Scared, she put her hand to her mouth and forgot that Olga was even in the room.

''Aunt . . . Elizaveta?'' Brushing away her tears with the back of her hand, Olga got up.

The old woman was at a loss. She shook her head and clenched her arthritic hands. ''I can't . . . can't remember why I boiled the water!'' She was frightened. She looked at her niece, begging for help. ''I can't remember why I boiled the water.'' Her moment of clarity had vanished.

Olga hurried to Elizaveta and put her arms around her. ''It's okay. Come on, sit down'' She directed her aunt back to the chair. ''Sit down. Don't worry.''

Her voice shaking with hysteria, Elizaveta said, ''But I can't remember, Olga. I can't remember!'' She let herself be taken back to the chair.

''That's it,'' said Olga, helping her down. ''Just sit. Everything's fine. Good. Just relax like you told me.'' She helped her get comfortable, and said, ''You didn't, Aunt Elizaveta. You didn't put on the water. I did. I wanted tea so I put on some water.''

Fully confused, Elizaveta gazed up at Olga. ''Really?'' She wanted very much to believe.

''Really.''

Biting a fingernail, Elizaveta tried to smile. ''Oh, yes. Sure. Of course. You . . . you put on some water. I . . . I think I'd like some too. Will you make some for me? Tea, that is.''

Later, as Elizaveta sipped the dark Georgian tea, a schoolgirl grin appeared on her aged and merry face. ''So we'll finally meet. I'm so flattered. I'm so happy.''

''It's best this way.'' said Olga. Calmed, she was relieved that she finally understood what needed to be done.

''I'll finally get to meet Mr. Miller.''

"So you'll be there?" asked Olga sitting opposite her at the table.

Elizaveta was shocked. "Be there? I can't wait!"

"With the documents?"

She grew blissful. "Yes, with the documents." Elizaveta noisily drank her tea. "Just think, Olga, the documents—they'll be in the West soon. And then the world will know that real religion has not been wiped out of the U.S.S.R. There will be lots written about the Church of the Catacombs." She shook her head, not able to believe it. "Two telegrams. That's all. Yet what a stir they'll make! Imagine what will be said when people find out that after all these years there is proof that the Tsar did perish. Real proof. Our telegrams. One . . . one from the very head of the Soviet government ordering the execution of Tsar Nicholas II and the whole royal family. Absolutely official. Absolutely undeniable."

"At last," said Olga, "the world will get concrete evidence that they are dead."

Elizaveta looked up sharply. "Concrete proof that they were murdered! Murdered like my father. And like my father's, their bodies were never found either. Officially there has never been anything conclusive. People surmised that they were killed, but until now the world has never known for sure." Elizaveta gazed into her cup of tea and drifted back in thought. "And the other telegram, the second one, sent from Ekaterinburg confirming their deaths—the deaths of the Tsar, the Tsaritsa, the Tsarevich, and the girls."

Olga had seen the documents only once, when Elizaveta had brought them out to show Bishop Tikhon. All this, thought Olga to herself, for such old documents.

Such risk. Such danger.

"It was so long ago," said Olga.

Elizaveta shrugged. "Yes, but I remember." Then she became defensive. "They might make a difference. They might not. In any case, we simply can't let the Soviet government rewrite such important history. It is our duty, Olga, to tell the world what really happened out there in Ekaterinburg and who . . . who ordered it." She leaned her head back. "First the Bolsheviks had them hidden, then the Tsarist generals—they kept the documents secret so that their armies would think the Tsar was alive and that there was still reason to fight. And then . . . then me. But you're right. It has been a long time. I've had them locked away for so many years. It's hard to believe that after all this time the end is here." Elizaveta became worried. "I just hope people in the West will take notice. Pray, Olga, pray."

"Of course." She would pray that both she and her aunt would survive the next few days.

"Oh, and I want to invite Bishop Tikhon, he—"

"No!" interrupted Olga. Very serious, she sat forward. "We cannot invite Bishop Tikhon."

Elizaveta was hurt. "But . . . but why? He's the head of the Church of the Catacombs here in Kiev. He could do a little service. That would be so nice and very appropriate, too."

"No." Olga was absolute. "It just wouldn't be good." Her dark blue eyes shifted back and forth. "Too many people. I don't want to scare Nick with too many people. Please. Please. Do you understand?"

She really didn't. "I . . . I suppose."

Olga reached across the table top for her aunt's

hand. "I know you'd like to, but we mustn't tell Bishop Tikhon until it's all over."

"Oh . . ." Elizaveta could not conceal her disappointment. "But—"

"Promise me you won't," said Olga, squeezing the old woman's hand. "I don't want to frighten Nick and . . . and I don't want to hurt Bishop Tikhon's feelings either. Really, it'll be easier to explain once it's all over."

"Well, if you insist."

"I do."

"Then I won't," said Elizaveta, resigning herself to Olga's decision. "I promise I won't tell Bishop Tikhon until it's over if it will make things easier for you and Nick."

Olga was relieved. "Thank you." She patted her aunt's hand. "It will be much better this way." Olga stood. "I should be going. Is everything all right?"

"Absolutely. Just imagine. The documents in the West." She looked fondly at Olga. "And don't worry. Everything has passed. I'm fine. I just get these moments every now and then." She tapped her head. "It's age, nothing more than age."

"You just get some rest." Perhaps, thought Olga, she'll have one of these fits when she meets Nick. How convenient it would be if Elizaveta didn't remember a thing. "And don't go carrying two buckets of water. You'll hurt yourself."

"Now, now . . ." Elizaveta dismissed the warning. "Just tell me where we'll meet."

"I'll get Nick and then we'll meet you at the Church of Saint George. That will be safest."

"How nice." It was in a secret tunnel not far from

the Monastery of the Catacombs. "That was our first church, the first one we set up after the Revolution. We even named our group there. The Church of the Catacombs." Elizaveta frowned, thinking of how the congregation had been declining over the years. Only a dozen or so members were left in Kiev.

Olga crossed behind her seated aunt. She ran her fingers through Elizaveta's brittle, gray hair. "Good-bye. I'll check with you tomorrow. Just have the documents ready." She bent and kissed her forehead. "I love you."

Elizaveta pulled her niece around and with tea-warmed lips planted a kiss on Olga's cheek. "Don't worry. I don't know why, but I have this feeling that everything will be all right. Just have faith in God."

"Yes." Olga wished she could be optimistic. "I'll have faith." She took off her slippers and put on her shoes. Standing at the door, Olga said. "You're sure you're fine?"

Elizaveta nodded defiantly, squinting and smiling.

"Good-bye, then."

Olga shut the weatherbeaten door behind her. From her vantage, she could see the meandering Dneiper River below. Several barges slowly made their way upstream and far in the distance greasy black smoke slithered into the sky.

Olga began to make her way down the hill. Before, she thought she could do it. Before, they were merely words and promises. Now, however, the realities of the situation were obvious. Yes, she was different from Elizaveta. She had different goals, different realities. Nonetheless, she had never intended to hurt her aunt. Only to spare her. She had rationalized earlier that it would be necessary to betray her aunt in order to protect her. Tonight, though, Olga had realized how much simpler the matter really was: betrayal was simply betrayal.

She reached the bottom of the hill, nervous but glad to have regained her sense of what needed to be done. Now it was time to act. Without Mayakovsky's knowledge, she would meet with Nick tomorrow night, introduce him to Elizaveta, and fully explain the situation of the documents. Whether or not he would indeed transport them to the West would be his decision.

In any case, she would warn him of the Kremlin's intention to arrest him.

XVIII

Shivering in the cool night, Yezhov took a deep drag on the cigarette as he checked his watch yet another time. Eleven o'clock. Briefcase at his side, he had been sitting on the bench in the ragged courtyard for over an hour. He nervously tapped his feet in the dusty dirt. When his eyes again returned to the ninth-story apartment, he found that the one light, the same light, remained on.

It flicked off.

Yezhov's heart jumped but he did not get up. Zipping his lightweight jacket, he knew it would be best to let things settle for a few minutes. With his hands in his pockets, the cigarette hung from his lip and he puffed slowly on it. When there was nothing left but a stub, he spit it out and ground the butt into the earth. He did not want to hurry into the darkened apartment, however, and he lit another Marlboro. It tasted disgusting, though, and he threw it to the ground. Finally, unable to stand the badgering cold, he grabbed his briefcase and headed in.

The building's entry was damp and poorly lighted. Straining to see, Yezhov searched the wall, then found and punched the button. Opening, the elevator doors scraped against one another like fingernails being laboriously dragged across a blackboard. He got in and flinched as they repeated their noise with mechanical precision. The lift, with dark green graffiti-ridden walls—Sasha, Yura, and Misha had each scratched their names into the paint ten times—shook and rattled all the way to the ninth floor. Yezhov winced when, to his dismay, his arrival was fully announced by the cry of the opening doors. The dim corridor was empty and quiet, though, and he cautiously made his way to the third door on the right.

He waited for the elevator doors to make their clumsy closing, and took the long, thin key out of his pocket. Holding it up to the light, he made sure it was rightside up, then slipped it into the lock. There wasn't a sound and he placed his other hand on the doorknob. In one surgical-like movement he turned both hands and the door opened as if on command.

The apartment was black and quiet and lifeless. Nothing. Apparently the occupants were asleep and undisturbed by Yezhov's entrance. He inched the door forward, stepped through, and, with both hands, shut it quietly behind him. He stood still in the darkness. Unable to see a thing, he knew there should be a corridor directly in front of him. He raised his foot, then froze. There was a subtle squeak of wood against wood. Sensing movement other than his own on the parquet floor, he reached for the door. If he hurried, there was still time to get out.

With a disturbing click, the hall light burst on and Yezhov shielded his eyes.

"Good evening."

It was Sonia, his ex-wife, with her robe tightly wrapped around her. Anticlimatically, Yezhov cast her a disgusted look, took off his coat, tossed it on a hook, and went into the kitchen. He set the briefcase beneath the table and, fumbling for his cigarettes, pulled out a stool and sat down. Hesitant at first, Sonia came in.

Standing in the doorway of the kitchen, Sonia said, "I waited up for you but it got to be late. I haven't seen you in days."

He tossed the pack of American cigarettes out on the table so that she'd know what she'd be missing.

"I've been eating and drinking with the Americans after work," said Yezhov, even though he had been making it a point to wander around until he was sure Sonia and her parents were asleep. They were gone to work before he got up in the morning. "Very nice people. Some attractive girls, too. If you know what I mean," he added with a laugh.

Looking sickly without all her make-up, Sonia said, "The wedding's set. Two weeks from Saturday."

Yezhov eyed her through his glasses and grunted, trying to make it clear that he didn't care.

"I . . ." She caught herself. "It's cold out . . . the first frost will be soon. You look chilled. Want some tea?"

He nodded indifferently and turned to the window. The other buildings were dark and bleak. Only accordion music and drunken clapping from another apartment broke the stillness. A wedding party, perhaps.

Sonia kept her distance as she crossed to the small

stove. Striking a wooden match and lighting the gas, she quickly looked over her shoulder as if she expected him to strike her.

Nervously filling the kettle, she said, "Found a place yet?"

He hesitated, thought better of it, and said, "Of course." He had not, however, found anything else besides the filthy room a widowed *babushka* was renting near the center of Kiev.

"Where?"

"What business is that of yours?" he snapped.

"Curious. That's all."

Yezhov lit the cigarette. He couldn't stand her and was glad to be leaving.

"It's in the center of the city, a short walk from work. Very convenient. A room," he said. "A very large room in an old apartment. Tall ceilings, large windows, balcony. Rather elegant I'd say. And clean. Some *babushka* is renting out part of her apartment. Used to belong to some member of the nobility."

"Oh. Expensive?" Her words were strained.

"A real treasure and a real steal."

Sonia turned to him and at that moment saw his briefcase beneath the table. She knew what was in the case, and, her eyes fixed on it, she said, "I . . . I—"

"Oh, really," he said with disgust. "Don't bother saying anything. Don't even bother with the tea. Let's not make things any more complicated than we have to. Just thank God we don't have any children."

"Yes." Ashamed, she bent her head. He did not know of her three abortions—two while they were married, one after—because she could get no other form of birth control.

"No children and you're getting married. Lucky me. I don't have to forfeit twenty-five percent of my income for alimony." He blew a smoke ring. "What a relief. The other fellow's going to have to take care of you now." He took off his steel-frame glasses and put them on the table.

Unable to stand it any more, she turned off the gas. "You can get your own damned tea. I want you out. I want you out of here as soon as possible." Trying to maintain control, she walked briskly out of the kitchen.

"With great pleasure, Sonia. Don't worry, I'll leave in two or three days. I'd leave tonight but I believe I'm paid up all the way through next week. Or do you owe me? Did we ever settle for the nylons and perfume I got you? Or the jean skirt—you know it goes for two hundred rubles on the street."

His words were wasted. She had already hurried into the bathroom and turned on both water faucets. Above the noise, however, he could still hear her sniveling.

So, he realized, he'd have to take that room the *babushka* was renting out. It was cramped and unclean, and the woman herself was a haggardly old thing with warts on the right side of her face. But what choice had he? Instead of hunting for another place, it was best for now to concentrate on the exhibit and to just go ahead and take the room. He'd contact the old woman tomorrow and perhaps move in the next day. There'd be time to find a better place on his own later, or if he could get something on one of the Americans, surely he'd be allocated an apartment.

The bathroom door opened and he heard her shuffle down the hall.

"I hope you sleep like the dead," he said full of sarcasm.

If he were going to gain anything by working at the American exhibition, he had to act. There was no time to waste. Perhaps he could frame the guide from Kansas who had given him the carton of cigarettes. Or maybe he could somehow compromise the guide from Seattle with whom he had exchanged records. Compromise him with narcotics?

Yezhov shook his head and snuffed out his cigarette. That would never do. Such small stuff. Groping for such small stuff. He could never get the recognition and the compensation he needed out of that.

Colonel Mayakovsky's warning rang clear. But as long as he was careful, what choice had he? Besides, he was a lieutenant in the KGB and he did have some responsibility, some authority. He was not ignorant by any means, despite the way Mayakovsky treated him—and everyone else.

Yezhov just had to be slow and cautious and deliberate. In that way if there was anything to report on Miller, he'd certainly get the credit he deserved.

XIX

She had long, blond hair. It was thick and flowed profusely from her head, onto her shoulders, and she frequently pulled it back with one hand. Her face was Slavic—a soft, clean complexion, wide cheeks with well-defined features, and a hint of Asian ancestry. Her build was large and sturdy, not fat. Her hips were broad, suggesting a strong maternal nature. And Olga had . . .

"Shit," said Nick, shaking his head as he walked from the guide lounge to the irrigation stand, his mid-afternoon break over.

He couldn't put her together. The picture of Olga in his mind was getting fuzzy. So obsessed was he with the sight of Olga overcome with fear at Saint Vladimir's that he couldn't quite remember what she looked like. In his memory he couldn't put the specifics together to produce one clear image. He could only recall disjointed highlights. It was as if he had played a videotape of Olga through his mind too many times and now it was worn out, only offering blurred highlights of what used to be there.

He paused at the gate that opened onto the exhibit floor. She had said that she was going to be working that night. Had she deliberately lied or had something legitimate come up? He cringed as he thought of Masha's warning: "Anyone who truly wants to get to know you also wants you to get to know them—and that includes meeting their friends and family." Olga, if she had any, had never even mentioned friends in Kiev. Her father was in Lvov—or was that a lie too?—and she had no family members in town except perhaps the great-aunt she had briefly mentioned. So was that her? Was the old woman in church Olga's aunt? If so, why had Olga not introduced him? Why, he asked himself again and again, had she run away from him?

Nick had a headache, and he didn't want to answer any more questions that afternoon. Pushing open the gate, he breathed in the warm, stale air. He didn't even want to be at the goddamned exhibit. It was so crowded, so cramped. He was sick of it. Though there were fewer than on the weekend, thousands of Russians milled about before him, whispering amongst themselves. There had recently been a slanderous article in *Pravda* about how only the rich could get educated in America. He thought he might go crazy if he had to explain one more time that there were twelve free grades of school available to all Americans.

Nick wanted to trust her. He even wanted to take the letter and package to her uncle. But now how could he? How could he ever straighten anything out with Olga? He made his way toward the irrigation stand.

Across the room he spotted the young Jewish couple

who had come the day before and, as indifferently as possible, asked about welders and manicurists in Los Angeles. Nick knew the game only too well and had played along while they asked how many square meters a California apartment had, if the typical family had a color TV, if people were afraid to walk the street at night, if Los Angeles were indeed a good city in which to live. Obviously, they were hoping to get visas to Israel and then, once out of the U.S.S.R., to emigrate to California. They had come again to FARMING U.S.A. to soak up as much information as possible. Nick avoided them and moved on. It was futile. They'd never be prepared for their resettlement in the West.

He passed the seeder display which plunked down kernel after kernel of corn on a conveyor belt, then crossed under an enormous section of a rotating irrigation machine. There was the typical crowd around the small working sprinkler encased in a plexiglass bubble; people felt the shooting water hit the bubble and grinned in disbelief.

Nick stepped onto the guide platform, knowing that if he ever saw her again, he would always doubt her. As things stood now, there was no way he would take the letter to her uncle in New York. Most bothersome, however, was the dawning realization that even if things did get straightened out, it really didn't make any difference. Tossing and turning in his fretful sleep last night, it had occurred to him that after a few short weeks he'd never see Olga again in his life.

"Molodoi chelovek." Young man.

Fuck, said Nick to himself. A short man in his late forties stood peering up at him. His clothing, apparently unimportant to him, was in disarray.

"*Molodoi chelovek,* how much does a pair of *jeanzie* cost in the United States of America?" The man wore thick broken glasses that magnified and disfigured his sleepy eyes.

Speechless, Nick gawked at the man. What was going on with Olga and why did he have to answer this question for the fiftieth time today?

The man, adjusting the glasses on his nose, drew closer and in a louder voice said, "I ask you, how much does a pair of *jeanzie* cost in the United States?"

Nick opened his mouth. He tried to speak but his throat was parched. Who was the jerk who invented blue jeans, anyway?

"You speak *Russki?*" The little man squinted in frustration.

No, thought Nick. I don't. I won't. "*Da.*"

"*Jeanzie,* how . . ."

Nick shut his eyes and blurted it out. "Anywhere from eight to twenty dollars. Some fashionable ones cost more."

The Russian scratched his head with quick motions and his eyes bugged in disbelief. "That's impossible. Why so cheap?" He lowered his voice as a woman approached. "My son just spent one hundred fifty rubles—well over two hundred dollars—for a pair of *jeanzie*! Can you imagine, that's almost two month's salary." He jabbed a finger up under his glasses and scratched his nose. Eying the woman as he spoke, he hesitantly asked, "What about books? Are they hard to get?"

The woman, with orangish-red hair and a staunch chest that stuck out as a single edifice, positioned herself closer and expressed disdainful interest.

"Well . . ." Sensing that the woman was about to go on the attack, Nick went on the offensive. "Books aren't hard to get in America. Actually, it's easier to get Soviet authors in the States than it is here." Sick of his job and the exhibit, to make his stab at the woman complete, he added, "Authors like Solzhenitsyn are widely available, too."

It was more than she could take, and she opened her lipstick-smeared mouth in a tirade. "Who wants to read Solzhenitsyn? Such trash, such lies! He belongs right down there with child pornography."

Fully knowing the answer and loathing it, Nick's question was simple. "Have you ever read Solzhenitsyn?"

Her eyes opened wide. "Well, well, no. I haven't read him because he's such a terrible author and that's why his books aren't sold here. He . . . he writes such lies and so poorly, too!"

Nick's entire body tensed. "So you only read what the government censors say are good books, is that it?"

"Of course. That is their job. That way we don't waste valuable materials, time, and money publishing bad authors." She smiled proudly. "Our government takes care of us and decides what we should read."

Nick didn't care if this woman was an agent sent to provoke him. "That's disgusting. How's there ever going to be peace and friendship in the world if you don't even know what's going on in your own country? I mean, how do you ever expect to really understand what's going on in the U.S.?"

"Well, well . . ." She flushed red and became all huffy. "This is all very nice. So you have lots of books and newspapers, and from what the other guides say you have lots of material goods, too—*jeanzie, kosmetiki, avtomobili.* But when you have so many things and so much freedom,'' she said, redirecting the conversation as she saw fit, ''you are also free to have poverty, unemployment, discrimination, and so very much more. Can't you see there's no security in so much freedom?''

Nick slapped his forehead. ''I don't believe it.'' He wanted to call her a fascist, an insult that would surely land him in deep trouble. Instead, he put his face in his hands and closed his eyes. He couldn't take any more. ''Just leave. Just get the hell out of here. What you say is not only terribly wrong, it's terribly dangerous.''

''Besides, we don't have all the material luxuries because of the war,'' she said, batting her eyes and unable to stop herself. ''But you clearly can't understand that. Can't you see what a fine country this is? Can't you see that it really is better?'' Not granting Nick a chance to respond, the woman turned and indignantly stormed away.

Furious, Nick called out after her in English: ''You fucking redneck commie!'' He cut himself off, unable to believe his own words. What was happening to him? Back home he used to eat granola and participate in antinuclear demonstrations.

Upset, the little Russian man, still standing before Nick, reached out. ''Don't, don't,'' he said, taking Nick's arm. ''It's not worth it. Don't get upset about that woman. Forget her and remember me. Remember me to your countrymen and not that woman. Extend my warm greetings to everyone in America.'' He took Nick's hand and shook it, then hurried away.

''Yeah, but . . .''

Nick's attention was still focused on the woman. What would she do: leave the exhibit calmly or write a complaint claiming that Nick had argued with her and insulted the honor of the Great Soviet People?

No sooner had the little man with thick glasses left than Nick was approached by a group of collective farmers with the first agricultural questions of the day. Wearing dark, bulky clothing, they were sunburnt and their broad muscular bodies were evidence of their physical labor.

One of them waved his callused hand in the air. "*Molodoi chelovek!*"

As Nick looked for the voice, his eyes were caught by that unmistakable head of hair. He caught his breath in relief and nervous anticipation. Olga. She was lingering in the corner

"It says," began one of the farm workers, "on that panel over there that only four percent of your population works on the farm. How is that possible? Everyone knows that the United States is a great exporter of food, so how can so few feed so many? Is this some sort of fairy tale?"

Looking sincere and anxiously hopeful, Olga was smiling just with her eyes. Not coy, she had come to talk, to explain, and this much was clear. Slowly, reluctantly, she turned away and watched the seeder demonstration, then gazed at a television monitor as it showed shots of American wheat fields under irrigation.

His anger began to subside. She came back, he thought. She'd tell him what the problem was, why she had run away. He hadn't misjudged her after all. At least she cared enough to come back.

The collective farmers, bursting with questions,

closed in on Nick. He was overwhelmed by them, and when he checked back to where Olga had been, she was gone. He became apprehensive. Then he spotted her by the drip irrigation display, her image hazily reflected in one of the mirrored panels. What did she want? What would she say?

Facts. They wanted cold, hard facts. They wanted to know everything, from the average size of the American farm to the size of an American sow's litter to the frequency of tractor repairs. They interrogated Nick almost without end, and he impatiently answered each question, trying all the time not to lose sight of Olga.

"I don't know," said one of the farmers, full of skepticism. "American farmers have much independence but they are so insecure financially. They have to work from sunup to sundown, too, and still the crops might fail. No. No. I'm afraid our collective farmers would never consent to work on an American farm."

"Let me assure you," said Nick, searching for her, "that our farmers would never consent to work on a collective, communal farm. Our farmers are extremely independent and perhaps only more conservative than one other group in America—factory workers."

"Factory workers?" said one of them in disbelief. "But how can that be? Everyone knows the working class is the most oppressed under capitalism. Why should they support your government?"

"Nick, I must apologize." Again she was direct, though this time she was scanning the room to see if anyone was watching them.

They stood behind the drip irrigation display. He

wanted to reach out and hold her. Instead, he let his hand haphazardly swing out and brush her. Anyone would have thought that he had simply bumped into her.

"What was it?" His tone was demanding, but conciliatory. "Why did you run away?"

"I was afraid. I'll explain, but we can't talk here." She became nervous. "Can we meet tonight?"

"Olga, why? Why were you so frightened?" If only she could give him a sensible answer.

She looked into his eyes. "There's much I have to tell you. For now all I can say is that I shouldn't have been in church."

"I don't get it." He wanted to understand.

"I'll tell you more later." She saw, however, that she needed to divulge more. "It would not have been good for me to have been seen in church with an American."

He shook his head. "Damnit, is everything all right now?"

"Yes, it is," she said, stressing each word. "Just tell me, can we meet tonight?"

"Sure, but . . ."—he felt as if he were betraying her—". . . but I'll have to bring another guide with me."

Her deep eyes became narrow. "Must you?"

"Well . . ." He wanted most of all to talk intimately and be alone with her again. Recalling Masha's advice, he asked, "What will we do? I'd like to meet some of your friends or . . ."

"Yes," she said, seizing the chance. "My aunt. I want you to meet her."

He sighed with relief. "Your aunt?"

"Yes. She's very nice. Don't worry."

"Wonderful. Same time?"

"No." She glanced about the room, looking at everyone but him. "Nick, it would be better if you didn't return to your hotel. You have a special bus that takes you back, right?"

"Yes." He became hesitant again.

"Ask the driver to let you off in front of the farmers' market. Just tell him you want to buy some vegetables or something." She did not want to frighten him by telling him that he would pick up his tail if he returned to the hotel. "I just want to save time, that's all," she said. "I'll be waiting for you by the main doors and that way we can spend the whole evening together . . . with my aunt, too, of course."

"All right." He could not hide his concern. "There isn't any problem is there?"

She faced him directly. Smiling, softly she said, "No. Not any more."

Olga leaned over and quickly kissed him on the cheek. Then, without a further word, she melted into the crowd and was gone.

Nick watched her go. His eyes clung to her until she disappeared around the corner and into the dairy display. Thinking, hoping, that she might return, he kept staring at the spot. She did not come back, however, and Nick resigned himself to waiting a few more hours before finding out. Only if Olga could explain everything logically and clearly would he agree to take the letter to her uncle in New York.

XX

From the bench where Yezhov sat waiting, he saw her cotton print dress and blond hair as she emerged from FARMING U.S.A. Passing through and around the many groups of people scattered beneath the trees, she bore a serious, pensive expression and pulled her hair back behind her head with one hand. Yezhov was quite certain, however, that she was unaware that he had seen her enter the exhibit and seek out Miller.

Yezhov played with his East German glasses as she approached. To obscure his face further as she neared, he bent over and reached for his briefcase, which rested near his feet. He admired her rather shapely legs when she walked by only several meters from him, and when the blond woman had gone another ten meters, Yezhov calmly got up and started after her.

She was easy to follow. She did not check behind her once as she led the way past the Hall of Soviet Women's Art and the Hall of Soviet Ukrainian Educational Achievements. Keeping an eye on her and those around, Yezhov noted several of his colleagues. One posed as a retired man sitting on a bench and admiring the day; he noted those Russians who met with the guides during their lunch break. Another, a woman with a gift for remembering faces, served *piroshki*—meat pies—from a blue pushcart; she noted those who came repeatedly to the exhibit.

The blonde entered the central portion of the grounds of the VDNX. More than a dozen low, severely neoclassical Stalinesque buildings—inscribed with Lenin's sayings and surmounted by workers bearing sheaths of wheat and hammers and sickles—faced onto a rose garden and circular fountain. From there the woman walked around a small pond and toward the park's gates.

Yezhov was pleased that, to his knowledge, none of his colleagues were following the blond woman. That left her all to himself. Shifting his briefcase to his other hand—with his gun inside, on occasion he did find it heavy—he even managed a small grin.

While Mayakovsky had ordered him to stay away from Miller, the colonel had said nothing about this woman.

XXI

She was Sister Elizaveta of the Church of the Catacombs. And in her subterranean stone chapel, a handful of tapers and oil lamps burning before icons, she stood proudly dressed in her profuse black habit of nineteenth-century design. From a pointed crown of material on her head, the rich, black cloth flowed in a broad conical form all the way to the ground; stretched at its base, the gown measured a full two meters in width. The majority of her face concealed, all that was left exposed was an oval shape of weathered flesh from above her brow, around her eyes, to just below her mouth. Hanging from a chain on her chest rested a large, solid gold Russian Orthodox cross, which had belonged to her father, the priest.

Elizaveta kissed the cross, struggled to lift up the gown, and sunk to her knees. At once she started to paw at the earth flooring of her chapel with her bent, stubby fingers. She took her air in swallowed clumps, held it, and let it wheeze out of her weary body. Digging compulsively, her frantic pace slackened only when her splintered fingernails scraped the lid of the steel case. Full of reservation, Elizaveta dusted away the remaining dirt and pebbles before slipping her fingers underneath the lid. She was surprised by her own trepidation; at such a victorious time she hadn't expected anything less than joy.

As if she were tearing an adhesive gauze from her skin, she crudely forced open the lid of the steel case. There it was. The tin box which had held her life hostage for nearly forty years and which now held the hope of the Church of the Catacombs.

"No," she said, putting a dirty finger to her mouth. "It holds all the hope for all the religions in all the Russias." Leaving splotches of dirt where she touched herself, Elizaveta crossed herself once, twice, three times. *"Xristos Voskreseniye."* Christ has risen, she muttered.

She regained her breath, reached down, and took the box in her hands. Lovingly brushing away the last of the dirt, the old woman closed her eyes and strained to recall the day her father had presented the box to her. It had been a birthday present and had contained the very finest chocolates from the Abrikosova factory in Moscow. Through her worn fingers she felt the raised double-headed Imperial tsarist eagle on the lid and the emblazoned Russian lettering: MOCKBA. Moscow.

Elizaveta giggled and sat back on the ground, her nun's habit in billowing piles around her. She couldn't quite recall receiving the gift from her father, but now, over sixty years later, she could clearly remember going to her room and eating all of the chocolates in a single sitting. Then she had saved the tin box and used it as a special place for special things. An odd history, indeed, she thought. First it had contained fine chocolates fit for the Tsar, then notes and buttons and rings—even a love letter from a merchant's son (she strained her memory. Hadn't he fled to Paris after the Revolution?)—and for the last forty years it had been buried away with documents folded and tucked neatly inside. She raised the candy box to her ear and shook it. Yes, she could hear the telegrams rattling inside.

Elizaveta found the anxiety of success wearing and sighed. She had waited so long for this moment that it was practically anticlimatic. Under the weight and warmth of her heavy clothing, she moaned as she stood. Then, with her torn, black shoe, she kicked shut the top of the steel case which had held the tin box. She heard a noise.

The habit covering her ear, she cupped her hand to the side of her head. "Yoo-hoo, Bishop Tikhon?" she called.

Perhaps he was coming after all. Maybe Olga had changed her mind and asked the bishop to come. How wonderful it would be if he were there when she presented the documents to Nick.

"Bishop Tikhon!"

A bat fluttered into the chapel but was repulsed by the smoke from the icon lamps.

"Oi," she said, dismissing it with a wave of her hand. "Just another one of you."

Elizaveta frowned. So it wasn't the bishop. Well, perhaps Olga was right. She had said that too many new people might put Nick on edge, that it would be better if it were just the three of them. Nice and small, nice and simple. As Olga had insisted, Elizaveta hadn't mentioned it to Bishop Tikhon and she wouldn't until it was all over, either. The old woman only hoped that the bishop would not be offended at not having been included.

Elizaveta had spent the last hour cleaning and straightening her underground chamber. She had not, however, cleaned the monks' coffins tucked into the arches of the chapel and for the first time she admitted that she would die before she ever got around to cleaning them. Now her chapel glittered and glowed with polished brass, silver, and gold. She searched the drawn, somber faces of the icons. It was time to leave for the Church of Saint George.

"*Bozhe moi!*" My God, she exclaimed.

This was it. The end at last. Elizaveta couldn't tell whether she was happy or sad.

Next to Seraphim the Monk's coffin were several torches, their rag-wrapped tips soaking in fuel. Elizaveta took one by its heavy wooden handle, shook off the excess liquid, and held it over a candle. It burst into an oily flame and black smoke rose and stuck to the catacomb's stone ceiling. Torch in one hand, in the other she held the tin box. With two fingers, she raised the front of her long black habit. She had a good distance to go to reach Saint George's and with such precious merchandise she had no intention of traveling above ground.

"Heavens!" she said. "Anything could happen up there." She looked down at her garb. "Besides, what could be more conspicuous than a nun on the streets of Kiev?"

No, she would stay underground, in the world of the holiest martyrs, and the world she knew best. There was no need to risk exposure on the surface. The Monks' Tunnel led all the way from the nunnery near her house to the Monastery of the Catacombs, a passage that had once served as the perfect link for those monks and nuns who could not resist one another.

Elizaveta had to backtrack toward her house to get to the Monks' Tunnel. Following the labyrinthine passages that led from her sequestered chapel, Elizaveta went as far as the Great Hall. There, instead of traveling along the left side of the lake—the last waters of a once great underground tributary—she shuffled along the craggy path on the right bank, her habit dragging behind her. The cavernous Great Hall, soaring overhead, was faintly illuminated by her crackling and snapping torch, and Elizaveta was but a gloomy reflection in the lake's clear waters. A clump of bats hung in a niche above and, annoyed by the disturbance, flew away in a crying mass.

Elizaveta went directly toward an alcove hollowed out in the distant wall of the Great Hall. Once there, she made for the yawning fissure in the alcove's corner. From behind, she felt the air rush past her as she approached the opening and the flame of her torch hissed. The next moment the breeze came from the other direction, then shifted again, and so on, as if the caves were inhaling and exhaling. Her father had called it God's Breath.

Elizaveta shielded her torch from the wind as she passed through the fissure. She stepped into the broad Monks' Tunnel on the other side and paused. A millenium ago a rambling tributary swung wide of the Dneiper River and into the hills of Kiev, burrowing its way along and leaving in its place this smooth, gracefully arching tunnel. To her left the passage, which had once led to the cellars of the nunnery, was blocked. Elizaveta couldn't quite remember when that exit had been buried . . . whether it had been during the Revolution, the Civil War, in the midst of Stalin's purges, or . . . or . . . No, she was sure it had been closed for many years before the Fascist Occupation of Kiev.

She plodded onward to the right, toward Saint George's, which was located just off the Monastery of the Catacombs. Like a great subterranean road, the tunnel had a gravel flooring and was free of debris and blockage. Elizaveta traversed this passage rather mindlessly, clutching the tin box with its dear contents snugly against her bosom. It was damp, and all sounds to be heard were those of her crackling torch, her laborious steps, and her heavy wheezing as she breathed in and out.

"The Germans!" exclaimed Elizaveta, recalling the history of the documents. "I was so sure they were our liberators."

After the Revolution the documents had been hidden away, first by the Bolsheviks, then by the tsarist generals. Yet for their own self-serving reasons, neither organization told the world that the Tsar was dead; the first group did not want to claim responsibility, the second did not want to admit defeat. Then, after the Civil War, terror reigned and a clear route to Western Europe could not be found. Hidden in the Urals, the telegrams became all but forgotten as millions perished during Stalin's purges.

In the initial hope that the Fascists were their liberators, the Church of the Catacombs brought the telegrams to Kiev. The plan was to turn the document over to the Germans so that the whole world would know what Lenin and the Bolsheviks had done.

"But the Fascists were worse than the Bolsheviks!" said Elizaveta, simply. "They said they believed in God, but they killed just as many as the Communists."

That's when Elizaveta had hidden them away in her catacomb chapel, undetectable by either the Germans or the Soviets. She could not risk their falling into the wrong hands, and the safest place to put them was underground.

"But now the time has come."

They were going to send the documents to the West and show the world that real religion—not this official Soviet-sanctioned church that had kowtowed to the Politburo—was still alive and struggling. It was important, too, that somehow, somewhere, there be a written record of the Church of the Catacombs so that, if ever found out and terminated, at least the world would know they had once existed.

"We must give hope to the future generations, for without hope . . ." Elizaveta's voice trailed off.

And, as Bishop Tikhon had flatly stated, the documents had to be publicly presented in the West because, while he felt atheism was one issue, there was another far more disturbing: the deification of Lenin. Something, anything, the bishop had said, must be done to discredit this man who was worshiped as mankind's saviour throughout the U.S.S.R.

Lost in thought, Elizaveta trod on. But then she became aware of a noise behind her. Steps in the gravel.

She spun around, her habit billowing out. "Who is it that follows me?" she demanded.

She held the torch high and peered into the black. Nothing. She clutched the tin box into the folds of her gown.

"I know there is someone there, now . . ."

Her words were cut off by a growl, low and deep. It was an inhuman noise that grew with each moment.

"Oh, dear Lord!" gasped Elizaveta, stepping backward.

Into the very edge of the faint light hobbled the mad dog. The same dog she had come across before, it bore little recognition to any earthly creature. Rabid saliva bubbled like puss from its mouth and a broken front leg hung mangled. While one eye bulged forward out of the head, what remained of the other was nothing more than a mound of thick, black, scabby blood.

Elizaveta trembled and for the first time in her life wished she had a gun. She held the torch toward the creature, but it was only momentarily fazed by the light. Undaunted, it struggled forward on its three good legs. It was then that Elizaveta saw the rest of its mangled body.

"Ahhh!" cried Elizaveta.

The dog had found no rodents to dine on. But they had found the dog. And whatever it was—rats perhaps—that had feasted on the mongrel had torn strips of flesh like jerky from the dog's legs. White bones poked out at random through raw muscles that seethed with blood.

Elizaveta crossed herself. She had prepared herself for any type of human interference, but not for anything like this.

"Dear Lord, I pray that the devil be kept at bay for only a few more hours! Please, Lord, I beg you!"

The creature's lips shriveled aside, exposing deathly fangs, and it began a slow, awkward march toward Elizaveta.

She ran. Elizaveta scooped up her habit, turned and ran as if the dog were on her very heels. The torch whistled and flapped in the breeze, and she did not look back once. Hundreds of droplets of sweat emerged on her forehead and her lungs heaved and strained for air.

Finally, some ten minutes later, she reached the turnoff. Leaning on a large boulder, she struggled to regain her breath and stared into the black tunnel behind her. A chill of relief rushed through her when she realized that the mad dog, hampered by its smashed front leg, had not been able to keep up with her.

"Some . . . someone must . . . must," she gasped, "kill the dog before it . . . it kills."

She mopped her brow and stiffly raised her habit to her knees. With difficulty, she clambered over a small pile of rocks.

"Oh!"

She tripped and fell against a wall. Not wasting any time, she righted herself and made her way out of the Monks' Tunnel. She scrambled into a narrow shaft—its walls and flooring jagged—and continued through a series of mazelike passages into a damp grotto. She paused and listened. When she was sure that the dog was not behind her, she followed a path that rose and fell, made her way between two large boulders, and traversed another corridor until it deposited her at the very edge of a precipice. Quite sure of the way, Elizaveta never hesitated, having taken this route thousands of times in the last half-century.

Beneath her headdress, her ears perked and she

strained to hear voices as she approached the church. Looking ahead into the dark, however, she was disappointed, unable to see or hear anything. The tunnel she walked led to the side of the underground church and Elizaveta was dismayed not to see the glow of light leaking her way. She stopped to catch her breath when she reached the church's man-made outer wall. Where were Olga and Nick? Shouldn't they be here by now?

By the light of her torch, she found the latch on the small side door.

"Olga? Nick?" She opened the door and poked her torch through, holding it high in front of her. "Anyone?"

There was no response. Disheartened, she stepped into Saint George's ornate interior, furnished entirely with religious artifacts Elizaveta had rescued from the Bolsheviks. She glanced around. Nothing. No one. Only the mournful faces of the icons stared down upon her. Where was her Olga? Had something happened?

Next to the door were two buckets, one holding three more torches soaking in fuel, the other greasy water. Elizaveta placed the torch she had carried in a holder in the wall, then took one of the other torches and lit it. She crossed to the central column, carved out of rock and decorated with frescoes, and placed this torch in a holder. The Church of Saint George, its low ceilings arched as they bore the weight of millions of tons of earth upon them, came to life. Remarkably preserved in this underground room, the icons and jewels here were priceless. The iconostasis, which Elizaveta had carried piece by piece from a church in 1928, was sheathed in gold and dated "1450, Novgorod."

Clothed in her black habit, Elizaveta, the fear of the

mad dog still etched on her face, bowed her head and went to the iconostasis. She lifted up the heavy material, threw it upward, and as it filled with air, sunk to her knees. She crossed herself once and, bending forward, placed her hands flat on the floor. Chanting the Lord's Prayer over and over, she kissed the ground, rising and falling with her words.

XXII

"You'll understand everything once you meet my aunt," said Olga, clutching his arm. "I'll explain it all, don't worry. I just don't want to go into it out here on the street . . . in public. We'll meet Aunt Elizaveta and then the three of us will have dinner together."

Nick considered this. "Fair enough."

They stood in front of the faded yellow farmers' market at the intersection of Kreshatik, Shevchenko, and Red Army Streets, and pedestrian traffic was heavy. Nick glanced about anxiously.

"Come on, let's get out of here before someone recognizes me," he said.

Nick wanted to trust her as much as he wanted to find out. Questions, he decided, could wait until the appropriate time. During or after dinner, perhaps.

As they started off, he added, "But I want you to tell me everything, I want to hear it all."

Quite serious, Olga said, "As you wish, Nick."

With the issue resolved for the moment, both of them

relaxed, equally glad to be together again. He was enthralled and calmed when she took his arm in hers, embracing him briefly as she did so. Serene and silent, Olga led the way from the farmers' market directly to the main Metro station. From there they took the subway to Heroes-of-the-Arsenal Square, where they hopped on a bus.

After a short ride, they got off on Citadel Street. Finally away from the crowded streets, subways, and buses, Nick spoke.

"Olga, where are we meeting your aunt, at her house?" he asked, expressing his worry.

She motioned ahead as indifferently as possible. "No, at the Monastery of the Catacombs."

"What?" Nick slowed.

Straining to act natural and belie her concerns, Olga said, "That's where we're meeting her, of course." Seeing that this was not enough, she added, "Nick, she works there."

"Oh." He accepted Olga's words and his skepticism waned.

Approaching the State Museum of the Monastery of the Catacombs, Nick could see the tall golden onion domes towering high overhead. They came around the corner of the bright whitewashed fortress walls and before them stood the Gate Church of the Trinity. Though the radiant frescoes of its outer walls beckoned out, Nick's eyes remained fixed on the gilded cupola perched brilliantly atop. As they passed through the gate beneath the church, Nick realized that they looked like a nice couple out for a visit to one of Kiev's museums.

All that remained of what had been one of the richest

and most influential religious centers in the Russian Empire were a group of buildings and preserved ruins. Nick and Olga walked along the calm central street, a street which had once been swarming with busy monks who controlled hundreds of thousands of acres and tens of thousands of serfs. On either side were the low, white stone buildings with pitched green roofs. Originally they had housed the monastic cells for the church hierarchy.

They passed the preserved ruins of the Dormition Cathedral—blown up by the Nazis—and Nick could tell by the slope of the ground that she was leading the way toward the wooded banks of the Dneiper River. Visitors and tourists were gathered in random clumps in this central area, and Nick doubted that they would meet Olga's aunt in so visible a place.

Olga paused near the base of the Main Bell Tower. It rose in four many-columned tiers, culminating in a massive golden dome some ninety-six meters above. Nick knew the tower well for, perched high on the river's bank, it could be seen for miles.

"Isn't it odd," said Olga, craning her neck upward, "to think of all that has taken place on this ground. Monks began this monastery almost a thousand years ago. Then the Soviets came to power and closed it; they said that the monastery had lost the support of the people. The monks and priests who hadn't already fled were killed. Then the Fascist invasion . . . so much was destroyed. Yet the Revolution was scarcely sixty years ago and the Fascists were here just over thirty years ago. So little time. Our passing is a mere flash. Come," she said, pulling on him. "We must hurry. We must not be late."

"You're sure about this, huh?"

"Of course," she said without looking at him. She started forward. "You'll see."

"Wait," said Nick, resisting. "Before we meet your aunt I . . . I want to say that I was really upset about the other night. Olga, I want to trust you, but something doesn't make sense."

She drew close to him. "Nick, I want you to understand and I want everything to make sense." She embraced him, wrapping her arms around his back and squeezing. "Believe me, Nick. Everything will be clear when you meet my aunt."

What could he say? How could he not trust her? It was obvious she wanted to straighten out the situation. And, thinking of the evening ahead of them, he hoped that perhaps they would have some time alone together.

Past the central complex of buildings and churches was the old print shop. To the side of that, Olga led the way down a narrow cobbled street and through the massive fortress walls. They continued on this deserted street leaving the walled part of the monastery behind. To their left and across a ravine was another group of golden-domed churches, six- and seven-hundred-year-old stone structures clumped together in the woods. They passed a small decrepit stone house, on the stoop of which sat a fat, toothless *babushka*, wearing a long dress and kerchief and throwing bread crumbs to a clattering of free-running chickens.

"Xleb! Xleb! Xleb!" Bread, she cried, gumming the words.

The chickens pecked with frenzy, the woman threw more crumbs, and Nick was sure this was the way this place had looked a hundred years earlier.

"We're almost there," said Olga, motioning ahead. "The catacombs."

He grimaced. "You've got to be kidding."

Trying to belittle his concern, Olga said, "Nick, don't worry. It's just part of the museum."

Through the bent and drooping trees Nick could see another group of whitewashed baroque buildings. They were low and massive, detailed and clean, with arched windows and green roofs. The courtyard, obviously quite elegant in its day, was in disarray; a decorated well was crumbling, stone-encased flower beds were little more than overgrown rubble, and vines and bushes had encroached upon everything. There was not another soul about, and the only sound was that of a flock of distant birds.

They headed for a small building on the left. He assumed this was where Olga's aunt worked, and he envisaged meeting her, being shown around and, over an elaborate meal at the woman's house, learning why Olga and her aunt had been so frightened at Saint Vladimir's.

Olga waited for Nick to open the thick oak door, and the two of them entered a square room with high ceilings. It was free of furniture except for a wobbly chair on which, next to a smaller door, sat a complacent *babushka*.

"Good evening, children," said the old woman, smiling.

At last, thought Nick, Olga's aunt. The woman did not rise out of the chair, however, and Olga did not greet her. Instead, the *babushka* held an open palm toward the door.

"This way," the woman muttered.

Confused, Nick realized that this wasn't Olga's aunt. It did seem, however, as if they had been expected and that Olga and the woman had exchanged a knowing glance. But Nick shrugged this off. He had never been in a Soviet museum that didn't have a bored, motherly old woman seated in each room. He put this out of his mind further when he looked through the door and saw a narrow staircase that curved and twisted down.

"Olga . . ." said Nick, pulling back on her arm.

"Shhh," she said in a whisper. "It's just the entrance to the catacombs."

"You know," began Nick, noticing that his hands were shaking, "I'm a little claustrophobic. I mean, I don't take too well to small enclosed spaces. Especially . . . especially if they're underground."

"Shhh."

"But is it safe?"

"Of course, don't be silly."

She squeezed his hand as she led him down the winding rock stairs.

Angry at himself, he said, "Why do I always get myself into things I know I shouldn't be involved in?" He bumped his head against the low ceiling. "Ouch!" Irritated, he demanded. "Olga, where in the hell are we going?"

"You'll see," she said without stopping.

The smooth whitewashed walls were uneven and rolling, and naked light bulbs dangled at random along the way. The narrow passage, which was not wide enough for two people to stand side by side, grew cooler as they descended, and Nick shivered. Soon they reached the bottom and Olga, without hesitation, continued, taking Nick by the hand. He cautiously followed, running his free hand along the wall. He tapped his foot and discerned that the flooring was of iron slabs.

"Why didn't you tell me," said Nick, sarcastically, "that I was going to get the inside tour of the Monastery of the Catacombs?"

The initial passage wound on in one direction like a narrow one-way street. Several branches were boarded over and others were bricked shut; clearly only part of the catacombs was open to the public. The tunnel bent sharply to the right, and in this hairpin corner were four carved niches, each of which cradled a short coffin. Nick stopped, a mixture of surprise and revulsion on his face. One plaque read: NIKON THE GREAT. And another: SIMION, BISHOP OF VLADIMIR AND SUZDAL.

"They've been here since the eleventh and twelfth centuries," said Olga impatiently. "They'll be here later. You can come back when we have more time."

But his attention was caught by a small glass window just beyond the coffins. "What the hell?"

"Hermits used to isolate themselves in there," explained Olga. "The entrance was sealed shut, food was passed through the window, and they stayed in there until they died. Their bones are still in there."

"That is disgusting," he said shaking his head.

"Nick, they're Holy Relics." She started off. "Come, we must not linger."

The catacombs twisted along. They passed several small chambers, a post with chains where insane people were held, and more clusters of sarcophagi. Dug into the wall at one point was a small, ornate refectory. The clean narrow passage continued, periodically marked by boarded and bricked off tunnels.

Ten minutes later, deep within the catacombs, Nick and Olga reached a large, dark room, faintly illuminated by two bulbs. This was Saint Balaam's Church, the deepest point of the catacombs still open to the public; from here, the passage turned and wound back to the surface. Buried away in the outermost depths of the catacombs, the marble columns, the life-size icons, and the golden Royal Gate had remained untouched for six hundred years.

Nick was shocked when he saw Olga bow her head and cross herself in front of one of the icons.

"Olga," he said with relief, "are you a Believer?"

Confused, she pulled her hair back behind her head. "Nick, I don't know."

Though he was not particularly religious himself, he was comforted. It meant that she was on the other end of the spectrum from the Party.

"Is that why you were in church?" he asked.

"In a way, yes. I come from a family that strongly believes in God." She shook her head, both upset and unsure of herself. "I believe in something, Nick. I'm just not sure it's religion. In a way you could say I'm the strongest believer of them all. Militant even." She went to the side wall and began groping behind one of the icons.

He was still trying to digest her words when, startled by her actions, he asked, "Olga, what are you doing? What's going on?"

She moved the icon aside and an iron knob appeared. She turned it as one would a jar lid, and rusted metal screeched against rusted metal. Something popped loose and a portion of the wall quivered.

"People have always used the caves of Kiev as a place of shelter and hiding. First from the pagans, then from the Mongols. Later from the tsars, then from the Bolsheviks. Many partisans hid from the Nazis here, too. Likewise, my aunt has used the catacombs as a place of refuge." Olga pushed against the wall and it creaked. It moved a second time and dust came cascading down. "Help me, please."

He was paralyzed.

"Nick!"

Reacting to her request without thinking, Nick went to her side and together they pushed on the right side of a row of icons. With a tearing sound, a concealed portion of the wall bent backward from floor to ceiling, forming a false door. Shocked, Nick peered in. The catacombs, rough and unfinished, extended into the unknown darkness. His eyes wide open in disbelief, Nick stepped back.

"Olga," he said, gesturing with his hands, "what in the hell's going on? That's not part of the museum and you know it. What are you trying to do, get me sent to Siberia? Jesus Christ, I trusted you and . . ."

She paid no attention to him and stepped halfway through the opening. From an inside ledge she took two candles.

"Here," she said, handing them to Nick.

"No. Forget it." He lifted his hands upward, refusing them. "I want to know what this is all about."

She cast him an unpleasant look and searched her purse for a match.

Nick was fully aware that this was the point of no return, that from now on this venture was no longer an innocent visit to an old woman. Eying the passage through which they had come, he stepped backward. Now was the time to leave.

Then he heard it. He perked his ears. The sound, projected down the tunnel, was distinct but he didn't want to believe it. Footsteps. Nick could hear distant footsteps on the iron flooring. He was not sure if it was more than one person, but whoever it was wasn't wasting any time.

"Shit." He cursed himself for having come this far and, frightened, he said, "Olga, there's someone coming. A tourist or . . . or . . ." He didn't even want to think of the possibilities, he just wanted her to get out of the way so they could shut the false door. If they acted quickly they could still avert trouble.

"Quick, get in." She found a match and struck it.

Nick slapped his forehead with his open palm. "You can't be serious!"

"Get in. Hurry." She lit the two candles.

Nick did not move as the sounds grew nearer. Though they were subtle, and still distant, the steps were direct and fast.

"Nick," said Olga, impatiently, "I'm trying to help you. Come on."

He backed away. Olga grabbed his arm and squeezed it.

Desperate, she said, "Listen, Nick, you're already in trouble. Serious trouble. You've been followed everywhere in Kiev. In the other cities they wanted you to know they were watching you, but here you were supposed to be oblivious to it. And you were."

"Wh-h-at?" But he could believe her words all too easily.

The footsteps were growing closer. Olga was as blunt as she could be: "Nick, the KGB is planning to arrest you. I think I know how to get you out of it."

"You . . . you mean . . ." He looked back down the tunnel.

"This is your chance to do something, Nick. Help us," she begged. "You're the only one who can. You're an American, people will look after you, but without your help, we'll disappear."

He turned to Olga and he knew what he had to do. "You're right." This was his chance to go beyond merely saying what was right and wrong.

He crossed through the false door and he was Olga's accomplice. Whoever it was behind them was not far away. He grabbed the matches and one of the candles from Olga.

"The door," he ordered.

They couldn't leave themselves so exposed. He crammed the matches into his pocket, held the candle in one hand, and together he and Olga shut the metal door. They desperately hurried, bit by bit inching shut the rusty, screeching metal door. The footsteps bore down on them distinctly now, and in slow, careful movements they raced until finally the door was shut. Olga leaned her shoulder up against the door as she struggled to secure the latch.

"There." Perspiration forming on her brow, Olga said, "Quickly."

She started off, but Nick paused, able to hear the person approaching. Olga grabbed him.

"Hurry," she urged. "If we're found here there will

be trouble. It's safe farther in."

He hurried after her, quite a willing partner and determined to get away. Unlike the museum passage, this catacomb tunnel was black and rugged, neither lit nor whitewashed. Each held a candle high in one hand, cupping the flame with the other. Picking through the rubble, they stepped over crumbled rocks that littered their way and avoided craggy areas of the wall that jutted in and out.

"Nick!" Olga suppressed a scream.

First she, then he, became entangled in a massive cobweb that spanned the tunnel. Olga pulled globs of it from her mouth and he grabbed it away from his neck. Wispy, hairy cobweb sputtered and burned and shriveled as it touched the flames of their candles. Suddenly Nick hated this confining space lost beneath the earth's surface.

"Don't worry," said Olga, seeing the fear in his eyes. "This passage isn't frequently traveled, but it's safe."

They came to a junction and passed beneath primitive wooden beams. Olga, apparently having gone this route many times, turned right without hesitation. That tunnel in turn forked, and they headed left. Nick moved too quickly and his candle flickered. He stopped and faint noises reached his ears.

"What is it?" asked Olga from ahead.

Nick looked behind them into the absolute darkness. "I thought I heard something." There it was again. The distant, faint echo of screeching metal.

"It's right up there," said Olga, motioning toward some collapsed beams. "The turn off."

Nick asked no questions and followed her. When she

began to pull an old wooden beam to the side, Nick automatically helped her. The wood was somehow attached near the roof of the cave and the bottom, with little effort, swung freely to the side. A fissure just wide enough for one person appeared. Olga, holding the candle out in front of her, stepped sideways into the crack.

Nick held the beam. "I've got it."

She took no more than two or three steps and was already in a tunnel on the other side.

"Now you," said Olga, peering back through the crack at Nick.

"Crap, I hate this kind of stuff," he said, focused in the small space. "But . . ."

"It's easy," she said, challenging him. "Just hold the beam with one hand and step in. Then let go of it. The beam's made to swing back into place."

He took a deep breath. "What the hell," he said, shrugging.

Nick glanced up at Olga on the other side, and slid in. He closed his eyes and felt ragged rock poke into his back, the other wall was only inches before him and he scraped his knuckles against it. He still held the beam with his right hand.

"Just let go of it," said Olga. "Good. Now give it a nudge."

He did as she said and slowly the force of gravity pulled it back, blocking the exit. His heart pounding, he realized, however, that it had not returned to a completely vertical position. He clawed at it with the tips of his fingers but it wouldn't budge.

"Olga!"

Looking over his shoulder, she saw the problem and

dismissed it. "That's good enough, Nick. Come on."

"If you say so," he said, just wanting to get out of the crevice.

Two fast leaps, rock bruising his body, and he was out. He twisted his torso, relieved that there was nothing blocking his movement.

"Man, oh, man," said Nick. "I don't know what I'm into, but I'm into it deep."

She kissed him on the side of his dirt-smudged face. "It's okay now. There's a church not very far from here."

Holding their candles in front of them, they moved cautiously on. This tunnel was both wider and more free of debris than the others. Their pace quickened when they rounded one bend, then another, and a dim light appeared.

"Olga?" called out the voice of an old woman from up ahead. "Is that you?"

Smiling, Olga raised her voice and answered, "Yes, Aunt Elizaveta, it's us."

"Excellent, my children," came the response.

To Nick, Olga said, "We're here." In an attempt to reassure both Nick and herself, she added, "That was just a tourist back there."

"But what if I was followed?"

"Don't worry. You weren't. That's why we met at the farmers' market—so that you wouldn't pick up a tail at the hotel." For his sake she forced herself to relax, and said, "Besides, no one would be able to find us back here."

Of a different mind, Nick checked behind them. "Olga, I . . ."

"Bats." She blew out her candle, then Nick's.

"Yoo-hoo?"

"We're coming, Aunt Elizaveta."

The tunnel began to glow with light from the chamber ahead. An entry appeared, and into this opening stepped an old woman dressed in the heavy black habit of a nun. Although only her happy oval face was left exposed, Nick recognized her as the woman who had been with Olga at Saint Vladimir's.

"My children!" Clasping a small red box in one hand, she put the other to her face. "Thank God you've come." Lifting up her gown, she scurried forward into the tunnel and embraced Olga. "Thank God."

Olga kissed the woman. "Aunt Elizaveta, this is Nicholas Miller."

Elizaveta stood back and admired Nick. "Such a fine young man. My thanks to you, Mr. Miller. My thanks to you. Come, embrace me." She opened her arms.

Confused, Nick stepped forward only to find himself enfolded by the woman. She kissed him on each side of the face, squeezed him with surprising strength, rocked a bit, and hummed.

"Such a fine young man," she said, gushing. "But let's not stand here in the entry. Come, enter the Church of Saint George."

Nick was shocked by the grandeur and elaborateness of this subterranean church. The work was more rich and ornate than any he had seen in Kiev.

"Do you like it?" asked Elizaveta anxiously, the top of her habit rising up and down with her forehead.

"I don't believe it. It's incredible." He stepped farther into the church. With the only light coming from the two burning torches, Nick was awed by the beauty surrounding him. He looked at the old woman in her archaic garb—had he just stepped back two centuries in time? To her, a sly grin on his face, he said, "This isn't part of the museum, is it?"

Elizaveta laughed. "Oh, no. It's a working church." She motioned around with an open hand, the black material draping from her arm to the floor. "These are some of the most sacred and gorgeous icons in all of the Ukraine and Russia." She blushed with her confession. "When the Bolsheviks were destroying them one after the other, we smuggled these icons here for safekeeping."

"Olga," said Nick, "you didn't tell me your aunt was a nun."

Nick heard it the instant Olga did. Their moment of peaceful calm passed and they exchanged frightened glances. It was the dull sound of wood scraping rock. The vertical beam that covered the crevice. Someone was moving it.

"Aunt Elizaveta," said Olga, trying not to panic, "did you tell Bishop Tikhon."

"No," she said, unsure of what she was being accused of. "You told me not to. I . . . I promise I didn't."

The sound came again, faint and low.

Elizaveta, unable to hear anything, said, "What? What is it? Olga, is something . . . ?"

Olga grabbed her aunt by the arm. "I don't know. It may be anything, but we'd better not take any chances. The back way, Aunt Elizaveta, where is it?"

She hugged the tin box against her chest and wrapped it in the folds of her habit. "That way." With her head she nodded toward the small entrance through which she had come.

They all heard the sound of loose pebbles rolling.

In English, Nick said, "Oh, no." He prayed for it only to be a bunch of rats. He knew, however, that it wasn't.

The three of them hurried across the church. Olga took the torch from the central column.

"In there," said Elizaveta, pointing to the bucket of water. "Douse it in there. We'll take the other one."

Elizaveta took the torch by the door and Olga dropped the other into the water. It hissed, smoked, and steamed.

"Here," said Elizaveta, feebly pointing to the wall. "That's the door. Oh . . . oh . . . dear Lord, grant us success and safety." With the tin box in one hand and the torch in the other, she attempted to cross herself.

Hearing distinct noise from the tunnel behind them, Nick lunged at the door, found the handle, and yanked it open. Elizaveta bent over, ready to exit first.

"Hurry!" urged Olga, hearing footsteps.

"Oh, my God," said Nick.

He had his hand on Elizaveta's back, nudging her forward as fast as he dared. Olga was crowded behind him. They were all at the door itself when a mighty shout burst forth.

"Stop!"

From across the room it was a deep, thundering order that left no choice but to obey. The three of them, still facing the door, froze.

"Gospodi pomilui!" prayed Elizaveta, voice trembling.

It was everything that Nick had feared all along. God, how he had gotten into this? They had him. Arrest. And then imprisonment. For how long? Forever.

"Nick," whispered Olga, pained. "I'm sorry. Truly I am."

He turned around expecting nothing less than a full squadron of *militsiya*.

"My God!"

It was Viktor Yezhov, the tall crowd controller from the exhibit, the one with the steel-framed glasses. His briefcase was thrown on the ground behind him and in one hand he held a stubby candle. In the other hand, pointed at them, was a handgun.

XXIII

"Step forward and get away from that door," ordered Yezhov, waving the gun at them.

"I . . . I don't understand." Elizaveta, hiding the tin box in the folds of her habit, begged for an explanation.

"Shut up, old woman!" shouted Yezhov, his voice deep and severe. "Now step forward."

Olga, holding the flaming torch, moved cautiously away from the door. Nick and Elizaveta inched forward in small steps.

"What's going on?" demanded Nick, trying to pretend as if he were not afraid. He pointed to the gun. "Put that thing away. We haven't committed any crime or broken any laws." He felt Elizaveta's withered hand grasp his wrist. "You're going to have to answer to your people as well as my government. I'm an employee of the U.S.—"

"Yes," said Yezhov, interrupting. Smiling, he was not intimidated. "An official employee and that is all."

His shirt grimy and sweaty, he edged farther into the church. "I have no idea what it is you all are up to down here, but under persuasion, the old woman at the entrance told me that you," he said, aiming the pistol at Olga, "were connected with some church movement."

"Bozhe moi." My God, said Olga, letting her eyes close. *The babushka* was part of the Church of the Catacombs, placed at the entrance so that other members could slip into the catacombs. "What did you do to her?"

Yezhov was snidely indifferent. "Just enough to make her talk and show me where to find you—which she did, although she was a bit noisy. I'm sure she's run far away from the catacombs by now." He moistened his lips. "Plans have been made for you, Miller, and whatever you are involved in down here will only help matters up top."

"Oh, Lord," moaned Elizaveta. The surface meant that the documents would fall into the hands of the Soviet government and that all would be lost.

"Nick," began Olga. "I'm . . . I'm sorry." Though there was nothing but pain on her face, her mind was racing ahead and she was thinking of something much different.

Hot wax from Yezhov's candle splattered onto his wrist. He blew out the flame and tossed the candle to the floor.

"You," he said to Olga. "Give me the torch."

Her deep eyes perked up. She knew what to do, and glanced to the side for confirmation from Elizaveta. They looked briefly at one another in acknowledgement; this was the type of situation for which they had long ago prepared. Olga raised the torch and stepped forward. Just then Elizaveta began to grow and whirl.

"Oi, oi . . ." said Elizaveta, desperately clutching the heavy folds of her gown on her chest. "My heart. Dear God, my heart!"

Yezhov shifted his attention to Elizaveta, and Olga acted. Her arm recoiling like a heavy spring, she heaved the burning torch at Yezhov with all her strength. Dripping flaming drops of fuel, it spun through the air. Yezhov raised his arms in protection and the torch hit him full force.

"Run, Nick, run!" cried Olga. "Take my aunt and get out of here!"

Burning fuel soaked into Yezhov's skin and he cried out in pain. His shirt sleeve smoldered, threatening to catch fire. Battling the torch and the oily substance it smeared upon him, he dropped the gun. At the same moment the torch fell to the floor and the flame went out. In an instant the Church of Saint George was hopelessly black.

His heart pounding as if it might burst out of his chest, Nick tried to see something, anything. Any second he expected a bullet to go tearing through him. He had never experienced such absolute and intense blackness before. His eyes were wide open, yet he was blind, unable to see even his own arms and legs. And here they were buried beneath the earth's surface.

"Olga!" he shouted, stretching his hands outward into the void.

"Get out of here!" she demanded from nowhere. "Take my aunt and go. She has important documents, Nick. You must get her out of here!"

"Olga!" He couldn't leave her.

Something grabbed at him and latched on. Nick stifled a scream. It was Elizaveta's rough hand.

"The documents!" repeated Olga.

"Yes, yes," came Elizaveta's excited voice. "She'll stop the man. We've come too far to lose. We've got to save the documents!"

Rapid steps were converging upon Nick. Something was poking through the air. It was an extended arm, lunging for him. Nick swung his foot back and kicked. His hard shoe sunk into soft flesh, and Yezhov's deep, pained cry was evidence of the damage. He sensed Olga at his side. She apparently struck Yezhov with her fist. Then she turned to Nick and started pushing him away.

"Go, hurry!"

He heard her lunge in Yezhov's direction. A frenzied scuffle was evidence that they had connected.

The noise and turmoil were all around him. Nick didn't know what to do, where to go. Elizaveta pulled on him.

"We must leave!" cried the old woman.

"Olga!" What would happen to her? "Olga!"

"Nick, go! Go!" she screamed as she struggled with Yezhov.

The old woman pulled on his arm and he began to follow her. His hand in front like a shield, he touched the outlines of several icons. He understood at once what Elizaveta intended: they would escape through the rear entrance. He sensed that she was bending over and he leaned, but not far enough. The dull, cold wall tore into his forehead.

"Jesus . . ."

He braced himself to prevent falling over and, touching his forehead, felt ragged, sticky skin. Elizaveta continued to pull on him and then he was through the door and into a black void beyond. She released him and he heard her shuffle back and shut the door.

"Miller, come back!" Yezhov's words were muffled by the wall and made impotent by the darkness.

From within the church Nick could hear the crashing of icons and candelabra. Yezhov started swearing as he struggled. There was a pause as someone fell. Olga cried out. Olga? How could he leave her?

"Molodoi chelovek," whispered Elizaveta. "We must go." Sensing his hesitation, she said, "Olga can take care of herself."

"I'm here."

Nick, his arms outstretched, felt the empty air for Elizaveta as he stumbled across the dusty, rocky tunnel floor. He touched the heavy material of her habit and took hold of her arm. She set off at once, Nick at her mercy.

"Run, Aunt Elizaveta!" cried Olga from inside the church. "Get away!"

Her voice faded along with the scuffling as Nick and Elizaveta made their way through the black tunnel. Nick held one arm overhead. Grimacing, he turned his face sideways, fully expecting to collide with a jagged rock. In anticipation of stone and debris, his steps were large and clumsy. He was nothing more than a blind man.

"Just follow me. I know. I know," said Elizaveta, reassuringly, her voice coming out of nowhere. "I've spent my whole life down here." Just then she tripped over a rock. "Oi!"

Her fingernails ragged, she held his arm as she struggled for balance. She groaned, and he tried—where was she?—to help her. Then, just as he grabbed her, he too stumbled over the rock. She helped him, and once they were sure they were both standing, hurried on. She slowed a moment later and Nick heard the patting of her palm against the tunnel wall.

"Soon," she said. "We must be there soon. Ah, yes."

Nick reached over and ran his hand along the cold rock. Abruptly it gave way to nothing. A corner. Another passage.

"Yes, this way. This way," said Elizaveta. "We must be quick. We have a long way."

Her aged hand poked about the empty space until it landed on Nick. With the same fervor she took him and led the way around the turn.

"Wait," said Nick, suddenly hopeful. "I forgot. The matches. Olga gave me the matches."

"Good," she gasped.

His hands shook as he searched his pockets for them. The loss of sight accentuated everything and he sensed the blood pulsing through his body, frantic and somehow disjointed. And now that they were stopped he could hear something more fragile: Elizaveta's desperate, sporadic breathing. Only inches away from him in the interminable darkness, he listened as she dragged the air over her teeth and into her body. Her saliva gurgled as she wheezed.

Fearful of spilling the matches on the ground, Nick's hands trembled as he lifted the small wooden box from his pocket. He turned the box over and over in his hands, wondering which way was up. Nick felt for the opening, slid open the lid, and plucked out a match.

With its tip, he searched for the flint. He found the abrasive strip and struck. Nothing. He struck again. Nothing. A third time. The match hissed, sparked, and burst into flame.

Light. Nick's eyes recoiled from the brightness. The smell of sulphur filled the air and Elizaveta's worn face, wrapped in her black habit, appeared out of the darkness. Her eyes red and wet, her cheeks smudged and sagging, she looked at the flame, squinted, and then glanced at Nick.

"I'm so hot in this clothing," she said. "But we must not waste time. We must save the documents."

"Documents?" demanded Nick. "What documents?"

"They prove that the Tsar is dead! Lord have mercy!"

Without further word, the hunched woman turned and scurried on, black cloth dragging in the dirt behind her. Overwhelmed by the whole situation, Nick followed, holding the match high in one hand, cupping it and protecting it from the draft with the other. His eyes shifted from the tunnel floor back to the dry wooden match, whose diminutive flame offered no more than a few moments of light. He tried to catch up with Elizaveta and his brusque movements nearly extinguished the match. He slowed.

"Come, come." Elizaveta, sure of the way, did not pause. "I'm so hot," she said again. "This is not a dress to flee in."

The tiny flame stabilized and they moved on. Nick held the match by the very tips of his fingers.

Elizaveta's breathing became more labored with each moment. One hand grasping the tin box, the other pressed to her chest, she was forced to slow her pace. At the end of each long-drawn breath a momentary pause was followed by a high-pitched squeal. Nick, his attention focused on Elizaveta, did not notice the match burning down to his skin.

"Ouch!"

He dropped it reflexively and the match went out before it hit the ground. The tunnel again dissolved into blackness. Nick fumbled for another match.

"Just a second," he said.

Elizaveta, trying to regain her breath, did not respond. His fingers in the matchbox, Nick could tell that there were less than a dozen matches remaining. As he took one out and searched for the flint, they heard a muffled cry in the distance.

"Olga!" said Elizaveta, trying not to sob.

Paralyzed, Nick and Elizaveta strained to hear something, anything. There was nothing but absolute silence until, finally, the stillness was shattered. Shattered by a muffled discharge of a gun somewhere behind them. Filling the caves around them, the blast grew louder and louder like the deep, reverberating grumble of an approaching sonic boom. Then it burst into their tunnel and a harsh gunshot painfully pierced their ears.

"Olga!" cried Elizaveta. "My dear one!"

Nick couldn't light the match. He could hardly bring his two hands together. He shook beyond control. Olga. Was she dead? His eyes welled. He jabbed at the matchbox. The match caught fire and Nick looked up. Tears rolled over and down Elizaveta's cheeks. She hugged the box to her body and moaned.

"Such violence! What has the world come to?" She

crossed herself and trudged on. "Follow me," she said despondently. "There is another way out. I'll show you. Then you must return at once to the other Americans."

"But what about Olga? She might need us."

Nick raised his hand too fast and the match went out. Elizaveta was a few feet away from him when he lit another. She had taken her headdress off and was gumming it in her mouth. Her hair, damp with sweat and sparkling like silver, hung in disarray. When the material was wet, Elizaveta twisted it into a knotted mass.

"Maybe we should go back," began Nick. "I mean—"

"Light this," she said, not paying any attention. "It's not a torch, but it will last longer than a match."

"Olga might need our help."

Elizaveta held up the twisted scarf. "Light this," she said impatiently. And then, "What is done back there is done. We must save what we can."

Nick took the wetted scarf and held the match to it. It resisted, then reluctantly caught fire with a dull red flame. The foul smell of the burning cloth filled the passage.

"No time to waste." Elizaveta mumbled, "Oi, I'm so hot." Then suddenly she froze. "What was that?" she demanded. "Did you hear something? An animal?"

Nick was still, concentrating on what lay beyond in the black. "I don't hear anything."

Elizaveta shut her eyes and patted her chest. "Thank God. Come, follow me."

He headed after her as she hastened onward. They came to another tunnel, traversed it, and continued on a narrower, rougher one. Scrambling over the rock-strewn floor, Elizaveta's breathing worsened. She dragged the air in and out of her body, coughing at the end of each deep breath. The wheezing became constant and her movement slowed.

They approached a small boulder blocking the passage. Elizaveta lifted her long black gown, placed a foot on the rock, and stepped on, then over the boulder. It proved too much. She leaned against the side of the tunnel for support.

"Rest for a minute." Nick reached out to support her.

She placed a hand against her chest and struggled to speak. She eyed the boulder with fear.

"That's . . . that's not supposed to be there," she muttered.

"Rest." Nick tried to remain calm.

He searched in one direction, then the other. Nothing. A rough underground passage that led nowhere in either direction. Nick didn't have the courage to ask if they were lost.

She started off again without warning.

"Just take it slow," chided Nick.

Several minutes later the passage split and Elizaveta hesitated at the junction. She strained to see down one tunnel, mumbled to herself, and shook her head in disgust. She hobbled over to the other tunnel. The arched opening was wide and low. Again Elizaveta shook her head. She hurried back to the first tunnel.

"Light," she demanded.

Nick stepped up behind her, unraveled a bit more cloth, and held it to the entry. Elizaveta took one conclusive look in.

"Nyet. Nyet." She shook her head.

Without a second thought she entered the tunnel with the arched opening. Nick was right behind her.

Dust whirled around their feet as they entered this cave, and Nick realized that he could no longer hear the reverberations of their movements. Apparently they were now in a much larger cavern, and as the floor sloped downward, the roof vaulted out of sight and the walls disappeared.

Elizaveta raised her eyes and began wheezing again. She groped for support and Nick hurried to her side.

"I'm not sure," she gasped.

"Just get your breath. You'll be okay. Don't worry."

Elizaveta clutched the little tin box. Her irregular breathing became more desperate and gurgling sounds emerged from her throat.

"It's . . . oi . . . it's so hot!"

"Stop. Don't move. Don't talk." said Nick. "You're okay, Elizaveta. You'll be fine."

She began to quiver and sway. Her eyes closed in pain as she tried to breathe. She drew air in with great difficulty, making high-pitched squeals as she did so. Nick took her under her arm not a moment too soon. She could no longer stand.

"Li . . .ght! Light!" she managed to say, opening her eyes.

Nick held the burning headdress in front of her face. "Right here, Elizaveta. Here's the light." he said, trying desperately to convince her. "Come on, Elizaveta, the light's right here!"

But she couldn't see it and she fought harder for air. "Light! Light!" she screamed, though her voice was barely audible.

She spun from lack of oxygen, her face shriveled in pain, and her eyes fell shut. All at once her strength vanished. Holding her, Nick dropped the burning material to the ground. Her head fell listless to the side and only Nick's support prevented her from collapsing. She was heavy, and he strained to lay her gently on the ground.

"Elizaveta!"

She was lifeless and there was no response. One arm behind her, one arm in front, Nick labored as he lowered her.

"Elizaveta!" he screamed. "Goddamn it, don't die on me!"

Just as he got her to the ground, the material became unraveled and burst at once into a bright, powerful flame. And in that last pulse of light, Nick realized that he and Elizaveta were not alone in the subterranean cavern. Lurking in the shadows was an unrecognizable four-legged creature the size of a dog. Foam liberally dripped from its mouth and most of its hide was eaten away.

Terror so severe rushed through Nick that he too was unable to breathe. As Elizaveta's headdress burned out and the vast chamber dissolved into absolute blackness, the room reverberated with the deep, mad sound of an animal ready to attack.

XXIV

The shot startled them both so much that neither Olga nor Yezhov could tell who had been hit. Embraced in a struggle over the pistol, it had discharged and now they clung to one another mortally afraid to learn the truth. They stood rigid and tense in the blacked-out Church of Saint George, their hands desperately holding on.

The gun fell to the floor.

Olga was the first to relax her grip and Yezhov knew. The sound of bubbling liquid erupted from her throat, followed by several terse, pitiful moans. Her grasp on Yezhov tightened again, seemingly an automatic reflex as if she were pleading to life for life.

The strength vanished.

The bullet hole aiming upward in her chest was initially dry, the skin charred. Then the blood began to flow. At first a mere trickle, it soaked through her clothing and began to warmly seep onto Yezhov.

Olga was dead by the time Yezhov lowered her to the

ground. His hand, sticky with her thick blood, laid her head gently down. Reaching into his rear pocket, he took out the butane lighter one of the American guides had given him. He lit it and saw: glistening red blood staining her thick blond hair. Olga's eyes remained open and stared, immobilized, at nothing.

Yezhov pulled away in revulsion. He sensed warm liquid not only on his hand, but on his chest and stomach too. Examining himself, he saw the stains where Olga had hugged him. Frowning with disgust, he returned to Olga's body and used the lower portion of her dress to make himself clean.

He felt a pang at the very bottom of his throat and in his mouth tasted the nausea that had overcome him. He located the extinguished torch on the other side of the church and scrambled toward it. With the butane lighter he lit the torch and it burst into a whirling flame. Under this brighter light, Yezhov saw that the Church of Saint George had lost its regal air of piety. Icons were broken in half, candelabra thrown on their sides, and Olga's body, not the resplendent iconostasis, was the focal point.

The shock passing, Yezhov placed the torch in a holder and went to the door through which Miller and the old woman had fled. He opened it and, beyond, saw nothing but random and wild tunnels continuing into the darkness. It was useless. Yezhov knew he'd never be able to locate Miller and catch up with him. And even if he did, he'd never be able to find his way back out again.

A sense of reality returning, Yezhov realized what needed to be done if he wanted to salvage anything. Indeed, it occurred to him that he might accomplish more than he had ever intended. He crossed back to the other side of the room and picked up the pistol. Holding it by two fingers, he used the dead woman's dress to wipe the gun completely free of fingerprints. Careful not to leave any fresh prints of his own, Yezhov rubbed the gun until it was shiny and then tossed it on the ground near Olga.

He stood and, looking down at her, was not filled with remorse but with acceptance. He was surprised at himself. She was the first person he had killed, and after the initial shock, her death meant nothing to him. An expenditure, that's all she had been. And now that he had determined how to handle the affair, he was quite pleased. He jabbed the tip of his shoe into the side of her body. Yes, she was dead.

The blond woman had screamed about documents and Yezhov hastily searched the church for anything possibly related. Kicking aside a few icons, throwing open the Holy Gates, he found nothing. They had to be important papers, of that he was sure, for the young woman had given her life for them.

There would be time for a thorough search later, though. It was more important to get the other matter underway. He would backtrack his way out of the catacombs where, once on the surface, he would telephone Colonel Mayakovsky. The search for Nick Miller was certain to begin right away and would continue, both in the caves and in the city, until the American was apprehended.

Pleased with himself, Yezhov straightened his clothing, adjusted his glasses, and gathered his briefcase. This would be very beneficial for his career. He was going to give the Kremlin precisely what it wanted: a valid reason to arrest Miller. Colonel Mayakovsky and the Kremlin would eventually learn the real truth. That would be after Miller had spent a few days in prison, however, and after the U.S. government and the Western press had learned of the charges. And even if the Kremlin wanted to, Yezhov was certain that by that point they would not be able to back down and admit an error of such gravity. Rather, they would most likely laud Yezhov and generously reward him for his services to the Fatherland. All the Kremlin wanted, after all, was a legitimate reason to arrest the American and Yezhov was simply going to give them more than they had ever anticipated: an employee of the United States government to put on trial for the murder of an innocent Soviet citizen.

Light. As the creature's growl grew closer and closer, all Nick could think of was light.

He felt his pockets. Nothing. The ground. Nothing. The matches, where were the matches?

He touched his shirt pocket again and found them. His body too tense with terror to shake, Nick reached into the pocket, took hold of the box of matches, and lifted it out.

Throaty, animal snarls filled the cavern. Louder. Closer. Its sound reflected off the tall ceiling and bathed Nick's ears from all directions.

This had to be a dream. A deathly nightmare. Not even an ember of light. Only something stalking, closing in on him.

Nick struck a match. A small cluster of fire filled the room, so bright that it caused Nick to squint and it caused the creature to hesitate. It was right there before him, some five or six meters away.

Without turning away from the animal, Nick groped to his side. He felt the fat at her waist. He reached higher and sensed a flabby breast. Higher still he found her face. He jabbed at her, poked her.

"Elizaveta!" he demanded. "Elizaveta!"

She was lifelessly quiet.

The dry match burned swiftly. Nick dumped the box on the ground before him. He fumbled for another one and lit it from the flame, the hissing noise causing the creature to flinch.

Nick grabbed his shirt sleeve and ripped it. Wasting no time, he tore it all the way to his shoulder and held it over the small fire. Slowly, surely, a warm yellow flame overtook the shirt sleeve.

"Elizaveta, damn it all!"

Still nothing.

At the brighter light, the creature took a hesitant step backward. Then it froze. A deep guttural growl emerged from the animal's tortured body. It opened its mouth and quickly, sharply, snapped in the air. Turning its one eye that was nothing more than a black, rotten hunk of dried blood toward the light, the creature resumed its forward movement. On its three good legs, it moved one step. Two steps.

"Elizaveta!"

Breathing hard and fast, Nick ripped off his other sleeve in a series of frantic movements. He lit it and stood. Holding a mass of burning material in each hand, he searched the cavern for a rock or a log or any kind of weapon. The stone room, however, was clean and smooth, totally free of debris.

In a famished growl, the creature whipped its head from side to side. A thick string of rabid saliva flew from its mouth like water from a fountain. As the animal began to tolerate the light, it moved yet closer.

Nick stepped between the creature and Elizaveta. Balls of fire in each hand, he knew only moments remained before these, too, burned into blackness. Reflexively, Nick took a challenging step forward. He held the fire toward the creature's face. It froze and turned the blind eye toward the flame. Before it could move again, Nick charged forward, swung back his foot, and kicked. He caught the animal, unable to see out of its rotten eye, in its fleshy throat. Thc creature stumbled to the side and gasped and growled. Nick threw a ball of material at it. The animal turned away and Nick charged again. He kicked, his foot sinking into the side of the animal's head.

Thick, black fluid spurted from the animal's head. In one last act, it snapped viciously into the air. Part of the flame struck the remaining fur, and hairs shriveled into putrid, oily smoke. Weak and defeated, it cried out, the first doglike sound it had made. Like a helpless puppy, it yelped in pain and stumbled from side to side.

Nick could not stop. He kicked his heavy shoe again and again into the soft side of the dog's head. Then the dog's cries ceased and it stumbled and fell to the ground. Unable to control himself, Nick jumped on the dog's head, stomping it underfoot, crushing it until the dark fluid ceased pumping from the body.

His face ashen, Nick moved away from the dog's carcass. The burning material in hand, he turned around. There lay the other black body on the cavern floor.

"Eliz . . . Eliz . . . Eliz . . . a . . . veta . . ."

One step at a time, he recklessly plodded to her side and sunk to his knees.

"Elizaveta, can you hear me!" he cried.

He nudged her, shoved her, but she did not respond. Then, ever so slightly, he could see her chest rising and falling.

Squeezing her arm, he said, "I'm going to get help. I'll be right back."

Around her neck was a piece of material, and he tore it loose. Nick lit the cloth—it burned in a cool, steady flame—and he made for the cavern's opening some forty feet away. When he reached the entry through which they had come, he turned around. Elizaveta lay there, unconscious, in the center of the cavern. The dog's bloody body lay not too far from her.

Nick clutched at his chest, which felt tight—tight as if a piece of wet leather were wrapped around his lungs and shrinking with every minute. He turned right, leaving the cavern behind. Was this the way they had come? He stumbled along. He had to get out of the catacombs.

Olga. Was she dead? And what about Elizaveta? Would she die, too? Die in that cave alongside the mad dog? He had to escape the caves. He had to find help for Elizaveta. He needed daylight and fresh air.

Nick reached a fork in the passage. "Help!" he cried. "Anyone, help! I'm lost!"

No one. He prayed for the police. For the KGB. And he turned left. A craggy tunnel, black ahead, black behind. Would he stumble along for hours, days, and go mad like the creature he had just killed?

His body beaded with sweat. He had to remember where Elizaveta was. If he couldn't find his way out, he could return to her. Christ, what if she woke while he was gone? She had no light, there was no one near . . .

He grabbed at his throat. It, too, was constricting, becoming painfully smaller. He stumbled into another tunnel.

"Help!"

Not even an echo. And not one of the Americans knew where he was. They didn't even know about Olga. And now they'd never know. He'd just disappear. Like his throat, the tunnel grew smaller, narrower. He stumbled against the sharp, rocky wall.

"Please . . ."

He turned down another passage. Ten feet later that in turn split. There was no way. No way he'd find his way out. He ran into a stone wall. A dead end.

Elizaveta. He had to get back to Elizaveta. The flame was burning low and he had to reach her before there was no more light. He spun around, his breathing short and quick. Something was crushing his chest. Something was choking his throat.

He burst into a run. Which tunnel? Right—no, left. He had to reach Elizaveta while he still had light.

"Elizaveta!"

Bitter perspiration dripped into his eyes. It stung like acid. The walls were closer, denser. He ran. The flame struggled for life. Life. He wanted the earth's surface. Kiev. The whole city was above him. Up. But he could not get there. He was lost. Buried alive in the catacombs.

He ran past an opening. Something tore out at him. A bat. No, a whole mass of bats. He screamed and ducked. But it was not a bat. It was another creature and it grabbed him, took hold of him. Nick screamed and struggled and fought. He dropped the flame and yelled.

But this thing had him in its grip. Firmly, it would not let go. Nick was spun around. He shut his eyes. Something struck him on one side of the face, the other.

"Stop it!" demanded a voice. "Stop it!"

Nick opened his eyes. A large man in a KGB uniform had Nick by either shoulder.

"I . . . I . . ." began Nick.

"The old woman," demanded Colonel Mayakovsky. "Where is she?"

Nick peered into one voidlike tunnel, then into another, "I . . . I don't know."

XXV

Followed by four men, Colonel Mayakovsky climbed to the apartment building's second floor. It was seven o'clock in the evening and, via the monitoring device attached to their phone, Mayakovsky was aware that Boris and Masha Lupin were just finishing a supper of cabbage soup. He also knew that Masha's parents were still out of town at their dacha and that her grandmother, Baba Genya, had finished listening to the "Voice of America" and left only moments earlier.

He paused outside the door, the men on the darkened steps behind him. He had made numerous such trips before and he clenched his hand into a solid fist. He raised that fist and brought it down on the apartment door in an unrelenting series of heavy knocks. Again and again, firmly and evenly spaced. The greeting of the KGB, it allowed no option but to open that door.

There was abrupt movement from within the apartment. A spoon dropped into a nearly empty bowl of soup. Absolute silence followed as the young couple listened for the sound they did not want to hear. Between knocks, a chair scraped against the floor.

Just then, at the bottom of the staircase below Mayakovsky, a tired woman entered the building. Carrying a string bag of eggs, a glass bottle of milk, and some black bread, she wearily mounted the steps. Hers had been so tiring a day that she did not notice Mayakovsky and his men until she had climbed halfway up to the second floor. Though the men startled her, she understood the situation at once.

"Oi!" she said under her breath with horror.

Mayakovsky's harsh glare conveyed it all: this will be you if you are not out of here immediately. Trembling, the woman understood and began backing down.

"Ex . . . excuse me," she was able to say. "Excuse me for interrupting."

She turned and hurried down the stairs and out the door, anxious to disassociate herself with the unpleasantness as soon as possible. Through a cracked window, Mayakovsky saw her run across the courtyard. He was sure that she would run—terrorized by the memories of Stalin's days—to a friend's, call her husband to make sure he was all right, and finally be grateful with the bread and milk she did find in the stores and that her family had not been hauled away to prison.

Mayakovsky resumed his confident knocking. He heard movement, then again nothing. He could guess what had happened. Most likely holding onto one another in fright, the young couple was unsure what to do. Mayakovsky, through experience, knew the simple words which would help them.

"Open the door!"

Someone stepped forward and a quivering man's voice spoke out. "Who . . . who is it?" he asked not wanting to hear the answer.

"Colonel Mayakovsky of the Committee for State Security."

The man whispered all too loudly to his wife: "KGB!"

"Open the door at once," ordered Mayakovsky.

Without further hesitation, the man obeyed and began nervously fumbling with the lock. He opened the door, and Mayakovsky, not seeking permission, walked directly into the apartment. Boris retrcated to Masha, and the two of them stood huddled together in the entry to the kitchen.

Mayakovsky, wordless, strode boldly into the living room, the two small bedrooms, and pushing Boris and Masha aside, into the kitchen. He was satisfied only after he had also inspected the bathroom. He shouted to his men out in the hall.

"Search it!"

The four men, rugged and dressed in dark, indistinguishable clothing, stormed in. One went for the kitchen, another the living room, and the other two took the bedrooms. They crudely tore open every drawer, rummaged through every cabinet, inspected every corner. As they sifted through the Lupin's possessions, it was evident not only that they were after something specific, but that they had done this many times before. Mayakovsky, like a proud landlord, did not lay a hand on anything. He merely surveyed, sure of his authority, while his subordinates did the work. He noticed that Masha was wearing the blue jeans Nick had given her.

"Take off those pants!" he snapped.

She edged backward into the kitchen, one hand to her mouth, the other groping for Boris's protection. She shook her head, unable to believe that this was happening to her. Tears filled her eyes and she began to sob.

"Now! Here!" demanded Mayakovsky, his boyish face glaring with anger.

Trembling with fear, salty drops of water, black with mascara, rolled down her cheeks. Masha undid the top button of her pants, lowered the zipper halfway, but could go no further.

"Boris!" she cried.

Without so much as raising an arm, Mayakovsky took a daring step forward. Automatically, Boris moved in front of his wife, staring at the colonel in challenge. Just then a shelf of pots and pans fell to the floor behind them as one of Mayakovsky's men emptied the kitchen cupboard.

Retreating slightly, Mayakovsky said to Boris, "Get her something else to put on. Just have her take the jeans off and put them on the table."

Boris went into the bedroom only to find another of the men rifling through the wardrobe closet and throwing what was not of interest on the floor. Boris grabbed a skirt from the pile of castaway clothing. Paralyzed with anger he dared not express, Boris stood in the corner of the bedroom until he heard Masha crying. He tore back to the kitchen. Backed up against the wall and naked from the waist down, she held her left hand across her thighs and was wiping tears from her eyes with her right. The Levis jeans were strewn on the table next to the half-finished bowls of cabbage soup. Boris went to her and helped her into the skirt.

The men began to emerge several minutes later, each one of them bearing an item from the United States: a second pair of blue jeans, Marlboros, an *America Magazine*, a Joni Mitchell record, and a brochure from FARMING U.S.A. Mayakovsky inspected all the goods and approved their confiscation.

"Get your coats," he said flatly to Masha and Boris.

"What for?" protested Boris. "We haven't done anything."

"Young man," said Mayakovsky both confident of himself and intolerant of any further delay, "either you get your coats or you don't. Regardless, you will come with us."

Boris knew that there was nothing else to it and that for now it would be best to comply. Submissively, he went to the bedroom and sorted through the clothing littered on the floor. With no idea of when they would return and with stories in mind of those who had been arrested and held for months, he picked out a shirt, sweater, and coat for each of them. At least they would be warm. When he returned, Masha was pleading with Mayakovsky.

"Why?" she begged, motioning dramatically to their ransacked apartment. "Why all this?"

"Take the things and wait for me in the hall," said Mayakovsky to his men. When they had obediently filed out, he turned back to Masha and Boris, his tone smooth and calm. "You are being arrested because of your association with the American."

"You, you mean . . ." Boris was afraid to say his

name.

"Yes, because of Nick Miller." Mayakovsky waited a moment. "He has committed a most serious crime."

"Nick?" Masha couldn't believe it. "What could he have done?"

A subtle smirk appeared on Mayakovsky's face. He was as blunt as he could be. "He shot and killed one of our own Soviet citizens last night." Mayakovsky was pleased with the effect it had on them. "That's right, he murdered someone. There was a search and we found him in one of the caves near the Monastery of the Catacombs."

"No . . ." Masha shook her head. "No, that's impossible."

"Oh, but it's quite true. He's in jail right now." Almost flippant, Mayakovsky clarified their situation to the point of simplicity. "You are fortunate, though. You have a choice: either testify against him or be charged as his accomplices." With his hand, he indicated the men in the hallway. "The American goods we have taken—your connection to Miller will have to do with foreign items being sold on the black market."

Boris and Masha were so stunned that they could not utter a word of protest. They were helpless and they knew it. There was nowhere to run, no one to turn to for help. No matter the truth, everything would be as Mayakovsky had said.

"Oh, yes," said Mayakovsky. "The phone. I almost forgot."

He went to the telephone, took it firmly in his hands, and ripped it out of the wall in a single jerk. He neatly coiled the dangling cord in his hand.

Pleased that all had gone so smoothly, he went to the door and held it open. With a slight smile, he said to Masha and Boris:

"Well, that's everything. Shall we go?"

XXVI

Hands clasped behind his back, Colonel Mayakovsky gazed out the large window from his sixth floor office in the center of Kiev. With high ceilings, it was a spacious office, handsomely appointed with an expansive mahogany desk and a tall leather chair. Two telephones rested squarely on one side of the desk, and each pen and each piece of paper also had its proper place. Adorning the wall behind were two retouched photographs, one of Derzhinsky, the other of Lenin, both in hand-crafted frames.

In the basement level of the same building, Kiev's KGB headquarters, things were not as pleasant; a lesser quality issue of Lenin's portrait hung there. It was one of the detention areas, and the windowless cell in which Nick Miller was imprisoned provided only a hard bed and cold water. The American had been there for two days now, ever since Colonel Mayakovsky had found the old woman and him deep within the catacombs. Masha and Boris Lupin were in separate cells on the next level down.

There was a quick rap on the door.

"Da."

Vishnyak, his aide, stepped in. "The agent being sent to the technology fair just arrived, Comrade Colonel."

With the events of the past few days so hectic, Mayakovsky was confused. "Technology fair?"

"Yes," said Vishnyak, typically well briefed on the colonel's pressing affairs. "The agent from Minsk to be sent to Vienna—for the technology exhibition—he is here."

Mayakovsky wasn't interested. "What about—"

"Lieutenant Yezhov just arrived, too," said Vishnyak with typical efficiency.

"Send him in. The other can wait."

Bathed in sunlight, Mayakovsky did not turn away from the window. A moment later, out of the corner of his eye, he saw Yezhov enter, wearing a tunic, olive green uniform, and polished black boots.

"Be seated, Lieutenant."

Yezhov chose the most well-padded chair. "You wished to speak to me, Comrade Colonel?"

Still facing the window, Mayakovsky pensively moved his head up and down. "The past few days have been rather hectic."

Adjusting his glasses, Yezhov could not restrain his pride. "There have been many things to see to, many developments."

"Yes, there have been." Mayakovsky examined the quiet street below. "The Kremlin, Lieutenant, is very grateful for the recent turn of events."

"Well . . ." he began with feigned modesty.

Mayakovsky raised his hand, signaling silence. "They are pleased to have such a significant charge brought against an American and, in particular, against an employee of the United States government. Because he lacks diplomatic immunity, we will be able to bring him to trial. Yes, as you've probably heard, there will be a trial, and it's sure to attract a great deal of attention. International attention. After all, we publicize very few incidents of this nature." Officially, serious crime did not exist in the U.S.S.R. "As a matter of fact, the story has already made front page news in London, Paris, Tokyo, and in every major American city. Because our own citizens will hear of it on 'Voice of America' this evening, we have decided to report the scandal in *Pravda* either tomorrow or the next day." Indifferent, he shrugged. "Anyway, it will be substantial propaganda for us: 'Soviet citizens—beware of contact with persons from the violent capitalistic societies!' " Mayakovsky took a deep breath and exhaled. With his back still to Yezhov, he continued. "Not only do we have an American with a most serious charge against him, but we are able to provide concrete proof why our citizens should avoid future contact with foreigners. Undoubtedly, it will also help secure the release of our colleagues imprisoned in Connecticut."

"Let us hope so."

"As you are aware . . ." said Mayakovsky, annoyed at the interruption, "our press wishes to paint you the hero. They would like to portray you, I believe, as the daring young KGB lieutenant who tried most desperately to save the life of your comrade citizen. Again, nice propaganda—this time for us. There was even talk of claiming that you knew the dead woman

. . . that you were prominent Komsomols together or something."

Yezhov flushed with pride and satisfaction.

Mayakovsky cleared his throat and slowly, deliberately turned around. His face drawn and irritated, his words were measured. "But we both know who killed that woman, don't we?" he said as if he had rehearsed the entire scene a number of times.

Caught off guard, Yezhov said, "I . . . I . . ." There had been nothing but praise ever since he had called Mayakovsky and reported that he had seen Miller shoot the woman.

"I know it, you know it, and so does the Kremlin," said Mayakovsky, taking several steps toward Yezhov and unable to restrain his anger any further. "Don't take us for fools, Lieutenant. We were aware of it from the start." Mayakovsky had had a series of long debates over the telephone on how best to handle the situation. "While the Kremlin is pleased to have such a shocking charge brought against an American, they are rather indifferently disposed toward you and your part in all of this. I, on the other hand, deplore the whole business." Fury in his eyes, he stared point-blank at Yezhov. "You killed that woman!"

Yezhov, twisting his hands together, tried not to panic. "So . . ."

"Silence!" demanded Mayakovsky. He leaned on his desk toward Yezhov. "The gun was your gun, issued to you and signed for by you. Lieutenant Yezhov, you defied my orders, interfered where you were not supposed to, and committed an act of murder against an innocent victim."

He looked up. "Innocent?" said Yezhov, defensively. "She would have killed me!"

Mayakovsky slammed his fist against his desk; the placid telephones shook. He couldn't bear to look at Yezhov anymore. In an attempt to control his rage, he stormed over to the window. Yezhov still had no idea whom he had killed nor of Olga's connection to Mayakovsky.

"Lieutenant Viktor Yezhov," began Mayakovsky, forcing himself to be calm, "I called you here this afternoon to inform you that there will be no story in *Pravda* regarding you, that you will receive no glory regarding this case, and that you are hereby given a month's leave of absence from your duties here and at the American exhibition. We will inform you when we are in need of your services."

"But Colonel Mayakovsky," protested Yezhov, rising to his feet, "what of Miller's trial? What of the Western journalists? I was there, I was the witness!" Realizing this could be the end of his career, he became desperate. "You'll need help with Miller's interrogation. I can help, Comrade Colonel. Please, you can't do this to me."

Gazing out the window, Mayakovsky said, "Of course we can. The Kremlin is very pleased with what has come of all this, but I have no need for an officer who is unable to follow orders. Should we be in need of a witness, we will make one."

Yezhov demanded: "Whose decision was this?"

Disgusted, Mayakovsky said, "That is not your concern."

The lieutenant sat down again. He took off his steel-frame glasses and, rubbing his eyes, racked his brain for some sort of leverage. "But . . . but what about the documents?''

Mayakovsky froze. Over his shoulder, he said, ''What's this?''

''You see,'' insisted Yezhov, putting his glasses back on. ''There's still a great deal I can do to assist in this matter. You can't dismiss me now. The woman mentioned documents. That's why Miller and the old woman ran. You were the first to find Miller, surely there must have . . .''

''That's odd,'' said Mayakovsky, concerned. ''I found nothing.'' He turned toward Yezhov. ''What else do you know about these so-called documents, Lieutenant?''

''Well, I . . .'' he stammered. ''Didn't you find anything.''

''No.'' The colonel was absolute. ''Nothing.''

''There must have been something. Something on Miller, perhaps, or on the old woman.''

Puzzled, Mayakovsky shook his head. ''That's very interesting, but there wasn't. However, I will certainly check into it.'' Lost in thought, he returned to the window. ''The old woman is in the hospital—I'll question her this afternoon.''

''And what about Miller? Surely I can be of assistance to you in his interrogation,'' added Yezhov, his voice deep.

Mayakovsky had little patience left. ''Lieutenant Yezhov, a specialist is coming from Moscow to interrogate Miller. I will contact you should your help be needed.'' He folded his hands behind his back, disgusted with Yezhov. ''Now . . . I have a number of things to see to today and I did not bring you in here to discuss the details of this case. I am in no need of your ssistance. I merely wished to inform you of your present work status: you are on a one-month leave of absence. Should you find it necessary to question this any further, your position will again be reviewed. And I can assure you that it will not be favorably."

Yezhov was silent.

Mayakovsky shouted: "Dismissed!"

Distraught about the turn of events, Yezhov hesitated before rising. Then, in a hurry, he got up and quickly left the room.

Mayakovsky heard his office door slam. He shut his eyes and exhaled with relief.

"*Bozhe moi.*" My God. The last thing he needed at this point was further interference.

"Vishnyak!" he shouted to his aide.

His office door was opened. "Yes. Comrade Colonel."

"Send in this other," he said with disinterest. "The agent we're sending to Vienna. And order my car."

Mayakovsky did not want to wait any longer. After he met with the next agent, he would head to the hospital to confer directly with Elizaveta.

Yezhov was furious. He gripped the back of his neck with one hand and squeezed tightly. It couldn't be true. Colonel Mayakovsky couldn't do this to him, couldn't negate everything that Yezhov had worked for. Only now, with his future called into question, did Yezhov realize how much of his career rested in the hands of a single person, a single person ill-disposed toward him. Only now did he realize how much he could lose should Mayakovsky so desire.

"Could lose?" said Yezhov, aloud. *"Nyet."*

He had already lost. Mayakovsky had taken away hi success, his achievement. There would be no glory, n promotion, and no opportunity for securing, amon other things, a decent apartment. If another witnes were needed, they would, as the colonel had said, sim ply create one. The KGB had no need for Yezhov. H was the loser in a struggle he hadn't realized he wa fighting. Mayakovsky, for his own reasons, had com to the conclusion that Yezhov was a hindrance and ha eliminated him.

A month's leave of absence. Yezhov knew what i meant. He was out. There would be no more upwar climb. Not now nor, as long as Mayakovsky was i command in Kiev, in the future. At best there woul be nothing higher than lieutenant. More likely, th month's leave of absence was just the beginning of th end. Even if he were allowed to return he would proba bly be assigned to some menial task, such as tran scribing endless, boring hours of conversation betwee foreigners and their inquisitive Intourist guides. H punched the button for the first floor and the elevato dropped. Never before had he felt so vulnerable. Muc more was at stake than just his career.

The entire situation, particularly Mayakovsky's ac tions, struck him as odd. He didn't care for any of it First he was reprimanded because he had followed Mil ler and the woman to her apartment. Miller hadn' been tailed, and he and the blonde had spent the entir evening together. Yet Mayakovsky found none of thi of interest except, perhaps, the aspect of the lights bein turned off. No damage had been done. No gran scheme ruined. Yezhov had brought relevant, potentially valuable information and Mayakovsky had acted as if . . .

The elevator came to the ground floor. Yezhov did not get out. It was too early to step aside. Too early to surrender. If he gave up now, all would be lost. Miller's interrogation. It was his last chance. His last hope. Yezhov could not risk being excluded from Miller's interrogation. Somehow he had to be part of it.

He pushed a button and the elevator plunged to the prisoner detention area.

Yes, the colonel had acted as if Yezhov had been intruding. But intruding into what? Yezhov's anger dissipated. If so, that would explain why Mayakovsky had dismissed him from the case. It would also explain Mayakovsky's lack of tolerance for Yezhov's actions and why he had appeared almost threatened.

The elevator doors opened and Yezhov stepped into a stark hallway. The corridor, dotted with naked bulbs, continued for no more than five meters before being interrupted by a thick, locked iron gate. In front of that barrier sat a middle-aged woman with hair dyed bright red. Over her staunch figure was a crease-free uniform, not marred by active movement; her only duty was to record precisely who passed in or out of that gate and the exact time of such movement. On the other side of the barrier stood an armed guard, also in perfect uniform. Beyond, in one of the cells, was Nicholas Miller.

Yezhov approached the woman, who examined him with the utmost disdain. She pursed her lips, smearing slightly her Red October Lipstick. In front of her, on her desk, sat a clock and the ledger in which she recorded all activity.

Yezhov bent down to the woman's ear level. He

spoke clearly and politely and in a voice that the guard could not hear.

"Comrade, I have a favor to ask."

The woman grunted and shifted in her seat. She sniffled and wrinkled her nose. She liked this position of power and she took an exaggerated amount of time to decide.

Several moments later, she said, "Guard, see what's wrong with the American down there. He keeps making noises of some sort."

When the guard obediently went to check on the noise that he hadn't heard, the woman turned to Yezhov.

"Yes?" she said, primping her unnatural red hair.

Yezhov took out a fifty-ruble note from his wallet.

"*Nyet, nyet.*" The woman was shocked and insulted.

Yezhov took out thirty more.

"Perhaps."

"There's one hundred more in it for you. And no danger."

The woman picked at something between her tea-stained teeth, glanced to see if the guard had returned, and then reached out her surprisingly long arm.

XXVII

His cell was a small room with a hard, narrow bed attached to the wall, a tap with cold water, and a sanitation hole in one corner. The walls were a dingy industrial green, and a low wattage bulb, encaged with heavy wire, hung in the center of the tall ceiling. There were no windows and the heavy steel door had only one vent at eye level that could be opened and closed from the outside.

He found no rest in sleep. He dreamed of Olga. He imagined that they were out for a stroll on Kreshatik—a very pleasant stroll—and then a taxi came roaring down the street, jumped the curb, missed him, and hit her. He woke up screaming. He woke up screaming again when he saw her at Saint Vladimir's. Though in the dream she was legless, somehow she ran away from him. She ran and collided with an enormous icon. She was absorbed by the icon, her face becoming long and drawn and hideously Byzantine. Then, once she was part of the icon, she turned into a cloud of incense.

Chasing after her, he burst into the cloud of smoke, was enveloped by it, and then awoke choking and gasping for air. Both asleep and awake, he heard her over and over screaming at him to run, to get away. Over and over he was awakened by her muffled scream and by the reverberating gunshot. And when he opened his eyes from fitful sleep, he thought he was in the catacombs and that he had to look for Olga.

Olga. They said he had killed her. He couldn't stand it. But the truth didn't make any difference. Not here, not in this subterranean jail, this man-made version of the catacombs, also removed from reality. Now buried away in this cell, the same damp, earthy coolness seeping into his bones, the only truth was their accusation. Here, where there was no sun and no moon—only the dim bulb which burned continuously—reality was whatever they chose.

By the end of the second day Nick could stand it no more. A light blanket thrown over his shoulders, he wore the same filthy and ragged clothing they had found him in, and he had washed only slightly in the frigid tap water. He had not been allowed to see any Americans nor even been told if anyone at the exhibit had been informed of his fate. And not a single Soviet representative had sought to question him. A senior officer, their colonel, was the first to find Elizaveta and him in the catacombs. They had hauled him out of the caves—leaving Elizaveta, still unconscious, behind—bluntly told him that Olga was dead and that he had killed her, stuffed him into a yellow and blue police jeep, and then finally shoved him back underground into this cell. Left totally isolated, no one spoke to him and it drove Nick crazy. In his sanest moments he knew they were in the process of deciding just what to do with him. At his weakest, years of Cold War propaganda against the horrible Russians came flooding in and he feared for his life.

Insane with anxiety, Nick ran to the steel door and began furiously kicking it. He screamed so loud that he thought his vocal cords would rip.

"I'm a foreigner! A foreigner, you fucking idiots! Do you hear me? You can't treat me like this! I demand to see someone from my embassy!"

A moment later a guard came to the door, opened the small window, and peered in. So freshly shaved that his face glistened, so well dressed that there was not a rumple in his uniform, the sight of this perfect soldier pointed all the more to Nick's poor condition. Nick ran his fingers over his prickly beard and stepped back.

"You must have a special cell for foreigners." Nick had convinced himself that there had to be. "Something more comfortable. Something with hot water."

The guard shook his head.

"But I'm not one of your citizens. I'm from a different country. I'm American." This had been his password to special favors throughout the U.S.S.R. It had to work now.

The guard shook his head again. He lifted his hand and pretended as if it were a gun. Then, against his strictest orders, he whispered the first words Nick had heard since his imprisonment.

"Bang, bang, bang!" said the handsome Russian soldier, laughing. "You killed her just like a gangster from Chicago!"

* * *

Nick fell asleep when he could cry no more. Death. Tossing and turning, there was nothing else rippling through him but death. Everything was temporal, particularly life. Nothing was permanent, with the exception of death.

Some hours passed before he was awakened by the sounds of a key in the cold, steel door. He opened his swollen eyes unsure of whether it was a dream or not, unsure if there really was a familiar person standing in the room.

By no means trusting himself, Nick said. "Mr. . . . Mr. Thomas?

"Congratulations, Nick," said the exhibit director, entering the cell. "You made Walter Cronkite."

Nick sat upright and rubbed his face with his dirty hands. "No kidding?" He pulled the blanket over his shoulders.

"I'm serious." Mr. Thomas, smiling, held a bulging plastic Marlboro bag under one arm. "Walter Cronkite."

"Wonderful. What does the Politburo think about that?" Nick couldn't imagine it; the U.S.A. and CBS seemed more like folklore. "Churchill said 'Russia is a riddle wrapped in a mystery inside an enigma.' Well, here I am locked in a cell buried in Mother Russia's bowels and I don't know why they're doing this to me." Nick looked up at Mr. Thomas, who was making a forced effort at being lighthearted. "You gotta get me out of here."

The older man stopped pretending. "We're trying, Nick." He ran his open palm over his bald head. "Honestly, we are. It's so damned complicated."

"Well, what in the hell took you so long to get here?

Where were you?" said Nick, beginning to unleash his anger at the situation. "I'm in prison! And I've been here for days. Where were you and what's the Ambassador going to do? Christ, I don't even know if it's morning, afternoon, or evening."

"Now, now," said Mr. Thomas, patiently trying to soothe Nick. "It's six in the evening and you've been here for almost two days. They didn't tell us about . . . about the incident until yesterday. And even then they contacted the embassy in Moscow directly. I've been trying to get in here ever since." He was at a loss. He held out the Marlboro bag. "I brought you some clothes. I figured you might need a change."

Nick spotted the bright plastic bag—the same bag he had used for bribing people throughout the U.S.S.R.—and said, "Next time you come, skip the file and chisel. Just bring me some more bags, some jeans, and a carton of cigarettes. That ought to get me out of here." Disgusted with everything, Nick got up, examining himself as he did so. "I look like shit. I feel like shit." He went quickly to the door. Taking the bars in his hands, he shook the door and screamed, "This place sucks, you fascists!"

"Nick!" snapped Mr. Thomas, grabbing him by the arm. "Stop it, stop it right now!" He shoved the bag of clothing into Nick's arms. "Take this and sit down. I don't like the situation any better than you do, but yelling obscenities is only going to make matters worse if it does anything at all. Now, sit down."

Frustrated and on the verge of breaking down, Nick threw the bundle of clothes onto the bed. He sat, put his head in his hands, and gave a disgusted groan.

"I didn't do it. I swear to God I didn't do it." Tears

filled his eyes. "I didn't kill Olga," he said, looking directly at Mr. Thomas. "I swear."

Mr. Thomas, slightly embarrassed, stuffed his hands in his pockets. "I didn't think so. No one does. Not even the Ambassador."

Nick, unable to hold it back any longer, began to recount the story in a monotone voice. "One of the controllers, Viktor Yezhov, followed us. He surprised us and started swinging a gun around." Relieved to finally tell someone, Nick felt as if he were letting excess air out of a drastically overinflated tire and that the dangerous pressure, with each word, was lessening. "Olga went after him. She told me to run. I didn't want to. I didn't want to go, but she told me to get out of there and take her aunt. And . . . and we ran. Through the catacombs. Then there was this gunshot. I—"

Mr. Thomas crossed the room and touched him gently on the shoulder. "Nick, I know you want to tell me, but . . ." He motioned around the cell, which was surely bugged, and put his finger over his mouth. "Someone from the embassy more versed on this type of matter is coming down on the evening flight from Moscow."

Nick understood. "Sure, I'll wait for him and then we'll talk." His answer was sober, though he didn't know how much longer he could go without telling someone. "Just stay clear of Yezhov. Don't let him back in the exhibit. He did it. He's the one."

Mr. Thomas nodded. Seeking to change the topic, he said, "You're okay, though, aren't you?" He spotted the bruise on Nick's forehead. "I mean—"

"No, they didn't rough me up at all." He touched

his head, then picked at his ragged shirt. "I ran into a wall and then tore up my shirt later on. But they haven't touched me. They've just let me sit and go stir-crazy in here."

"Nick," said Mr. Thomas, firmly. "You're doing fine and you'll be fine."

He shrugged off the encouragement. "No one has said a word to me. No one. From their side, I mean. And they haven't even asked me what really happened down there." Thinking about it now, he became more confused. "There's something else . . ." He didn't dare mention it, at least not while their conversation was being monitored. Colonel Mayakovsky was the one who had found them. Before anyone else had come, he took the documents from Elizaveta and stuffed them in his pocket. In a threatening voice he had warned Nick not to mention the papers to anyone. "It just doesn't make sense. None of it." Elizaveta, still unconscious, had supposedly been taken away to a hospital. Whether or not she was still alive, he didn't know. "You haven't heard anything about Olga's aunt, have you?"

Mr. Thomas shook his head. "The only thing they told us was that they were holding you . . . for . . . for murder and that . . ." Already he regretted saying this much.

"You mean there's more?" said Nick, incredulous.

Mr. Thomas closed his eyes. "And that there would be a trial."

"Oh, great." Nick stood up and started pacing around, gesturing with his hands as he spoke. "And you know what that means? That means they're going to convict me. Wonderful. Terrific. I'm never going to get out of this country. Never. And if they don't shoot me, in twenty years all I'll be able to say is that Kiev is a clean city, a green city. That, and 'Long Live the Decision of the Communist Party!' "

Mr. Thomas was at a loss. "Calm down." He didn't know how to handle Nick. "Just don't go get too excited. We're going to get you out of this. Don't worry, we will. Hell, the whole world is watching. Journalists are bombarding the embassy with questions and a few have even managed to get passes to come to Kiev."

Nick stopped pacing and, his back to Mr. Thomas, leaned up against the wall. He put his head on his arm and tried not to lose control.

"I didn't do it. I don't know what they want out of me, but I didn't do it." He choked on his words. "You know, I . . . I was still getting to know her, but . . . the only limits I saw in our relationship were the . . . the borders of the U.S.A. and the U.S.S.R. I really could have loved her."

XXVIII

Mr. Thomas's reassurances, the fresh change of clothes, and the news of Walter Cronkite brought Nick a temporary sense of relief. At least he hadn't been forgotten. At least he hadn't been abandoned. He had felt lost and helpless before, totally at the mercy of the Soviet system; rather, he imagined, like a Russian would feel locked up in his own prison system. Now, however, there was a powerful outside agent agitating on his behalf.

Curled up with his clean clothes on and a light wool blanket pulled over him, he slept soundly that night until his rest was interrupted by a series of powerful jabs in his ribs. He swatted at whatever it was. It struck again, bruising his muscles. A gruff male voice addressed him.

"Wake up," said the guard, striking Nick.

Nick rolled over, groaning. A uniformed guard stood towering over him.

As if to protect himself, Nick drew his arms and legs in. "What in the hell do you want? What time is it anyway?"

"Get up," repeated the guard. "Time for questions."

"What?"

Another uniformed guard came to the bedside. They ripped the blanket off Nick, took him by the arms, and roughly pulled him to his feet.

"Hey, you overgrown morons," said Nick in English, hoping that it would intimidate them. "Get your fucking hands off me. I'm up. I'm up."

He pulled away and, yawning and stretching, backed up against the wall. The overhead bulb burned continuously and for all he knew, it could be high noon.

"What time is it?" asked Nick.

One of the guards started out of the cell. The other came over and took Nick firmly by the arm.

"I want to know what time it is," he repeated.

"It's four-thirty in the morning," said the guard. "Come on, let's go."

"Oh, man," said Nick, irritated and still half asleep. The guard began to pull him. "All right, all right. I'm coming. Just get your hands off me."

The first guard led the way out of the cell and the other followed right behind Nick. Leaving his room, however, Nick did not experience any sense of liberation. He did not know what lay ahead. Interrogation could mean anything. His heartbeat increased and he quickly became more alert than he would have thought possible. Four-thirty in the morning.

"I can't believe it," said Nick, trying to quell himself. "I've never been up this early before."

The guards did not respond, and if others did speak down in the subterranean prison, Nick imagined that they did so automatically in a whisper. The guard's glistening black leather boots slapped against the cold concrete floor, the clean rhythmic sound broken only by Nick's shuffling. The first guard took some keys from his pocket and their rattling echoed off the walls. Metal struck hard metal when he inserted one key into the lock of a heavy gate. Then the gate was thrown open and Nick was shoved through. They paused briefly at a desk on the other side while a woman with flaming red hair, not saying a word, hastily recorded information in her ledger.

The woman nodded and the guards led the way to a sturdy, featureless elevator. They stepped inside the lift but, blocked by one of the guards, Nick could not see which button had been pushed. The doors closed swiftly and precisely; better, thought Nick, than in any foreigner's hotel he had ever been in. He was startled by the elevator's first movement and he reached to the back for support. Then, with great relief, he felt himself going upward. The last thing he wanted was to go any deeper below the earth's surface.

The elevator stopped when the number six lit up. The doors eased open onto a long, empty corridor. Reaching out, the guard took hold of Nick and pushed him forward

"I'm going," said Nick, disgusted and irritated. He shook himself free of the guard's grasp. "This is crazy. Questions at four-thirty in the morning."

The guard rammed his hand into Nick's back. "Walk."

Alluding to busy daytime activity were offices, meeting rooms, and other hallways. But now there was no one. The large building stood an empty carcass, and

Nick felt as if they were passing through a great void. Even the one window they did walk past provided no sense of time or place. All he saw outside was a purplish black sky that seemed more the work of a suicidal painter than it did of nature. A sky lost somewhere between late night and the first of dawn.

They followed one corridor, then turned down another. At the far end of this extended hall was a sharp, slanted beam of light which shot through a partially opened door and cut like a laser across the empty passage. Nick was led toward this light and he felt himself slowing the closer they drew to it. Without hesitation, the guards steered him directly to the light's source, a small room in the building's far corner.

Next to a single, straight-backed chair was a plain table. On the table was a bright lamp—the source of the piercing light—a steaming teapot, a bowl of sugar cubes, and two thin tea glasses. Otherwise the windowless room was featureless, its walls a flat gray. The guards deposited Nick in the room.

"Sit," said one of them.

So that was it, thought Nick. They were going to push and shove him around, humiliate him, and then question him when he was exhausted and at his weakest. Perhaps, too, they wanted to thoroughly interrogate him before he was allowed to talk with someone from the embassy. If that were true, that meant that he might be meeting with an official American representative in a few hours.

Questions. There would be many. Yet what had happened only a few days earlier seemed like the distant past. In any case, he doubted whether he'd be able to coherently recount the series of events. They were going to have to force it out of him simply because he was so confused. He closed his eyes. His fatigue was catching up to him in the form of a dull, throbbing headache.

The guards stood motionless outside the room and Nick, having seated himself, was only conscious of some fine dust particles floating in the lamp's beam. Somewhere else on the floor, a distant door opened, then closed. The stillness was shattered. The guards snapped to attention. The strong, sturdy sound of another pair of leather boots announced the impending arrival of the soldiers' superior. Each moment the steps grew louder. They did not slow, did not waver until Colonel Mayakovsky appeared in the doorway. Glaring down at Nick, the colonel's expression was hostile and intense.

Sinking slightly in his seat, Nick's hands took hold of the edge of the chair. He tried as best he could not to appear intimidated.

Without thinking, Nick blurted out: "I won't tell you anything unless someone from the American Embassy is present."

Mayakovsky shook his head in disgust. "You're even more immature than I had expected. Perhaps you need to be reminded of just where you are."

Nick was speechless. Cool drops of perspiration rolled from his underarm and trickled uncomfortably down his side.

Mayakovsky moved back into the hallway and out of Nick's sight. He obviously wanted Nick to overhear what he said to the guards.

"He's not going to give me any trouble," said the colonel. "At least none that I won't be able to handle.

The two of you are dismissed for now. Return to your stations below. If anyone should wish to speak to me, I'm unavailable. I don't want any disturbances. We'll be in here for three or four hours. Or . . ."—he paused—"or as long as it takes."

"Yes, Comrade Colonel," said one of the guards.

Matter-of-factly, Mayakovsky added, "Oh, and I'll escort Miller back to his cell unless, of course, he needs assistance in walking."

The guards' subdued laughter faded into the distance.

Mayakovsky entered the room and glanced briefly at Nick. His hands visibly shook as he closed the door behind him. When it was shut, he exhaled sharply as if he were under great pressure. He turned to Nick, his severity lessening with every moment.

"Pour yourself a glass of tea and drink it down. You'll need it," he said in a conciliatory manner. "Pour some for me, too."

Nick hesitated, but then poured two glasses of tea and quickly drank his. Like medicine it warmed and soothed his insides.

Mayakovsky took two steps and was at the table's side. He fumbled for three cubes of sugar and then threw them all at once into his glass. Nick flinched. Mayakovsky did not wait for the sugar to dissolve before taking several reckless swallows. Nervous himself for some reason, the colonel put his glass back on the table and returned to the door.

To Nick, a bit of the hostility returning, he said, "Not a word from you."

Mayakovsky opened the door carefully so as not to make any noise. He took a small step out of the room and looked down the hallway. He listened for something and was relieved not to hear it.

"Good," he said, opening the door further. "They're gone. Come on, let's go. But you must be quiet and do absolutely as I say."

Nick was at a total loss. "Go? Go where?" He didn't budge.

"Come on!" Impatient, blood surged to Mayakovsky's face.

Nick edged forward on the chair. "I . . . I don't get what's . . ."

"Quickly, you fool," said Mayakovsky, his voice hushed and intolerant. He couldn't believe Nick didn't understand the situation. "Can't you see I'm trying to help? Olga and I were in on this together."

XXIX

The obesc old woman stumbled to the phone. More asleep than not, she picked up the receiver and opened her mouth in a shrill outcry.

"What!"

"Give me Comrade Yezhov," said the woman's voice, impatient and muffled.

"Who?" demanded the *babushka*, scratching her toothless mouth.

"Yezhov. Viktor Yezhov."

"You want Yezhov? *Bozhe moi!*" My God! "What time is it?"

"Just after four-thirty. Now get him for me!" demanded the voice.

The old woman, a torn robe draped over her body, stumbled to the rear of her apartment. She threw aside a curtain and stomped into the small room. It was dark and the air smelled of dirty socks. Searching about, she spotted her new tenant asleep on the floor.

"Yezhov!" she yelled. "Aren't you ashamed of

yourself? How dare you! A phone call. A phone call in the middle of the night. My sleep has been ruined!"

Terrified by the screaming *babushka*, Yezhov bolted upright. "Wh . . . at? What . . . are you talking about?" He began to feel around for his glasses.

She shuffled through the mess. Standing over him, she shook her finger and further berated him.

"I rented this room to you and I won't have such a mess in here. Look at this—only your second night here and your room is a real pigsty." Her voice was high and piercing. "And I won't have you getting phone calls in the middle of the night. If you get any more phone calls like this, I'm going to throw you out. Throw you right out into the street, I will!"

Stunned by her sharp words and haggard face, all he could say was, "Phone call?"

"Yes!"

The *babushka*, complaining aloud the whole way, returned to her bedroom and slammed the door behind her. He put on his glasses, pulled on some pants, and sluggishly made his way to the phone.

"Da?" he said, yawning into the receiver.

"I'll take nothing less than one hundred and fifty rubles. If you won't give it to me, I'll report that you tried to bribe me."

Yezhov was suddenly awake. It was the red-haired woman from headquarters.

"Of course," he said, the excitement rapidly waking him.

"You said you wanted to know when they started to question him."

"Yes." The officer from Moscow who was to interrogate Miller was certain to find Yezhov of value. Not only could Yezhov's story be used to verify Miller's, but the documents—the missing documents?—had to be brought to attention, also.

"Well, two guards took him away not more than five minutes ago."

"But who's conducting the interrogation?" asked Yezhov. "It's not Mayakovsky, is it? Is the officer from Moscow there?"

"I don't know." The woman was terribly nervous. "Just remember, if you don't pay me, I'll turn you in."

"But—"

The line clicked dead.

XXX

His steps short and erratic, Nick followed Mayakovsky out of the interrogation room. He stopped still when he was in the hallway.

"What do you mean you and Olga were—"

Mayakovsky turned to him and sharply said, "Shut up! Not a word from you. I'll explain later."

None of the past few days made any sense, and Nick was too exhausted, too stunned to do anything but yield to Mayakovsky's authority. This might be some sort of ploy to further entrap him, but he didn't think so. Mayakovsky was too disturbed and his nervousness too genuine. But what was he disturbed about, and how had Olga and he been connected?

Even distant laughter would have been frightening in the awesome stillness of the building. The colonel locked the room behind them and hastily started off. Without checking to see if Nick were coming, Mayakovsky went to the door just across the corridor. He took the handle in his hand and paused, ascertaining one last time that there was no one else on the floor. When he was certain that there wasn't and that they had not been noticed, he opened the door and motioned Nick through to the stairwell.

It seemed to Nick that they made an incomparable amount of racket as they descended the cement stairs. No matter how deliberate they were, the sound of their steps echoed and ricocheted all about. Mayakovsky, seeming less like a KGB colonel and more like a fugitive with each passing moment, wasted no time. By Nick's estimation, they stopped when they had gone down six floors.

Mayakovsky turned to Nick and said, "Wait here, you'll be safe. Don't move and don't make any noise. I'll be back as soon as I can."

Mayakovsky partially opened the door, listened, and when he could detect no one, stepped out onto the building's ground floor. Nick watched as the colonel's hand pulled the door shut. Then Nick observed the doorknob barely turning as Mayakovsky, on the other side, slowly released it. Nick heard him pass down the hall, his movement short and quick. He came, perhaps, to another hall, checked, and turned the corner. His steps faded until they finally disappeared.

Nick shrunk back against the wall. He had always been terrible at waiting and once again he found himself squirming anxiously. His mind wandering, he anticipated discovery, only this time the game was not that of a child. He still didn't know what to make of it all—whether he should continue to follow Mayakovsky—and how Olga fit in with a KGB colonel. He could not imagine his release to be impending unless someone from the embassy was waiting outside, ready to whisk him away. But what good would that do? He'd still be inside the country and the Soviet authorities would ruthlessly search him out. If only this were Moscow; then he could be rushed to the embassy where Soviet law had no jurisdiction.

Or was Mayakovsky a good actor and this a setup? Nick leaned back against the cold wall and closed his eyes in fear. He envisaged the colonel returning with a handful of soldiers. They would claim Nick was escaping. Besides proving his guilt, that would authorize almost any action they wished to take. And he probably would run and they probably would . . .

Nick heard voices in the distance. The conversation was terse and concluded before Nick could catch any of it. Then he realized someone was coming, the movement growing more and more distinct. He tensed in anticipation and flattened himself against the wall. It very well might not be Mayakovsky. It might be someone just passing by or perhaps someone Mayakovsky had sent to "discover" Nick. His mind raced for some excuse in the event that he was found.

The steps slowed. Stopped. Nick, entirely focused on the door and who would step through, watched as the knob quivered, then turned. The door opened. Nick recognized the hand.

"We've no time to lose," said Mayakovsky leaning in.

Nick closed his eyes and took a deep breath. Mayakovsky was alone. There were no soldiers, no guards, sent to arrest him yet another time.

"Listen," he began, "I still don't know—"

"Quiet," demanded Mayakovsky, a mixture of frustration and fear on his face. "Follow me. We don't have much time. I've sent the guard away from the front desk for only a few minutes."

"But why should I trust you?"

"If you want to do something for Olga, then you will."

Mayakovsky was on his way again without further word.

At a loss, Nick moved into the hall. There was not the slightest hint of another person. This was the main corridor on the ground floor, broad and spanning the width of the entire building. Swiftly making their way through it, at midpoint they came to the building's foyer. Mayakovsky motioned for Nick to stop. The colonel took several bold steps into the lobby, looked around, and when he was satisfied that the guard had yet to return, signaled Nick. The two of them passed the empty guard's desk, crossed through the foyer and continued down the corridor all the way to the opposite end of the building. Mayakovsky's eyes twitching tensely, he ushered Nick into a small side hall at the rear of the building. He went straight to the second door on the right and, glancing behind them, motioned Nick into a small back room.

"In here," said Mayakovsky, flipping on the light switch.

It was a janitor's room. The walls were lined with supplies and the large, filthy sink had a mound of rags piled in it. There was a cracked mirror above the sink, and in the corner was a large waste bin containing, among other things, several apple cores whose fruity scent mingled with that of ammonia.

Mayakovsky locked the door and went to the wall of shelves. He moved aside supplies on the top shelf and reached in. From behind he pulled a pile of neatly folded clothes and a white plastic carry-on bag decorated with a colorful drawing of "Misha the Bear" and the inscription: "Moscow Olympics, 1980!"

"Take off your clothes and put these on," said Mayakovsky, handing Nick the clothes and expecting immediate compliance.

"Forget it. I don't know who you are or what you're up to," protested Nick. "You can't expect me to go along with something I don't know anything about."

Mayakovsky was taken aback. It was not his custom to explain his actions. He saw, however, that it would be faster to divulge something.

"Olga and I," he began, "were working together to get you to take some documents to the West."

Nick was stunned. "What about her uncle in . . . in New York?"

"There is no uncle, nor has there ever been."

Nick said, "Are these the same documents that—"

"Yes, Elizaveta's documents," said Mayakovsky, bursting with impatience. "Now do as I say. Put these clothes on. We must not waste any more time. I'll explain once we're out of here."

That he would be leaving KGB headquarters was encouragement enough. Nick unbuttoned his shirt and threw it to the ground, he kicked off his shoes and dropped his pants. Though he didn't know what it would accomplish, the guise began to make sense. Each article of clothing was fabricated in a Soviet-bloc country. The white cotton shirt was from Rumania, the dark baggy shirt from Poland, and the thick-soled, red-tinged shoes from Moscow's Lenin Shoe and Boot Factory. Once dressed, Nick examined himself in the broken mirror above the sink.

"My God," he said, a smirk on his face. "I look like I've lived here all my life. All I need are a few gold teeth."

Mayakovsky paid no attention. He picked up Nick's American clothing and deposited it in the trash can, meticulously burying the items beneath day-old trash. When he was satisfied that no one would find them, he washed and dried his hands. He then took a small bundle of papers from his breast pocket and handed it to Nick.

Predominant was the hardcover Soviet passport. Nick opened it and was shocked to see his own black and white photograph glued into it.

"Christ, that's me." He tapped the photo and glanced up. "How did you get my picture?"

"From your file, of course."

Officially embossed and completely filled in, the passport read; Berzinch, Vadim; Nationality, Latvian; City, Minsk. In addition, there was a work book with a detailed employment history written into its pages.

"You have a slight accent," said Mayakovsky, "and Baltic accents in Russian most closely resemble American. So you're Latvian, but you've been working as a computer scientist in Minsk for the past six years."

Not knowing what he was involved in, but fully aware that this was anything but official, Nick asked, "How dangerous is this?"

Mayakovsky was blunt. "Very." He handed Nick the carry-on bag and unlocked the door. "Come on, I'll explain more in the car."

Suddenly reluctant to give up his identity as a foreigner, Nick grew angry. "What in the hell is this all about? Where are you taking me?''

''Let's go,'' said Mayakovsky, opening the door. ''I picked Elizaveta up at the hospital a few hours ago. We have a quick stop to make at her house.''

Nick was paralyzed with confusion. ''Elizaveta's house? Really, I . . .''

Mayakovsky could no longer restrain his temper. ''Perhaps I misjudged you, Mr. Miller. I assumed that you would help us with the documents for Olga's sake alone. Otherwise, it seems, she will have died in vain. Then again, maybe we were all wrong about you. Maybe you can't act, even though without your help an achievement of great historical and political value will be totally lost.'' Burning with indignation, he said, ''Perhaps you would rather stand trial for Olga's murder?''

Nick wiped the sleep from his eyes, took a deep breath, and said, ''Come on, let's get the hell out of here.''

XXXI

Disturbed by what he had just witnessed, Yezhov did not move from the secluded corner in the foyer.

After he had received the phone call, he had hurried to headquarters, unsure what to expect but not expecting anything like what he had just seen. He had somehow hoped to become part of Miller's interrogation and in that manner, at least partially, to regain some of the recognition he felt he deserved. Instead he had walked down the street, the early morning sky charged with yellowish-orange light, and up the granite steps of the KGB's Kiev headquarters. But just as he entered the building's foyer, only to find it oddly empty, he heard someone quietly making his way down the hall. Suspecting that it could be one of Mayakovsky's people, Yezhov sought cover.

He then moved with haste behind a large, decorative pillar. But the person who had entered the lobby was not one of Mayakovsky's sergeants, nor even Mayakovsky's aide. It was Mayakovsky himself. And from his secretive spot, Yezhov watched in surprise as the colonel signaled someone and, seconds later, Miller appeared. The two of them then wasted no time in crossing through the lobby and to the rear of the building.

Mayakovsky's and Miller's steps having just disappeared, Yezhov, still positioned behind the pillar, heard more steps coming from another direction. Yezhov remained motionless. Within the minute, a young guard entered the foyer and returned to his desk. Yezhov spoke when he was sure that the junior officer was alone.

"Comrade." Yezhov, his voice threatening, moved into sight.

The young man, who had thought he was alone, gasped and quickly raised his head.

"Where were you?" demanded Yezhov. "Why were you not at your post?"

"Colonel Mayakovsky," said the young man defensively, "thought there was someone on the second floor who shouldn't be. He sent me to check on it." He shook his head. "There was no one."

Yezhov took a handkerchief from his pocket and cleaned his steel-frame glasses. Gazing pensively in the direction that Mayakovsky and Miller had gone, he knew what needed to be done. Should he be wrong, he and his career would be ruined forever. Should his suspicions prove correct, the promotions would be many.

XXXII

Kreshatik Street was for the most part empty, its six lanes free of vehicles except for one slow, nearly empty trolley bus and several delivery trucks. The first of the morning's workers were beginning to appear on the sidewalks, and lights were on in both Gastronom Number 21 and Central Milk and Cheese Store.

Slumped in the passenger seat, Nick tried not to look conspicuous as the black Volga sedan sped along. He felt anything but anonymous in the Soviet bloc clothes and he was certain someone would recognize him.

"This is the first time I've seen the sun in days." But he couldn't stand it any longer. "What do you mean you and Olga were in on this together?" He raised his hands. "In on what?" Looking out at the sun and the new day, he shook his head, still unable to believe it. "She's dead. Christ, Olga's dead."

His hands firmly on the steering wheel, Mayakovsky did not respond at once. "Yes." His voice was choked with emotion. Blankly he said, "I knew she couldn't go through with it.''

''Damn it all, through with what?'' demanded Nick. ''And after Elizaveta's, then where are we going to—''

''She couldn't go through with blackmailing you,'' said Mayakovsky, interrupting.

Nick sat up. No, that couldn't be true. Yet . . . ''From the very start?''

''Yes.'' Mayakovsky nodded slowly and deliberately. ''That's why she approached you and asked to meet.''

It was difficult for him to speak. ''Are you saying that . . .'' Nick didn't want to believe it. ''No. No, it wasn't all a setup.''

Mayakovsky shifted gears. ''It was all part of a much larger plan.'' Looking at him out of the corner of his eye, Mayakovsky said, ''How much do you know?''

His mind still on Olga, Nick asked, ''About the documents?'' He shrugged. ''Not much, only what Elizaveta shouted to me. She said they'd prove that the Tsar was killed.''

''Yes, actually they're telegrams ordering his execution. You'll see them soon enough. . . .'' He noticed a light green taxi behind them and his voice trailed away. His eyes on the rear view mirror, Mayakovsky accelerated and said, ''I'm part of it . . . part of the same underground group.'' His concentration was focused on the taxi. ''We had been looking for a way to get the documents out of the country when I learned of the Kremlin's intention to arrest you. You were to be the second American.''

''Two for two,'' said Nick, disgusted. ''Only juveniles and governments play like that—we have two Soviet spies in the U.S., they want two Americans here.''

They passed the main Metro station on Kreshatik and Nick's eyes lingered on the familiar plaza. The public space was now empty, however, save for one old woman with a short broom.

"The Kremlin wanted an even bargaining position." Mayakovsky turned and reprimanded him, saying, "You made yourself an easy target—you said the right things that provoked the wrong people." He checked the mirror again. "Our original idea was merely to get you to take a package to Olga's relative in New York. Our hope, of course, was that you wouldn't have known what you were taking. We were going to conceal the papers in the false bottom of a box and you would have sent them to our contact at the Russian Orthodox Monastery in the state of New York. In exchange for this, we would have notified your embassy that you were the next target. We presumed that they would have prevented—one way or another—your arrest."

"But the bottom line was blackmail," stated Nick, bluntly. "Or should I say still is? Look at me," he said picking at his clothes. "I'm a damn Sov. What are you going to do with me if I cooperate—drive me to the embassy in Moscow? And if I refuse, then what? Will you just shove me out the door and let them pick me up again?"

Mayakovsky, growing uneasy about the car behind them, reached into his coat pocket. "I trust this will be persuasive." He handed Nick an Aeroflot plane ticket. "There's a flight to Vienna at nine. With any luck you'll be on it."

Nick examined it and was incredulous. "Is this some kind of joke?" he said, holding up the ticket as if it were worthless. "I've got a Sov passport, I'm wearing Sov clothes. Since when can Soviet citizens travel freely? Really, this place is the world's biggest prison camp and you think I'm just going to go and—"

"Please . . ." said Mayakovsky, waving a hand at Nick. His attention was fixed on the long bouncing antenna on the taxi lurking somewhere behind them. "Your name is Vadim Berzinch and you are a computer scientist from Minsk. Try to look smart. You're supposed to be one of our top computer people on your way to the technology fair in Vienna."

Nick was shocked. He ran his hand through his hair and looked nervously out the window. "My God, but—"

"It should work. I've sent agents out before and I was to send one to Vienna tomorrow. The passport you have is his passport. I've already phoned the customs officials at the airport and told them that there has been a change of plans. I told them that agent Berzinch, who is a minor master of industrial espionage, was leaving today instead and that they should facilitate his exit. Let's just hope no one finds out until you're over Austrian territory."

Working through it in his own mind, Nick fell silent. He had to put things in perspective, and that included being put on trial for Olga's murder. He opened the ticket and noted the flight's destination: Vienna. Nick leaned back, throwing his head over the top of the seat. What choice did he have? After all, it might work.

"So . . ." he began, "how much of this did Olga know?"

"She knew it all," said Mayakovsky. "But don't confuse the issue. She did care for you. Truly. Yet if that had been all there was to it, she still could have done it,'' he said, concentrating on driving the black sedan. ''She could have still blackmailed you no matter how much she felt for you. She was, in a word, dedicated.''

He turned his head toward Mayakovsky. ''But?'' If he did get out, this would be his last chance to learn the truth.

''But there was the aspect of Elizaveta, to whom Olga was extremely devoted. You see, Elizaveta didn't know anything of this KGB business or of our intent to blackmail you. Olga insisted that Elizaveta not be told, not only because Olga knew her aunt would disapprove of the whole affair—and possibly not give up the documents—but to protect her aunt should something go wrong. That was Olga's main desire—to shield her aunt.''

''Which is exactly what she did—to the very end.'' Nick recalled the incident at the Church of Saint George and shuddered. ''She threw the torch at Yezhov and yelled at us to run . . . no warning or anything. She just did it.''

Mayakovsky passed a yellow Icarus bus and crossed onto Komsomol Square. Nick slumped further in his seat, his eye on the Dneipro Hotel to the right, and tried to imagine what things had been like at the exhibit since his arrest. Surely the guides were now asleep in their hotel rooms.

Mayakovsky made a broad circle around the ring of photographs in the center of the square. He steered the car toward the road that led down to Podol and suddenly the pavement gave away beneath them. They headed down the steep incline and descended from

Kiev's high bluffs to the lower town, the road at the bottom snaking back and forth. As far as Mayakovsky could tell, the taxi was no longer behind them.

"It was the incident at Saint Vladimir's Cathedral," volunteered the colonel, "that brought things to a head for Olga. She ran away from you because she knew you were followed. You see, whenever just the two of you met, I called off your tail." They passed through the center of Podol and crossed Krasnaya Square. "By acting as she did in the cathedral, we knew Olga had lost your trust. It was decided then that you should meet Elizaveta, a member of her family."

Nick recognized the advice and sat forward. Angry, he said, "That's exactly what Masha and Boris told me. They're in trouble because of me, aren't they?"

Mayakovsky nodded indifferently. "Eventually the dust will settle and they'll be fine." He did not want to upset Nick further by telling him that his friends were already in jail and would likely be there for some time to come.

Nick could not hide his disgust. He pulled away and leaned up against his door.

Going on, Mayakovsky said, "Olga was one of the few people whose actions and beliefs were in harmony. She felt it was necessary to get the documents to the West and she justified deceiving you by believing that she was actually helping you—helping you to avoid arrest here." He turned the car down a side street flanked by low buildings. "When she saw that this wasn't true—that she could do more harm than good—and when the decision was made to involve her aunt, she changed her mind. Her final realization was that she had to be honest both to her aunt and to you, or else it wasn't worth it. There was too much risk involved, otherwise."

"Didn't you know this?" said Nick, placing the blame on Mayakovsky. "She's dead. Couldn't you have done something? Didn't you see what she was doing? Maybe she wouldn't have been killed if—"

"That's right!" shouted Mayakovsky, unable to hide his own guilt. "If only I'd been there, if only I'd have seen what she was doing. But I didn't and she didn't tell me. . . ." He shook his head. "Oh, I was aware that she couldn't go through with it anymore. That much was obvious. I saw it in her face and I was making alternate plans. I just didn't suspect that she would act on her own so quickly. And then Yezhov . . ." Mayakovsky checked the mirror. The taxi had reappeared in the distance.

"Olga told me something about her mother," said Nick. "Do you know anything about it?"

"Some, not much. She was murdered, that much I know. She also was part of the Church of the Catacombs," said Mayakovsky. "Olga would never talk about it, but her mother was murdered by the KGB for her religious activities. That's why Olga wanted the documents out."

"And that's why Olga was willing to do as much as she did . . . in retaliation, I suppose." He understood still more about her. Nick turned to Mayakovsky. "So you're part of it, too. Part of the Church of the Catacombs."

Mayakovsky humbly nodded.

His voice snide, Nick said, "I don't understand how a KGB colonel can be involved with a church." He shook his head. "So what about you? What's your reason for wanting the documents in the West?''

''Atheism is one issue, but there is something more disturbing in the U.S.S.R. today.'' More concerned about the vehicle behind them than his words to Nick, Mayakovsky's tone lacked sincerity. ''People by nature need something to believe in, some 'opiate' as Marx said, to relieve the pain. And there exists in the Soviet Union such an opiate: Lenin. Plainly, I fear that Lenin is becoming a god in his own right—his pictures and quotations are more omnipresent than church materials ever were. You can't escape 'Uncle Lenin' here, and I feel something, anything, must be done to discredit him.''

Nick didn't accept it. ''Isn't that a pat answer. Sounds like a nice sermon you've rehearsed a thousand times.''

Sure of it now, Mayakovsky turned to Nick and sarcastically said, ''I'm sorry I can't give you my full attention, but at the moment I'm more concerned about the car that's following us than what you think about me.''

They parked on the dirt road beneath Elizaveta's house and proceeded by foot up the hill. Mayakovsky led the way and Nick, knowing that they were being observed, felt his stomach twist into a painful knot.

Under his breath, Nick said, ''I can't believe you want them to follow us.'' The carry-on bag hung from his shoulder.

''Of course I do. Better now than lead them to the airport and have them pull you off the plane,'' said Mayakovsky without turning around. ''It's Yezhov and one or two others, no more. Just don't look back. I don't want them to know that we are aware of them.''

Digging his feet into the ground, Nick said, ''But what if they've notified someone?''

''I don't think they will have. Not yet, anyway. I doubt they'll do anything until they're sure there's something wrong. They are all subordinates of mine, after all. In any case, no one will look for you at the airport. Now, if only we can elude them . . .''

Up ahead was Elizaveta's small wooden house perched on the side of the steep hill. The early morning sun broke through the trees, casting angular beams of white light on the structure. As they neared the house, Mayakovsky reached into his coat and took out a handgun. He then took off the coat of his uniform and draped it over one arm.

''I won't be needing this anymore,'' he said of the coat.

When they were within a few meters of the house, the front door opened and Elizaveta appeared. Looking pale but healthy, one side of her face was struck by a bolt of sunlight. More accustomed to the dark, she squinted painfully and moved into a shadow. She wore her old house dress, gray with faded roses, and opened her arms to them.

''Nick!'' said Elizaveta, the pain of the past few days evident in her face. Then she turned to Mayakovsky, bowed her head, and bent to kiss his hand. ''And Bishop Tikhon.''

XXXIII

"Bishop?" said Nick, incredulous. "I don't believe it."

Unaccustomed to having his authority challenged, Mayakovsky was angered. To Elizaveta, he said, "Better go inside." Glaring, he turned to Nick. "Spare me your judgments. We haven't much time."

The three of them entered the main room of the house. Elizaveta immediately went to the bedroom.

"I'll get the documents right away," she said, calling over her shoulder.

Placing his gun and coat on the table, Mayakovsky went to the side of the window and, with his back against the wall, carefully looked down the hill. The light green taxi was parked down the road beneath a tree.

"Elizaveta," he said when she came back in the room, "do you feel strong enough for a quick walk through the catacombs? Unfortunately, we've been followed."

She pressed the red tin box against her chest and stopped still. "Oi. Not again. How terrible. When are they going to leave us in peace?" She shook her head. "But I'm . . . I'm fine. This dress is much cooler."

Mayakovsky motioned to Nick for help, and the two of them lifted the heavy wooden table out of the center of the room. Mayakovsky proceeded to the large fireplace, issuing orders one after the other.

"Elizaveta," he said, speaking fast, "we need candles, matches, and I need a black cassock. I left one here, didn't I?" His words to Nick were blunt. "You . . . go to the window. Don't let them see you by any means. Just keep an eye on them and let me know if they start coming. They should be on their way soon. If there's something illicit going on, they'll want to discover it while it's going on, not after."

Nick at once crossed to the large window. Through its bubbly glass he spotted the light green taxi and the dull figures of two or three men. He could not, however, stop thinking about the catacombs. He wanted sun, fresh air, and unlimited space. The caves were the last place he wanted to be. He shut his eyes momentarily, only to be overtaken by the memory of Elizaveta's unconscious body and of the mad dog.

At his side, the old woman said, "Nick?"

He was startled. "Right here."

Hers was a face that had witnessed many births and many deaths, weathered as much by age as by life and its tragedies. With a gentle smile, she handed him the red tin box.

"The documents are in here," she said. "They're your charge now and . . . I have great faith in you. I'll explain more once we're out of the house, but—"

Accepting them, he said, "If I get out of the country, I'll make sure they get to the right place. And I'll make sure that they get as much publicity as possible. I'll do all I can, I promise."

Standing on her toes, she reached up and kissed his cheek. "Thank you, dear Nick, for taking the documents. Olga would have been very proud." She turned away and covered her eyes. She went to a cupboard by the sink, fighting back tears. "Olga, my precious one . . ." She reached for some candles. "She was so young. I've lived three of her lifetimes . . . why couldn't it have been me?"

"Elizaveta," said Nick, "I . . . I . . ." Turning the box over in his hands, he wished he could do more than just take some papers to the West.

On his hands and knees in the fireplace, Mayakovsky was striking a metal object with his fist. Ashes whirling about, he reached into the back and pulled on some sort of lever. Within the minute a large sheet of iron came loose in his hands. Gritting his teeth, he lifted the covering aside and exposed a hollow space behind.

"There." He stood and brushed off his hands. "Anything from the car yet?"

"No," said Nick. "They haven't moved at all." He stepped away from the window and anxiously examined the opening in the back of the fireplace. "Wonderful, more caves . . ." he muttered.

"Yes, another entrance."

"This city's riddled with holes." Full of trepidation, Nick unzipped his carry-on bag and set the red tin box inside. "And then what?"

"We'll detain them," said Mayakovsky, hoping that it was possible, "until your plane takes off."

Elizaveta held up several boxes of wooden matches and four candles. "Here."

"Good." Mayakovsky's mind was racing ahead. "Leave some matches on the table in plain view. Take the rest of them and the candles with you. Now my cassock, Elizaveta, where?"

The candles bundled under one arm, she went to the bedroom and pulled a long black robe from an ancient trunk. She brought it into the main room and, holding it open at the top, helped Mayakovsky into it. He pulled the garment over his head and worked it all the way on. The robe, full around the legs, reached the ground, concealing all of his clothing except part of his white shirt around the collar. It was a tailored fit and the large man appeared quite at ease in the black cassock.

"How convenient," said Nick, gesturing with his hand. "Out of one uniform and into another."

Mayakovsky dismissed the remark and turned to Elizaveta. "How many torches are inside?"

She thought for a moment. "Four."

"All right," he said. "Now you've got the matches and candles. I'll help you in and then you can start off. We'll catch up in five or ten minutes."

Lifting his robe, Mayakovsky squatted and stepped into the fireplace. In another movement he was through the opening and into the caves. Reaching his hand out, he helped Elizaveta as she bent over and crawled in.

"Oi . . . oi . . . oi . . ." she moaned.

Left alone in the house, Nick nervously moved away from the window. He spotted the two of them, only their legs visible, just inside the caves. There was a burst of flaming light when Mayakovsky lit one of the torches and handed it to Elizaveta. Nick heard them converse, the specific words indiscernible, as Mayakovsky related his plan to Elizaveta. Shortly thereafter Elizaveta started down the rugged tunnel, burning torch in hand, and descended into the depths of the dark catacombs. Mayakovsky reemerged, his black robe smudged with gray ashes.

"Any sight of them yet?" he asked.

"No. None." Nick could not take his eyes off Mayakovsky. In his uniform only minutes earlier he looked like the perfect KGB colonel. Now, in his long, black cassock, he looked like one of the head monks at an ancient monastery. "How could you claim to be a representative of God and do the work you had to for the KGB?"

The sunlight entering the room made Mayakovsky squint. "Don't forget that because of my work I might be able to get you out of the country."

"Yeah, but . . . we're talking integrity."

"No, survival. The KGB has had their own infiltrators in the Church of the Catacombs, so why shouldn't we have our own moles in the KGB?" He reached for the gun and slipped it under his robe. "We are criminals by Soviet law and outcasts from the official Soviet-sanctioned Russian Orthodox Church. To protect my congregation, many years ago I decided to enter the heart of the enemy's camp. Frankly, I never expected to have such a 'successful' career in the KGB. It seemed to have almost happened on its own . . . I just never stopped it." He made sure the matches were in plain view on the table.

Nick forgot about the car below. Checking the window, he said in a nervous voice, "They're getting out. Three of them."

Mayakovsky motioned toward the caves. "Go on, get in. Light one of the torches and wait for me."

Nick scratched his unshaven face. "I suppose I don't have any choice."

"No, you don't." He handed him some matches. "Go on."

Nick crossed the room, took a deep breath, and crawled into the fireplace. Holding the carry-on bag to prevent its dragging through the ashes, he edged his feet along, then stepped through the opening and into the caves. The familiar cool dampness surrounded him. He found the bucket and took the heavy wooden torch. Striking a match against the rocky wall, he lit the torch and it burst into a black, oily flame.

"Are you set?" called Mayakovsky.

Examining the tunnel, Nick said, "As ready as I'll ever be."

Nick got down on his knees and watched through the opening as Mayakovsky, his cassock flowing to the ground, stepped out the front door of the house. Caught in the bright morning sunlight, he cupped his eyes, spotted the three men, and then hurried back in the house. He left the door wide open behind him and ducked into the fireplace.

"I didn't want to leave any doubt in their minds," said Mayakovsky, a contemptuous grin on his face. "They shouldn't be too far behind us."

The carry-on bag looped over his shoulder, the flaming torch in the other hand, Nick said, "Listen, I don't want to get lost down here a second time. I hope you know the way." Nick adjusted the collar of his dark

Polish suit.

"We won't get lost, they . . ." He checked back in the house. "Quickly, now. We must go."

"Into the caves and then what?"

"There's another way out. You can get a taxi and you should just make your flight."

Leaving one in the bucket, Mayakovsky took the third torch and stashed it in a small crevice.

"We can do with one," he said, "and that's all I want them to have, too."

Mayakovsky set off, leading the way through a narrow tunnel with sharp, jagged walls. He was slow at first, not wanting to get too far ahead of Yezhov. The passage veered left and suddenly began to head downward. Nick carried the torch, holding it high, and took large steps down the inclined path. It began to twist, to wind itself deeper and deeper into the caves of Kiev. Mayakovsky paused at one point, disturbed not to hear anything. Then it came, a series of footsteps.

"Good." He reached down, picked up a handful of rocks, and threw them noisily to the ground. "They shouldn't have too much trouble. This passage is fairly simple."

"So maybe I'll make it to the airport," said Nick, glancing behind them. "But what's going to happen to Elizaveta and you?"

Taking Nick by the arm and urging him on, Mayakovsky said, "Part of the catacombs have been discovered, but not all. Together Elizaveta and I will be withdrawing from this world."

Nick was shocked. "You can't be serious."

"I most certainly am." He strained to hear if the others were still following. "Before the Revolution, monks lived for decades at a time without surfacing. And so shall we."

"But surely the caves aren't that big." Nick clambered over a pile of loose rocks. "They'll search the catacombs. You'll never make it."

"There are more caves farther down the Dneiper. And if they discover those, then we shall go elsewhere. Siberia is a very large place."

The tunnel continued its downward plunge, all the time growing cooler. Suddenly the sounds of the three chasing men caught up with Nick and Mayakovsky. At a junction of passages, fright constricted Nick's throat as a flurry of frenzied noise reverberated all around. Echoes bounced off the walls and shot off the ceilings like a series of ricocheting bullets. It was impossible to tell from which direction the sounds were coming and, the confusion evident on his face, Mayakovsky began to move faster. The torch's flame, leaving a coal black streak on the tunnel's ceiling, sizzled and cracked. The path fell away, precipitously dropping, and in a moment emptied into the enormous Great Hall, its craggy roof soaring high overhead like a demoniac cathedral. Across the broad, shallow lake and on the other side of the vast room was Elizaveta. At such a distance she appeared but a dwarfish figure with a small burning stick, her murky reflection grotesquely stretched out on the lake's still waters.

Nick and Mayakovsky clambered down the rugged path and to the banks of the lake. Breaking into a run, they hurried toward Elizaveta.

"They're faster than I expected," said Mayakovsky, the worry creasing his forehead.

The torch's flame bending backward, the bag slapping Nick's side, they sprinted to the safety of the other side. His heart racing, Nick glanced over his shoulder. The tunnel behind them began to glow with light.

"Get rid of your torch," ordered Mayakovsky.

"Forget it," said Nick, unable to escape the memory of being lost in the caves.

"Damn it!" Mayakovsky grabbed the torch from Nick. "Elizaveta's got hers. Run toward her. After this room we go by candles."

Bringing his arm back in one swift movement, Mayakovsky hurled the torch into the lake. A spinning stick of fire, it flew in a long arch through the air until it fell to the lake, hit the water's surface, and went out in a cloud of smoke and steam.

Mayakovsky reached for the gun in his robe. When they got to Elizaveta, he lit two candles from her torch and handed one of them to Nick.

"Any problems?" she asked, nervously.

"Not yet," said Mayakovsky, his attention focused behind them.

She took the other candle from him, handed him the torch, and started off. "To the nesting room."

Mayakovsky heaved her torch into the lake and the Great Hall darkened, the only light coming from the two candles.

"I sure as hell hope you know what you're doing," said Nick.

Abruptly the noise at the other end of the lake came to a crescendo and the three men, led by Yezhov, stormed into the Great Hall. They carried guns in hand.

"Mayakovsky?" Yezhov, torch in hand, called in his deep voice. "Come to your senses."

To taunt him, Mayakovsky shouted back, "In the Church of the Catacombs I am known as Bishop Tikhon. I would appreciate your so addressing me."

Elizaveta scurried into a small tunnel, Nick right behind her. Mayakovsky, his attention focused on the three men, lagged behind. A warning shot was fired, its bullet bursting from Yezhov's barrel with a snap of fire, then slapping into the cavern wall above Mayakovsky's head. Mayakovsky pushed Nick into the passage, took cover behind a rock, then fired two shots in return.

Carrying the candle, Elizaveta scurried through a straight tunnel, its walls smooth and round. Nick chased after her, Mayakovsky catching up after Yezhov had fired a second shot. The passage turned to the right, but was not crossed by any other tunnels or grottos. If by mistake this were a dead end, Nick realized that they would be cornered.

The frantic running of the three men in pursuit could be heard not far behind.

"Elizaveta, how far is it?" demanded Mayakovsky. "The nesting room—how far?"

"Just a ways." Once again her breathing was becoming strained.

"Are you all right?" asked Nick, cupping his candle with one hand.

"Fine," came her labored response. "And glad that it will be over soon—one way or the other."

The tunnel began to decrease in size until they came to a small opening that led into another chamber. Elizaveta stopped at the entry of this next room; the ground in it was covered with a strange dry, brown substance that floated around their feet.

"Ready?" asked Mayakovsky.

"Oh, yes," she said.

To Nick, Mayakovsky said, "Reach out and hang on to Elizaveta. We are going to pass through a large room and it is imperative that you do not talk and that as little noise as possible is made. We have to put out the candles—Elizaveta will guide us—and then we'll light them on the other side." He returned the gun to his cassock.

Nick's attention was caught by the commotion of the three men behind them. "The sooner," he said, blowing out his candle, "the better."

Puckering her lips, Elizaveta blew out hers and the caves became as black as the subterranean depths of the earth could be. Trying not to panic, Nick lunged his arm out and took hold of Elizaveta's arm. Mayakovsky's large hand grasped Nick's shoulder and, a line of three blind persons, they made their way through the small opening and into the next cavern.

Immediately, their feet sank into a warm, slippery, manurelike substance. Inhaling, Nick was overcome by the thick, foul-smelling air. Trying not to lose his balance in the slimy substance that oozed over his shoes and up his legs, at the same time he struggled to stifle an urge to both gag and vomit. Hot, moist, ammonia-filled breezes came in undulating waves, and Nick thought he heard something, something high overhead in the fathomless room. He tensed, gripping Elizaveta harder and feeling her brittle bones. A mysterious object seemed to whiz past his ear. Then another, back and forth. Nick forced himself not to scream. A creature chirped to one side, then another. A soft gush of wind folded over him, and Nick guessed what this room was. It was a nesting room full of thousands and thousands of bats. Another two or three of the creatures, their long bony wings cutting through the black air, swooped down. A dozen or so followed, checking out, it seemed, these human intruders. Nick wanted to speak out, to cry out. Only Mayakovsky's tight and obviously frightened grasp on Nick's shoulder kept him quiet. But all around, from every corner, Nick could hear the bats. An endless number of them blanketing the entire ceiling of the enormous chamber and, Nick knew, clinging to the walls in dense clusters. Their occasional high-pitched chirping, their bodies rubbing and ruffling, the musty stank of the guano all about—the presence of the bats could be sensed everywhere.

The cavern was extensive. When they reached the other side minutes later, Elizaveta began feeling about with her foot for a ledge. Apparently she was not right where she should have been. She continued to tap, carefully and with as little noise as possible, feeling for a smooth ledge that would lead to the passage out of the nesting room. She pulled to the left, then back to the right. Frustrated, she stuck out her hand. By accident she poked right into a mound of sleeping bats and they exploded into terrified flight. Elizaveta's arm recoiled and she shook with the scream that she dared not emit. When she had regained her senses, she pulled farther to the right, and here she found the ledge. With Nick's silent help, she stepped up. He jumped up behind her, anxious to get out of this room, and Mayakovsky followed at once. Above the subtle noises of the bats, however, they could now hear Yezhov and the other two men running through the tunnel. Soon light filled the opening on the other side of the room. Elizaveta had just reached the exit when Yezhov, holding the torch, appeared in the other opening.

"Maya—"

Yezhov cut himself off, realizing what room this was and what havoc a disturbance would cause. Flanked by the two junior officers, he stood absolutely motionless, staring at the bats and at Nick, Elizaveta, and Mayakovsky.

By the light of the torch, Nick could now see the room. All around—in every corner, every niche, every crevice, and all across the ceiling—were brown, hanging bats. So thick were they that their furry bodies appeared as one giant hide stuck pulsating to the cavern's walls and roof.

The bats became aware of a foreign presence and, aroused from their sleep, became disturbed. Hanging upside down by their claws, the bats began to roll their heads, their eyes glittering in the light. Huge pointed ears poked outward and leathery wings unwrapped and twitched nervously. Their anger growing at the intruders, one of the bats squealed a sad cry. Another answered. The ceiling began to move in waves like the sea. The walls began to throb with angry life. One of the bats let loose its hold. It took flight in a screaming frenzy. Another followed. Like flying, shrieking gargoyles, they flapped madly about the cavern.

Screaming to Elizaveta, Mayakovsky broke the stand-off: "Block the opening?"

At the same instant, his hand in his robe, he shot from his pocket without removing the gun. Startled as much by the bats as by the gunshot, Yezhov's eyes opened in paralyzed terror. The bullet struck him crudely in the shoulder. He fell to the side, one of the men grabbing the torch from him. Mayakovsky fired again. This time the bullet struck its target in the neck and Yezhov collapsed.

The roof dropped before another shot could be fired, and the mass of furious bats fell and took flight in a screaming rage. Diving, spinning, the blinding blizzard of bats filled the cavern so densely that it was impossible to see. A deathly scream from Yezhov pierced the atmosphere.

Around him, on top of him, Nick sensed the bats. He ducked, covered his head, and then felt his guano-covered feet slipping out from under him. Mayakovsky was gone, having disappeared somewhere in the black cloud of flying creatures. Barring the entry, Elizaveta stood like a martyr, her arms flung outward. Like bees around honey, bats swarmed to her, trying desperately to get out their usual exit.

Then, in a great swell, the bats located the other entry. The message spread and all at once, rising and surging, tens of thousands of bats dove toward it. Above the deafening roar the two junior officers screamed as their tunnel filled like a flooded sewer with bats. Caught in the deluge, they could not run fast enough and were washed away as the entire nesting room funneled out the opening, over Yezhov's body, and into the caves of Kiev.

Nick raised his head. In the blackness above him he could hear the last of the bats beating their wings. A sullen cry broke from one side of the room, answered by another. Nick guessed there to be no more than two dozen left in the entire chamber.

There was a squeak just to his right and before he could duck something fuzzy skimmed the left side of his face. He jerked his hand up, but it was already gone.

He felt a swoosh of cool air on the back of his neck, slapped into the darkness, and struck nothing. Then he sensed a handful of bats diving and swooping disturbingly close. He threw his head down and covered himself with his hands. The air rose and fell. Something sharp scraped his knuckles.

Then it was over. He heard the last of the bats flutter off to the left, out the opening, and into the caves beyond. The bats were gone and Nick lifted his head. Though reassuring silence surrounded him, he could see nothing. He dared not move for fear of falling.

"Elizaveta!" called Nick. "Mayakovsky!" They had to be here, had to be somewhere in the room.

There was a deep cough from below. "Yes . . ." came Mayakovsky's choked response.

The old woman did not respond.

"Elizaveta?" shouted Nick into the black void.

At first there was nothing. Then, a feeble voice. "I . . . I—"

"Where are you?" demanded Nick.

"Here . . . here," she managed to say. "I'm . . . fine."

Nick quickly took a match from his pocket and lit it, the small flame a bright yellow. He groped for the candle, and when that was burning, the nesting chamber filled with a soft light. Above him, cradled in the opening, was Elizaveta. Taking several deep breaths, she had her hand on her chest and struggled to sit up.

"Oi . . ." she said painfully. But then a smile of relief emerged on her pudgy face. "The men . . . they're gone."

Below Nick, Mayakovsky stood and wiped the mire from his long, black cassock. Clearing his throat, he coughed deep and hard. Across the room he spotted Yezhov's body, several bats hovering about.

A faint grin emerging on his face, he looked up at Nick and smiled. "Are you all right?"

The candle in one hand, Nick picked up the carry-on bag with the other, and came to his feet. He brushed off his Soviet-bloc clothing and sighed.

"Me?" said Nick, more calm than he would have thought possible. "I'm okay, but I've got a plane to catch."

XXXIV

Vienna's airport sparkled.

It shimmered with color. Not to be found were the faded yellows of old tsarist buildings or the deep reds of the Revolutionary banners, but glistening blues, greens, pinks, oranges, and endless hues in between. Even purely functional benches jumped with life and vibrancy.

Diversity. There were different colored people, too: Europeans with rosy, white skin; blacks with rich, dark skin; and Asians representing every Oriental country. And like the people who wore it, clothing came in every shade and shape imaginable. Short skirts, long skirts, plaids, checks, light business suits, white pants, silk ties. But very few kerchiefs. Some of the people roared with laughter, others cried. Still others talked so loudly that their conversations could be totally overheard. Yet they didn't care, it didn't matter if others knew what they both said and thought.

The airport was filled with stores, tiny and large.

Spotlights beamed down on such varied merchandise that it would have taken days just to look at every item. The store clerks were polite and friendly, too; they didn't shout, they didn't bite. And there were food stands, cafés, and restaurants dotting the halls, the aroma of their delicacies—meats and fresh fruits and fresh vegetables—pleasantly scenting the air. The people that served the food did not wear white hats and white robes, nor was the service rude and slow.

Wearing the dark Polish suit and the reddish shoes from Moscow's Lenin Shoe and Boot Factory, Nick sat in a white room so neat and clean that he knew beyond a doubt that he was in Austria. Seated in a padded chair with chrome legs, he felt out of place, rather like a Russian at the exhibit. On his lap was the carry-on bag. In the bag were the documents. Nick nervously played with the carry-on's zipper, twiddling it in his fingers, anxiously pulling it back and forth.

At the large desk in front of Nick was a neatly uniformed Austrian customs official, his suit coat and pants navy blue, his freshly laundered shirt a perfect white, his dark hair and well-trimmed mustache speckled handsomely with gray. The man's hands were soft and white, and he sat meticulously thumbing through Nick's Soviet passport. Perplexed by the whole affair, the Austrian was not certain what to do with Nick.

Ripping the bag's zipper open in a nervous twitch, Nick said, "Really, I'm not a Soviet citizen."

"Oh?" The very formal official was quite cautious. "But all your papers here are in order. There doesn't seem to be any problem. If you're not Soviet, then may I ask just what country do you belong to?"

"The United States." Nick was thrilled that the

Austrian treated him so indifferently and that there was no special treatment for foreigners. "I guarantee you, I'm as American as . . . as Levis jeans." Nick couldn't restrain a ridiculous grin.

The official failed to see the humor. "Oh, really, is that a fact?" He obviously doubted Nick. "Is . . . is there perhaps something else?" he said, courteously.

Nick laughed out loud. "No, honestly, there isn't. I'm not defecting. I swear on Lenin's mausoleum that I am not defecting. Look," he said, opening his mouth. "This is American dental work. No gold. Believe me, I'm not Sov. Just call the American embassy. They'll know all about me." He searched the room. "If you've got a newspaper besides *Pravda* there's probably an article in it about me."

The Austrian was not impressed with Nick's behavior. He returned to the Soviet passport, examining each page with great care. When he had gone through it thoroughly, he examined the cover. Then he took a silver pen from his coat pocket and, in small, neat writing, recorded the passport's number.

The official raised his head. "If your name is not Vadim Berzinch and you are not from the Soviet city of Minsk, then just what is your name?"

"Nick Miller," he said, emphatically. "I promise I'm Nick Miller. Please, just call the U.S. Embassy. They'll know me. They'll claim me."

The man groomed his mustache with his little finger. From his desk he took a sheet encased in plastic and, running his eyes down the list, found the number.

He picked up the phone, saying, "You'd better hope they claim you, otherwise . . . otherwise we may have to put you on the next jet back to Moscow."

Nick's body began to quiver. He tried to stifle it. He bit his lip, covered his mouth. But he couldn't hold back. Nick bent over, his head touching his knees, and the laughter burst out of him. He laughed until he cried, tears coming to his eyes and dropping onto his Soviet-bloc clothes. He laughed and cried with joy and relief. Mayakovsky and Elizaveta had fled and were now hiding somewhere in the caves of Kiev. Olga. Olga was dead. But at least he still had the memory of her. That part lived and would live, and that would have to be enough. He had the documents with him, too, right in the silly carry-on bag. Christ, he'd made it out of the Soviet Union, papers and all. And after he'd explained to American officials what had happened and how he'd gotten out of the U.S.S.R., he'd get things underway. Yes, he'd make certain the documents got to the right place and got the proper coverage in the media. He'd make certain even if it took years.